"Pastor Kevin Holt has blessed tl. [...]
years of his pastoral and preaching ministry. His new book, "An Anchor for the
Soul", is an excellent guide for our daily Bible reading. He has masterfully
blended the Old and New Testaments in such a way that numerous questions will
be answered. This book will give you a fountain of faith which will enrich your life
daily."

Rev. Charles E. Crank | Former Indiana District Superintendent Assemblies of
God, Retired

"Dr. Kevin Holt, has provided a must-read masterpiece entitled, "An Anchor for
The Soul." As you read this life-changing book your faith will hear the words,
"this hope, as an anchor of the soul, a hope both sure and steadfast and one which
enters within the veil." In the New Testament era, if the tide was out when the
ships came close to the harbor, they would cast their anchors into the harbor.
Then, when the tide came in, the anchor would go deeper, pulling the ship safely
into the harbor. Our anchor, however, did not go down into an earthly harbor, but
it went up and is fastened within the veil of the Holy of Holies. As you read this
powerful devotional, you will come to know that this anchor of the soul is pulling
us daily, closer to our Lord, in the midst of the storms of life. You will learn that
this anchor is your steadfast Savior, who brings balance to your spiritual boat, no
matter what is taking place in our world. Your tide is coming in!"

Dr. James O. Davis | Founder/President | Global Church Network

"Few people can unpack the biblical narrative in a way that consistently points to
the gospel of Christ like Pastor Kevin. I have been an admirer and student of his
teaching for years and am so thankful that others will now have the opportunity to
be blessed by his unique ministry."

Peter Heck | Teacher/Pastor, Speaker/Author

The quality of our relationship with God is directly related to our willingness to
engage with God's Word consistently. My friend Kevin has provided us a practical
and powerful tool to help us engage with the greatest book of all. Kevin loves
God's Word and has given us a lifetime of learning and reflection to glean from. I
highly recommend this book.

Wayne Murray | Senior Pastor, Grace Assembly of God, Greenwood, IN

An Anchor for the Soul

Hope to steady us in an upside down world

Rev. Kevin J. Holt, D. Min.

PREFACE

"This hope we have as an anchor of the soul..."—Hebrews 6:19

I have been a senior pastor since November of 1985. I was 21 when I began and I have just concluded my 37th year in ministry. In the nearly four decades I have pastored and the three congregations I have been blessed to lead, I have experienced and seen so much change. Church music has experienced a revolutionary change, the frequency of church attendance has declined drastically, church dress (even in the pulpit) has undergone a complete metamorphosis, and the issues of our culture have become more and more complex. It is a different world today in 2022 than it was in 1985.

With all that has changed, one thing has remained constant. The truth, reliability, and power of God's Word. Jesus said when He warned of changing times and seasons, *"Heaven and earth will pass away, but my words will not pass away." Matthew 24:35 ESV* That, my friends, is a source of great comfort. We need something that is unchanging when everything around us is unsettled— God's Word is just that.

The focus of my pastoral ministry for 37 years has been the expository teaching and preaching of Scripture. Not only is it the one constant of our rapidly evolving world, it is a living Word that is able to set free and transform hearts and minds. Beyond that, and because of its unchanging nature, it provides a fixed point, an anchor of sorts to our soul, the very seat of our emotions. It steadies us when we drift or slip and it holds us close to God when we feel anxiety or fear.

It has been my practice for many years to read through the Bible every calendar year. In 2020, I began as a daily discipline, posting a short devotional thought from my own personal reading and quiet time, on social media (Facebook and Twitter). It served to discipline my schedule, help me write thoughts succinctly (Twitter only allows 280 characters and that is hard for a preacher), and hopefully it has been a blessing to those who have read and reflected upon them.

Last year I decided that I would take many of those and expand them into a full devotion, unpacking in a paragraph or two, the nuggets of truth from God's Word that I feel God had shown me. That effort has led me to this 365-day devotional, all formed around my daily tweets and posts for the last three years. Each is a page long and designed to be read along with a daily reading section of Scripture that if followed, will lead you through the Bible in a year.

Our world today is tottering, and things that we would have never imagined are happening right before our eyes. This is truly an upside down world. In a world such as this, we need an anchor to steady us. That anchor is the Word of God and the hope that emerges from the truth it contains. Corrie Ten Boom said, *"In order to realize the worth of the anchor we need to feel the stress of the storm."* It is my hope that this devotional will be a source of encouragement, faith development, and challenge to you.

Most of all I pray that while the world around us rapidly changes, my reflections on God's Word will help quiet your restless heart and serve as an anchor to steady your soul when you feel the stress of the storm in this upside down world. —Pastor Kevin J. Holt (November, 2022)

"In order to realize the worth of the anchor, we need to feel the stress of the storm."—Corrie Ten Boom

DEDICATION

In September of 1982 my mom and dad drove me to Lakeland, Florida to enroll in my first year of college at Southeastern College (now University), an Assemblies of God Bible College. I had been to Florida a time or two, but was born in Muncie, Indiana and had lived there my entire life. I had no car in Florida, just a 10-speed bicycle, and within 24 hours my parents were headed back north. I was in a brand new world and feeling very much out of place and alone.

As part of God's great master plan, I was paired with a young man from Columbus, Georgia, a red-headed, southern talking, ministerial major as my roommate. His name was Gerald (Chuck) Harvey Griffith. I cannot overstate to you how thankful I am for that part of God's plan. I spent only one year in Florida, then I transferred to Central Bible College in Springfield, Missouri where I graduated in 1985. I only roomed with Chuck for one year, but in that one year, a friendship was forged that would remain undaunted for the next almost 40 years. Chuck became then, and remained my best friend.

Space will not allow me to say too much (I could write a book about our friendship instead of a dedication page), but I am forever grateful for this man of God that I was privileged to call my best friend. In that year in Florida, we laughed, learned, strategized, theologized, and solved the problems of the Church universal together. We were two very different people. Chuck was a neat freak and "germaphobe" and I was not. Picture Chuck (Felix Unger—Tony Randall) and me (Oscar Madison—Jack Klugman) and you will get a sense of our relationship.

Our friendship never wavered, although through the years our ministry paths (in different parts of the country) kept us from connecting often. For a few years Chuck and his family did move to Indiana so we were in the same district, but a southerner at heart, Chuck moved back to Georgia to pastor in his home town of Columbus.

Our families vacationed together when our kids were young, and no matter how many months or even years we were apart, when we met up again, the connection was immediately there and we would pick up like we had last seen each other yesterday. I have laughed and cried with Chuck more than any other friend, and his love for the Word, the Church, and for Jesus has inspired me. His integrity was unmatched, his gifts limitless, his humor (often self-deprecating) epic, and honestly, and it's hard to say, but his love and respect for me was humbling. He always made me feel more confident and always made me feel like my ideas mattered and were good. Such individuals are few and far between.

When our kids were grown, we always looked forward to three or four days between Christmas and New Year's. Sheila and I would meet Chuck and Sherry in Nashville, Tennessee and would spend that time shopping, drinking lots of coffee, eating out, and staying up late talking about life in the ministry. It was the few days of the year that I ALWAYS wished would hurry up and arrive, and then always felt like passed too quickly. But every year we would pick up right where we left off.

I received a call from Sherry on September 14, 2021. She said she was following the ambulance that was carrying Chuck. She asked me to pray. Chuck, she thought, had suffered a heart attack. For several days we prayed, trusted, fasted, and believed. On September 23, 2021, the faith of Gerald (Chuck) Harvey Griffith became sight. At the age of 57, he was with Jesus.

Chuck left behind a wife that he cherished and who adored him. Chuck and Sherry ministered perfectly together and complemented one another in ways that were truly remarkable. He was so loyal and so devoted to her and his girls. Maci and Cami were what put a spring in his step. He was so proud to be the dad of these beautiful young ladies, both who were raised by a godly daddy who taught them to love Jesus first and most. And they do!

Chuck was so thankful for Matt, his son-in-law, who with his daughter Maci gave him two adorable grandchildren, Charlie and Griff. Chuck was a very blessed man but his family was so blessed to have this man who loved being a husband, daddy, and papaw! I dedicate this book to my best friend in ministry. 40 years was not enough but I consider myself to have been blessed to have known him that long. He loved the Word as much as I do, understood it and articulated better than I could, and would have cheered me on and made me feel way better about my writing than I deserve. Thank you Chuck for being my friend for the last 40 years! Looking forward to seeing you again one day!

ACKNOWLEDGMENTS

There are many people I wish to thank, without whom this project would not have been possible. First, my son, Kyle, is responsible for the reading guide that accompanies each day's devotion. He worked with nearly 1200 devotions helping match them with the reading segment for the day, so that this book serves the dual purpose of reading guide and inspirational encouragement. Hayley Williams, our programming manager at Glad Tidings, is responsible for the graphic work and I am grateful for her beautiful work.

Proofing a book of this magnitude, when so much of the writing is marked by personal style and theological focus, is no easy task. Paula Mangus, our director of operations, and Amy Cooper, our communications and data manager, and my sister, provided proofing assistance; and Lori Ramsey, my assistant since 2004, also proofed and did all the formatting, layout, and submission of the final version. All of these individuals are amazing, and I am so appreciative that despite their hectic workloads, they found time to work on this project as well. Thank you so much.

I also want to thank my friends, Dr. James Davis, Peter Heck, and Pastor Wayne Murray, for their willingness to add their kind words to this volume. No greater honor could be given to me than to have Reverend Charles Crank, one of the finest preachers of our day and my district superintendent for more than half of my pastoral ministry, adding commendation to this volume. He is deeply respected, and I am so grateful for his support to me, especially in my early years of ministry. Finally, a word of thanks to those who have encouraged me by leaving comments and messages in response to my posts.

I trust this devotional volume will be a blessing to you all!

Kevin

Day 1 | Honest with Our Hearts

January 1—Read Genesis 1-4

It is far easier to criticize another and assume their blessing is ill-gotten than to honestly consider our OWN motives and the condition of OUR heart. We must allow the Spirit to convict, chasten and cleanse us so that we may be like Him and blessed of Him. Genesis 4:1-16

It seems clear that the great disparity between the sacrifice of Cain and that of Abel was an issue of the heart. Cain's was a sacrifice that was thoughtless, without great cost, and emptied of the deep heart devotion that was expected by God. Abel, on the other hand, offered a sacrifice that was acceptable to God and pleasing in His sight. God rejected the sacrifice of Cain and gladly accepted Abel's. Cain, instead of regarding his own emptiness and heart deficiency, became envious. He was angered at the thought of Abel, and ultimately killed his brother and committed the first recorded murder. All because he preferred to criticize his brother, rather than check his own heart and motive.

This is an important lesson for us. It is easier to criticize someone else and convince ourselves that their blessing is a result of some impure motive, than to place our own hearts on the scale of His righteousness. Ours is not to question the heart or motives of another. We must place our own lives before the discerning eye of the Spirit and honestly allow Him to convict, chasten, and change us.

Day 2 | He Remembers Us

January 2—Read Genesis 5-8

"But God remembered Noah"—Such beautifully wonderful words. Noah trusted God through sinful times, but still Noah was a sinner invited onto the ark of salvation. If we are heaven-bound, it is not because we are special. It is because God, in His grace, remembered us. Genesis 8:1

The opening words of Genesis 8 should not be overlooked: *"But God remembered Noah."* The author does not mean that prior to that, God had forgotten Noah. It means that He was moved toward him, that His heart acted toward Noah in a way that demonstrated His grace. Noah had sinned and would sin again, but his soul longed to be holy in the midst of a decadent and godless culture. So God remembered him—He acted upon him in grace and saved him from destruction through flood and through the ark of salvation.

We have the hope of eternal life and the assurance that we will be with Him, but not because we have impressed Him with our holiness or wowed Him by our effort. On the contrary, that hope and assurance is a result of His undying love and remarkable grace. While we were yet sinners, He died for us. Though we were worthless and inept, He loved us. Though we were written off by the world and even possibly by ourselves, He remembered us and demonstrated His grace by revealing the depths of His heart at Calvary.

Day 3 | Creature Not Creator

January 3—*Read Genesis 9-12*

Babel should remind us that while humanity is incredibly endowed by God, capable of great feats and amazing exploits, we are still creatures—HE is Creator. Temporary progress may appear to tout human superiority but we must not be fooled—God will have the final say. Genesis 11:1-9

Humanity's potential was clearly seen at Babel as the people built an extravagant tower and lavish city that testified of the divinely endowed gifts, intellect, and creative genius of humanity, created in the image of God. This was no ordinary city or unimpressive tower. It heralded their great potential as the crowning jewel of God's creation. Still, no matter how great they had become, they were still the creation, not the Creator—man, not God.

In a world that has become so technologically savvy and intellectually advanced, it is easy for humanity to become blinded by their own pride and somehow oblivious to their utter dependency upon their Creator from whom they draw life and breath. This was the issue with Babel and this is the reality of our world today. We must not be fooled. Any advancement we make or achievement we gain is nothing less than an unmistakable witness to the fact that God empowers the weak, and without Him we can do nothing that is sustainable.

Day 4 | God is Unhindered by Our Doubts

January 4—Read Genesis 13-15

Often we doubt and limit the promises of God. Without a child, Abraham doubted that God could ever satisfy his longing—God showed him the stars, saying, "so shall your descendants be." Trust confidently in the God who does immeasurably more than you ask or think. Genesis 15:1-6

Though blessed with great material wealth, Abraham was painfully aware that the true longing of his heart and the divine promise—A SON— still eluded him. His longing, he was certain, would never be fully satisfied. His personal desires and overwhelming emotions placed a lid on the capability of God. Years later, he would find that limitations on the power of God exist only in the faithless hearts of humanity and never in the divine reality.

When it seems that the longing of our heart will never find us, it is easy to lose hope and begin to focus our attention on what we do not have. While our human vision looks elsewhere and our hope becomes withered, the promise and capabilities of God are often forgotten, and His power seems beyond our reach. In these moments, we must rehearse the promise of God and remind ourselves of His power. His abilities are not limited by our imagination and His reach is not hindered by our doubts. His blessing of Abraham transcended his fondest dreams, and His work in our lives will surpass our most passionate expectations!

Day 5 | Don't Limit God with Your Expectations

January 5—Read Genesis 16-17

Don't ever assume that God is finished working in your life or that His promise in you is both fulfilled and filled-full. Abraham thought Ishmael was the fulfilled promise but found God was able to do exceedingly abundantly above all he thought or asked. Genesis 17

Having a child at his age made no sense at all to Abraham, or Sarah for that matter. It was their assumption that Ishmael was their heir and that the promise of God was fulfilled in him. There was no further expectation that God would give them their own son or that any great miracle was to occur. Their hope was satisfied and their expectation was lowered to fit their reality. But God was not limited by their expectation.

Too often we settle for what we can do or what we can make happen instead of trusting God for that which exceeds our expectations and wildest dreams. He is not limited by what we can imagine and certainly not hemmed in by what we can make happen. He who spoke the world into existence and upholds creation by the power of His Word can do in and through us more than we can ever imagine.

Day 6 | A Sacred Calling

January 6—Read Genesis 18-20

When chosen by God to carry His promise and reveal His blessing one will also experience spiritual insight into His purposes. This gift carries with it the responsibility of bearing an intercessory burden for the lost and broken. Genesis 18:16-33

God richly blessed Abraham with a promise that through him and his Seed, all the world would be blessed. It was granted to him to be the father of all nations and from his offspring would emerge the Savior of the world. With that great promise came the grand privilege of being one in whom God would place great trust. God was willing to share with Abraham His divine purpose and counsel. He did that when He was preparing to bring judgment on Sodom and Gomorrah and wanted Abraham to know. That knowledge possessed by Abraham led him to passionately intercede for the people of the land that were about to be destroyed as a result of their sin.

Those who have been mercifully blessed with God's favor and calling must not rest in that calling and forget those to whom they have been called to serve. Knowing the holiness and love of God, as well as His judgment and wrath, should stir in those entrusted with both a divine call and discernment, a spirit of intercession for those with whom they labor and serve.

Day 7 | Resisting an Attitude of Entitlement

January 7—Read Genesis 21-23

Abraham, to whom was given unmatched influence and a great name, refused to take the property of Ephron, instead insisting on paying for Machpelah. Too often an attitude of entitlement among Christian leaders undermines the opportunity to influence people for Christ. Genesis 23

Few were as wealthy, prominent, and influential as Abraham in the ancient eastern Mesopotamian region. Where he traveled, there were always those who feared him and sought to appease his needs and accommodate his wishes. It would have been easy for Abraham to embrace and abuse that respect, and demand a catering to his needs and desires. Yet, he took great care to resist that attitude, and instead humbled himself among all people.

One of the great detriments to the cause of the Kingdom today is an entitlement attitude that grips and controls so many Christian leaders. When we feel we are too important to tend to the smaller tasks or stoop to the level of a tiny child, broken believer, or messed up sinner, we have betrayed our calling and done a disservice to the very cause to which we say we have devoted ourselves. Godly leaders will sacrifice themselves and their resources to shed the best light on the Kingdom they proclaim.

Day 8 | A Cup of Cold Water

January 8—Read Genesis 24-26

Rebekah had no idea that her simple act of kindness would bring such blessing, allow her to become the mother of Jacob, and place her in the lineage of Christ. Even a cup of cold water given in the name of Christ yields eternal reward. Genesis 24:10-21

Unbeknownst to Rebekah, when she went to the well to fill her jug with water for the day, Abraham's servant had asked Yahweh for a sign. The one who would give him water to drink would be the one chosen to be the bride for Isaac. Being Isaac's bride would lead to being Jacob's mother and the grandmother of Judah, from whose line the Messiah would come. A simple drink offered led to royalty and an act of kindness yielded divine favor.

Too often we count as nothing the simple things, the kind gestures, or the acts of service. Whatever our hands find to do should be done as unto the Lord and with all our might and passion. We never know when that act, kind word, or simple expression of compassion might lead to an unparalleled experience of divine favor or an outpouring of God's grace.

Day 9 | The Penalty of Playing God

January 9—Read Genesis 27

Trying to make happen what God has promised through our own wisdom or ingenuity will always lead to broken relationships, painful outcomes, and cumbersome burdens. We may still end up owning the promise but our influence is tainted and our lives forever scarred. Genesis 27

Rebecca knew from the promise of God that Jacob was to be the son of promise and the one to carry the blessing. There is no doubt that she had passed that word on to Jacob, and he had grown to expect a day when he would be the carrier of God's call. Together, however, they plotted to ensure that he would receive his father's blessing and worked craftily to make certain that nothing of that blessing was lost. The outcome was catastrophic and resulted in family division that would never be fully healed, a world that was forever changed, and years of pain and suffering for Jacob, who despite the blessing of God, spent his life wrestling and laboring for every moment of joy.

It is important for us to learn from the life of Jacob. Even when we know the plan that God has promised to us, we must be careful not to force that into existence. He will accomplish and make beautiful all things in His time. To play God and try to make His plan come to fruition more quickly is to invite disaster, pain, and hardship and to put the fullness of His promise at risk.

Day 10 | A God Who Stands Over Our Failures

January 10—Read Genesis 28-30

Jacob, though alone in the dark with nothing but a rock upon which to lay his head, and a mind racing with memories of past failures, found that God's presence stood over those failings, would never abandon him, and provided still a hopeful future. Genesis 28

Jacob's deception and lying had forced him to flee from home, fearing that the hatred of his brother, Esau, could lead to his death. Esau was determined to kill his brother, who had stolen from him his birthright and his father's blessing. Jacob's first night alone and on the run was life-changing. While trying to sleep with nothing more than a rock for a pillow, and tormented by the memories of his sin, Jacob encountered the presence of God. God had not come to kill him, condemn him, or threaten him. God revealed Himself to Jacob as the One who watched over him, would transform his failure into blessing, and would fulfill His promise in him.

Often we are overwhelmed with guilt and recurring memories of our failures. Rest eludes us and an uneasy sense of worthlessness dominates our thinking. We are certain that God cannot use us and we fear that soon all will know just how wretched we are. God stands over our failures and promises to redeem even our deepest disappointments. He has plans for us and promises to work those in us as we learn to walk with Him toward that promised future.

Day 11 | The God of All My Days

January 11—Read Genesis 31-35

When I wander from the place He called me, and distance myself from the revelation of His presence that I first encountered, there He watches and protects me, waiting for the day that I return. MY seasons change, YOU stay the same. You're the God of all my days! Genesis 31:13

The revelation that Jacob experienced at Bethel and the encounter he had with God's presence was life changing and stamped indelibly on his heart and memory. But for the wandering fugitive, his life had changed, his surrounding had been altered, and the pressures of life were much different. Times were different, but he was running again, this time not from his brother Esau, but his father-in-law, Laban. There God again showed up and reminded him of His promise and His unchanging character.

Our lives are often a rollercoaster of emotional and spiritual moments of delight and frustration. At times we find ourselves so low that the memory of God's promise can easily escape our minds and set us up for depression and hopelessness. Even in those moments and those places, His presence is there with us. He always seeks to remind us of His unchanging nature and His steady hand that leads us.

Day 12 | Disrupted Vision

January 12—Read Genesis 36-38

Joseph's dream was for dominion and rule, but his reality became slavery. How often we must endure the challenge and disruption to the vision God gives us before we experience its fulfillment. Genesis 37

When Joseph was only a teen, he experienced dreams promising that God would someday use him in a magnificent way and that he would exercise dominion over his family and others. Little did he know that the dominion promised would be to save for his father, Jacob, a posterity. But before that dream would be realized, instead of dominion, he would experience rejection, false accusation, and even prison. Only when he endured that would he experience the fulfillment of his dream.

So often we become frustrated and even disillusioned when the divine promise we believe to be ours does not materialize, or at least not in a timely fashion. It is not unusual at all for God to take us through the difficulties of trial and frustration before we experience the fulfillment of His promise. This calls for patience and trust as we await the realization of a vision that has experienced disruption.

Day 13 | Faithful at All Times

January 13—Read Genesis 39-40

The presence of the Lord was with Joseph and prospered him in Potiphar's house, and was also with him when falsely accused in prison. God showed Joseph His faithful love. God's presence, faithfulness, and love are never diminished by our present circumstances. Genesis 39

Despite the amazing and heartening dreams concerning his future, the life of Joseph certainly did not go according to his hoped-for script. Instead of a place of honor, Joseph found himself as a slave. As if that was not bad enough, false accusations left him in a cold and dingy prison, despised by his false accuser, forgotten by the outside world, and seemingly without hope. God, however, had not forgotten Joseph. He granted him favor while a slave and caused him to prosper when he was in chains. That dream, though delayed, would ultimately be realized.

Each of us has a plan, a dream, a script we think our life will follow. When that plan seems to be misplaced or has gone awry, it is easy to think we have been forgotten. Yet, the life of Joseph and indeed all of Scripture reminds us that God is faithful at all times, and even in the detours of life, His presence, love, and faithfulness can be experienced.

Day 14 | The Purpose of Our Pain

January 14—Read Genesis 41-43

When Joseph revealed his dreams to his brothers, there was no mention of God. After the pit, Potiphar's house, and the prison he testified that it was not him, but God, who could give an answer. Trials serve to humble us so that we can decrease while HE increases. Genesis 41:16

Joseph was seventeen when God first revealed to him, by way of two dreams, His plan for using him. That revelation, though a surprise, seemed to have created some level of arrogance, or at least misguided enthusiasm, in Joseph. As he shared his dreams with his family, he made no mention of God but only the place of exaltation he anticipated he would one day have over them. After two decades of hardship, that changed. When faced with a need to interpret dreams, he gave God all the glory and all the credit.

It often takes trial, chastening, and hardship to meld our character and shape our holiness. No one arrives at Christ-likeness without passing first through the fire. Don't despise the trials, shun the challenge, or resist the chastening. They are all working for your good and making you like Jesus.

Day 15 | Surrendering Our Pain

January 15—Read Genesis 44-46

Joseph refused to rehearse the sin of his brothers against him, but instead he saw the hand of God that would bring reconciliation with his brothers, preservation of his family, and the renewing of his father's hope. This is godly maturity—giving thanks in all things! Genesis 45:1-11

This text hails back to that great moment when Joseph was reunited with his brothers after years of separation. They had hated him, sold him into slavery, and concocted a bogus story, saying he had been tragically killed. His dreams, they thought, had been forever snuffed out. But God had other plans and preserved Joseph that he might ultimately save his family by feeding them in Egypt. Joseph could have remained bitter, treated his brothers with angry vengeance, and exacted justice. Instead, he forgave and saw God at work in his pain.

What pain and frustration are you feeling today? Who has hurt and mistreated you? How you handle that is up to you. You have a choice. You can nurse and rehearse it, or thank God for it and see what He might do with it and whose life might be blessed by your surrender.

Day 16 | Restored and Fruitful

January 16—Read Genesis 47-48

God is not only able to restore what we thought was lost, but to enable that which is restored to bear fruit! Then Jacob said to Joseph, "I never thought I would see your face again, but now God has let me see your children, too!" Genesis 48:11

When Jacob was presented the coat of many colors that he had given to Joseph, ripped and allegedly soaked with the blood of his son, he was sure that he had lost Joseph and would never again see him or embrace him. Later, when he learned that he was alive and was able to reunite with him, he was blessed to see not only Joseph but his grandsons who had been begotten by his beloved son. Not only had God restored what he feared was lost, but he was able to see the fruit of Joseph as well.

Often we feel as if our lives are wrecked and forever broken with failure and distress. But, we serve a God who is able to restore, and beyond that, cause fruit to emerge from our brokenness. Truly the ability of God transcends even our potential to hope and believe.

Day 17 | Pursuing the Promise

January 17—Read Genesis 49-50

Joseph was 17 when he was carried away into Egypt, and 110 when he died there. All his life was spent outside the promised land, yet he longed for it and labored so others might experience it. Even when the promise eludes us, it should be our passion and pursuit. Genesis 50:24-26

Joseph was the great-grandson of Abraham, to whom had been given the promise of Canaan. It was the family's promise: the inheritance of the patriarchs and their offspring. Yet, Joseph was carried away from his home and became a slave in Egypt. Except to bury his father, Joseph would not again see the land of promise. That reality, however, would not prevent Joseph from longing for the land of his fathers and sacrificing so that others might experience that blessing. Indeed, it was through the sacrifice and pain of Joseph that his family was preserved and ultimately enabled to return to their promised inheritance.

Often, we do not get to experience the promises of God as we would hope—but our loss does not negate His promise. To passionately pursue all of the promises of God, even if we do not experience them, is the life of faith to which we are called. As the writer of Hebrews reminded his readers, some died not having received the promise (Hebrews 11:39) but their reward was far greater and eternal. We must strive for the promises of God, and work, pray, and sacrifice so that others may receive those promises, even if our reward must wait until eternity.

Day 18 | Called Out of Comfort

January 18—Read Exodus 1-2

Though content and comfortable in Midian, Moses' people suffered deeply. God saw their pain and called Moses out of comfort to save them. We must not allow our contentment and comfort to deafen our ears to God. He hears the cry of the hurting and calls us to act. Exodus 2:23-25

After 40 years of comfort in the wilderness of Midian, 80-year-old Moses was ready to settle down and enjoy the final years of his life in quiet comfort. But his people were in great distress and cried out for a deliverer to free them from their imminent peril. While minding his own business and tending his sheep, God called Moses to leave his comfort and respond to His call to provide hope and deliverance to the Israelites. He argued—but ultimately relented and brought them out of Egyptian bondage.

God still sees the pain, brokenness, and bondage of those for whom He died. He also watches us settle into safe comfort, enjoying the security of our salvation while a lost world cries out for an answer. As with Moses, God calls us to denounce the comfortable contentment of our safe lives, forsake the pursuit of ease and selfishness, and respond to His call to bind up the broken hearted, declare hope to those languishing in darkness, and proclaim salvation and freedom to the lost.

Day 19 | The Call to Burn

January 19—*Read Exodus 3-6*

The burning bush that so intrigued Moses is a picture of God's call on him and all who would follow. We are called to be ablaze in the power of God's Spirit. We will be consumed by something, either the passions and lusts of this world or the beauty of His holiness. Exodus 3:1-6

Such an amazing sight Moses beheld as he routinely led his sheep through the Midian desert—a bush ablaze, yet not being consumed by the fire. As he approached the stunning sight, the Divine voice beckoned him to pause, remove his sandals, and listen. In the next few moments the trajectory of his life would forever be changed. The bush that burned brightly was a metaphor for what God expected from him. He was being called to burn with the passion of the Great I AM, stand before the great dictator of the world in that day, demand the release of the people of God, and then lead those same people to liberty.

We, too, have been called to burn ablaze with a message–a message of hope, freedom, and redemption. Today many are consumed by the burning flames of sensual lust, worldly passions, or earthly power. We are invited to draw near to God and hear His voice. We are invited to engage the presence of God and burn with the holy fire that sets our hearts ablaze and ignites our world for Jesus.

Day 20 | The Word Will Perform

January 20—Read Exodus 7-10

As Moses approached Pharaoh, he was equipped with the Word and power of God. But Pharaoh's heart was hardened and he refused to believe. The response of others to God's faithfulness does not reflect negatively on our faithfulness or on God's power. Exodus 7:10-13

I wonder what Moses was thinking as he climbed the steps to Pharaoh's palace, a space with which he was very familiar: being the home of his childhood. This time he went to speak to Pharaoh on behalf of Yahweh, the God of Israel. He was equipped with God's Word and God's power, but still the heart of Pharaoh was hardened. His magicians duplicated the miracles of Moses and Aaron, and he rejected the message of Moses asking him to let his people go. I am sure that the failed mission was a huge disappointment to Moses.

There are many times that the message we share is rejected, sometimes even by those we love. This is not because God is unfaithful or lacking power, nor does it mean that we have failed. In fact, it means that God's Word has accomplished its purpose. His Word either convicts and transforms, or it hardens a disobedient heart.

Day 21 | Substitute Required

January 21—Read Exodus 11-13

The children of Israel had survived nine plagues that God had poured out on Egypt, but they could not survive the last plague without a substitute. If there was no substitute, death would come, but if a bloody substitute was found, they would be free. Exodus 11:1-12:28

Over the course of several weeks, the people of Israel had stood by while the Egyptians were pummeled by the divine plagues intended to turn the heart of Pharaoh. Each time he dug his heels in deeper and refused to give in. Egypt was the unfortunate recipient of Pharaoh's stubbornness, but Israel was unharmed. The last plague, however, could not be survived unless a substitute's blood took their place before the angel of the Lord passed through. No one could escape this judgment unless something or someone took their place.

While God protects His own from His wrath, no man can stand before the righteous judgment of God. The Apostle Paul was clear that all humanity was equally guilty of sin and that the penalty for all was death. Death, that is, unless we embrace Jesus, the Lamb of God Who became our substitute so that we could be free, standing in the righteousness provided by His substitutionary death at Calvary.

Day 22 | Stand Still in Him

January 22—Read Exodus 14-15

When we find ourselves facing impenetrable barriers and unfavorable odds, panic can erode our faith in God's plan, causing our trust to crumble. Yet, He invites us to peace in the midst of the storm—calm in the face of chaos—to stand still and see Him work for us. Exodus 14:1-14

The dramatic exit from Egypt after four centuries of bondage was a time of great rejoicing for Israel, following their reluctant leader Moses. It was a time of great anticipation and anxious hopefulness as they made their way toward the land of promise. All hope was squashed when they looked behind and saw that Pharaoh had changed his mind. He was pursuing them from behind and the un-crossable Red Sea stood before them. Their fears fostered complaints and their relentless cries threatened the faith of Moses.

It was in this moment that God spoke. He invited Moses to stand still and trust Him. God would work for him and stop the enemy, silence the complaints, and still the struggle in his heart. What a magnificent hope we have in Jesus and what glorious promises we find in His Word. When the storms are great, the seas are fierce, and the enemy is in hot pursuit, we can stand on His Word and in His love and see Him work on our behalf!

Day 23 | Grateful for His Faithfulness

January 23—Read Exodus 16-19

The Manna miracle reveals God's faithfulness and humanity's fickleness. We may complain that His provision isn't good enough, hoard resources today while doubting His faithfulness tomorrow, take His provision for granted, or assume He no longer cares if provisions are scarce. Exodus 16

Israel chronically complained. Within two weeks of their deliverance out of Egypt and across the Red Sea, they began griping. Their complaints about God's provision quickly stirred the anger of God and the frustration of Moses. Still, God provided them with manna from Heaven every day of the week except the Sabbath, when they were to gather enough for two days. Even with that provision, they were still prone to critical complaining.

Besides revealing God's faithfulness, the manna exposed the weakness and fickleness of humanity. No matter how generous the provision of God, human flesh is never satisfied. No matter how powerfully God provides today, we wonder if He can do it again. God's ongoing faithfulness is often met with an ungrateful heart that takes Him for granted, and sadly, when difficult times arise, we often fail to remember just how faithful He has always been. Have you expressed your gratitude to Him today for His unmatched faithfulness?

Day 24 | A Simple Altar of Earth

January 24—Read Exodus 20-24

While God longs to fellowship with humanity, He wants us to know and be persuaded that access to such fellowship is not enriched, indeed only deterred, by our foolish attempts to impress or entice a God Who is both holy and like no other. Exodus 20:22-25

As part of the Law, delivered to Moses by God on Sinai and then transferred to the Israelites, God gave many instructions. None were more crucial than the ones that pertained to worship. Israel was to worship by means of a very plain, unimpressive altar of earth, unadorned by earthly jewels. Their sacrifices were to be made on the altar of earth so that their focus could be on the One they worshipped, not their approach to Him.

Much could be learned by the contemporary Church. It seems we have bought into the notion that we can enhance our communion with God though our methods, by our toys and tools, and with the aid of our gifts and abilities. Nothing could be further from the truth. God is not impressed. We must come to Him humbly, deny any thought of deserving to be with Him, and acknowledge that nothing we bring makes our access to Him better

Day 25 | The Place We Meet God

January 25—Read Exodus 25-27

As Israel journeyed though the wilderness, God met with them in the portable tabernacle, erected according to the pattern He gave to Moses. He could have set a temple in their midst, but chose rather to meet them in the place their offerings and service made happen. Exodus 25:2-7

The narrative of Israel's journey through the wilderness is fascinating. No detail of that journey is more telling than God's instructions regarding the building of the tabernacle. It would be the place that Israel would meet with God, where His glory would dwell among them, and where their worship would be manifest. This tabernacle did not suddenly appear supernaturally but was made through the freewill offerings and the physical labor of God's people working together.

There is a great and eternal truth that emerges from this wilderness tabernacle. So often God's people expect that true worship and powerful encounters with Christ can only be experienced in the mystical, the realm of the emotional, or in the super-spiritual and often humanly constructed worship experience. If the truth is told, God's glory and presence are most tangible and most easily encountered in our generous giving and faithful service.

Day 26 | At Calvary We Meet Him

January 26—Read Exodus 28-30

"I will meet you there." Sweet words from a holy God to His own. Inside the veil, a cloud of perfumed incense filling the air, at the mercy seat, "I will meet you there." To us He says, "at the foot of Calvary in the sweetness of your worship— I will meet you there." Exodus 30:6

God gave Moses marvelous instructions to prepare the tabernacle so that the people could draw near and worship. It was behind the veil leading into the Holiest place where the most intimate and sweet fellowship would occur. The incense that would burn continually just outside the veil formed a cloud that covered the High Priest as he entered, and hovered over the Mercy Seat where the blood for the people's atonement would be placed. Here God declared, "I will meet you there."

This powerful statement is a glorious picture of the cross, where the justice of God that necessitated divine judgment and mercy that revealed His eternal love for humanity kissed. There, at the cross, our sin was judged in Christ and forgiven by God, thus allowing us to draw near to His holy presence and gaze upon His beauty. Without the cross we would still be shut out, but at the cross we hear His amazing announcement, "I will meet you there!"

Day 27 | These Three Things

January 27—Read Exodus 31-34

Facing an uncertain future, Moses had three requests from God. "Show me Your ways!" "Lead me with Your presence." "Show me Your glory!" His ways are found in His Word, His presence is known in prayer, and His glory is experienced in worship. Exodus 33:12-23

The people had rebelled against both Moses and God, and God was ready to rid Himself of the Israelites and start all over again. The future for Moses and his people was uncertain. What would tomorrow look like, and would they ever enter into the land of promise? These were the concerns the great leader of Israel faced when he cried out to God. There were just three things he asked of God: he wanted to know the ways of God, be led by the presence of God, and experience the glory of God. These would give him what he needed to face life's uncertainty.

More than 3,000 years later, we still need the same three things. When life seems uncertain and the way before us appears to be unsteady, we long for what Moses desired. His ways can be known as we immerse ourselves in His Word, His presence will guide us as we seek Him in prayer, and His glory will be revealed if we will pause and worship Him.

Day 28 | The Priority of His Honor

January 28—Read Exodus 35-36

The chief aim of God is His own honor and glory, for when He is glorified, His presence becomes the pursuit of humanity and hope abounds. Since this is the divine priority, God calls, equips, and empowers those who are committed to His honor and revealing hope in Him. Exodus 36:1

The building of the tabernacle in the wilderness was the divine priority once Israel left Egypt. This was the case because with the tabernacle, His glorious presence would be experienced, His name worshipped, and His honor declared among the people. Because this was God's highest aim, He anointed Bezalel and Oholiab and every craftsman who was charged with the erecting of the tabernacle. God saw to it that His purpose would be accomplished so that His glory could be revealed.

The Church that is committed to the work of God and the divine priority of His honor and majesty will have no ongoing difficulty finding laborers to carry out that purpose. It is too important to God to be left unfinished, or for the ranks of Kingdom workers to be left unfilled. When hearts obediently desire to be used of God to ensure His glory and the worship of His name, supernatural calling and equipping will unfold. God knows that when His name is honored the lost will be found and the broken will be healed—so His honor will always be guarded.

Day 29 | Carriers of His Presence

January 29—Read Exodus 37-40

God's glory filled the tabernacle erected by Moses, per God's plan. But, when God said to move, the Israelites carried the symbol of God's presence on their backs through the wilderness. As God leads us through our wilderness, we must be carriers of His presence. Exodus 40:34-38.

Moses carefully observed the specific plans God gave him in erecting the tabernacle that would stand in the center of Israel's camp. When his work was complete, the shekinah glory filled the tabernacle and rested there. Times would come, however, that the cloud would move and the mobile Tent of Meeting would be dismantled and carried through the wilderness until Moses was told to stop.

We love the times when God's presence descends upon us and we can bask in His glory, feeling as if we never want to move away from that moment. Like Peter on the mountain, we want to just stay and drink in the sweetness of His presence. But that is not the plan of God. He calls us to move on, to journey forward, to proceed to the place and destiny to which we have been called. We do not leave His presence behind in those seasons, but instead, we are called to carry it.

Day 30 | The Unintentional Sins and the Cross

January 30—Read Leviticus 1-4

Unintentional sin is the focus of the "sin offering." Unintended sin which emerges from a heart not fully consecrated, attracted and attached to the world, and committed to self-preservation. Sin cannot be overlooked—it must break our hearts and stir in us a longing to be cleansed. Leviticus 4:2

This chapter of the Torah outlines the ritual to be used in preparing a sin offering, a sacrifice that was to be used exclusively for those sins committed unintentionally. Other means were used for other types of sins, but there was a unique manner in which the sacrifice for the unintentional sins was to be handled. In fact, it would be these sins that would become the most common that the priest would have to mitigate.

It is easy to become lazy in our spiritual walk and deny ourselves the "big and obvious" sins that are universally accepted as the breaking of God's law. But what about those sins that emerge from a heart that has still not reckoned with the sinful nature that continues to lurk? What about the sinful pride that rears its ugly head when someone else is noticed for their accomplishment and we are overlooked? What about the selfishness that plagues our decision-making and leads us to reject opportunities to serve because it demands too much from us? These unintentional yet frequent sins of the heart need the work of the cross applied and the root of self ripped out, and sometimes that work comes at a great cost and painful sacrifice.

Day 31 | The Fire That Must Be Kept Burning

January 31—Read Leviticus 5-7

The fire of God came forth FROM His presence and consumed the sacrifice (Leviticus 9:24). It was to never be extinguished so as to remind God's people of their need for Him and His ever-abiding presence. The evidential fire of God's presence must never be lost. Leviticus 6:12-14

One of the essential elements of old covenant worship was that the fire on the altar used for the burnt offerings was never to be extinguished. It was to be kept burning as a reminder of two things: one, that the people of God were forever and always dependent upon Him, and two, that His presence would abide with them forever.

The fire is most often representative of the presence of the Holy Spirit. This text calls us to faithfully maintain our personal relationship with the Holy Spirit—to let not even a single day pass without making sure that relationship is kept fresh and renewed. We need the Spirit's power, His abiding presence within us, and the glowing light of His person exuding from us to a world looking for hope. We must never let that fire be extinguished.

Day 32 | Anointed as Priests

February 1—Read Leviticus 8-10

This strange ceremony was blood-laden—an Old Testament picture reminding us that we are of no value without Christ's blood. Blood dabbed on the ear lobe, signifying the need for anointed hearing of God's Word, on the thumb—holy service, and on the toe—an upright walk. Leviticus 8:22-23

Many of the rituals of the law seem odd to modern ears and rightly so. It is hard to place ourselves in the ancient context and understand the full intent of the sacrifices, offerings, and priestly action. This text in Leviticus chapter eight is certainly no exception. What we do know is that the ritual was bloody and that this ordination of Aaron and his sons as priests by Moses was a sacred act that unveiled powerful implications. The ear lobe, right thumb, and right toe of each one being ordained as priest was anointed by the blood to signify that their hearing, their service, and their walk was to be holy.

We no longer set apart people for Christian service in such morbid ways, but the apostle Peter did tell us in his letter that as believers who have been washed in the blood of Christ, we are all to be priests in the Kingdom of God: that is, we are to tell others of Christ and bring them to Him (1Peter 2:9). As a priesthood of believers we must invite the Holy Spirit to anoint our ears to hear and obey His Word, our hands so that we may serve in genuine love and kindness, and our feet that we may walk in His ways and in His Spirit.

Day 33 | The Work of Our Heavenly High Priest

February 2—Read Leviticus 11-13

Israelites who might have leprosy were to go to the priest to be inspected. It was a disease that could spread, destroy them, and bring harm to the camp of Israel. Destructive sins and attitudes of the heart must be brought to Jesus to rigorously inspect and cleanse. Leviticus 13:9

Leprosy was lethal and would not only destroy the one infected, but also had potential to spread through the camp of Israel and bring devastating results. When one thought they might have the disease, they were to go immediately to the priest to be carefully inspected to determine a course of action. If infected, they would be quarantined so they could not bring harm to others. Inspection and cleansing were both crucial aspects of the Israelite community so that they could be spared the rapid spread of destructive death.

We must recognize that attitudes of the heart: bitterness, envy, and unforgiveness—can also spread throughout the people of God and bring spiritual devastation. God intends for His people to experience joy and peace. When we have these improper attitudes, we must surrender them to our Great High Priest who will with the light of His Word deeply inspect us and by His blood cleanse us from them.

Day 34 | Our Sins Laid On Jesus

February 3—Read Leviticus 14-16

As Moses laid his hands on the goat, confessing the people's sins, so the "Lord laid on (Jesus) the iniquity of us all" (Isaiah 53:6). No reminder by Satan of our sin can hinder us from drawing near—Jesus bore our sins and removed them as far as east is from the west. Leviticus 16:20-22

The Day of Atonement was a day full of excitement and heightened expectation. The high priest would slaughter a goat, place its blood on the Mercy Seat inside the Holy of Holies, and then move to the scapegoat. As he announced the sins of the people with hands on the head of the goat, the goat would symbolically take their sins, and be led into the wilderness where it would remain forever. Their sins would be forgotten—at least until the next year.

At Calvary, Jesus became both the slaughtered goat and scapegoat for us as well as the high priest that carried His blood into the heavenly throne room where he placed it on the Mercy Seat as a testimony before the Father that our sins were covered. There, the Lord laid on Jesus, not a goat, the "iniquity of us all," and then Jesus carried those sins away so that as far as east is from west, our transgressions have been removed. We need not remind ourselves of those sins, nor succumb to the enemy who would love to bring them up. We can come boldly into His presence and worship God with clean hands and a pure heart.

Day 35 | Exclusive Devotion

February 4—*Read Leviticus 17-18*

Under no circumstance was an Israelite to bring an offering or sacrifice to anyone but to the Lord. To a Church cozied up to the world, daily sacrificing what belongs to God at the altar of pleasure, entertainment, and status—this message must again be made clear. Leviticus 17:1-9

The instructions of the Torah that God gave to Moses to pass on to the people of Israel were filled with strong admonition to ensure that God's holiness and demands on His people were maintained. They were to have no other gods, and were to surrender their loyalty and their devotion to no other. The pagans that they would find in Canaan would sacrifice to many gods, and Yahweh wanted them to know, in no uncertain terms, that He alone was worthy of their sacrifice and surrender.

The truth of the matter is that this kind of holy devotion is greatly lacking in the Church today. It seems that God is only one item on a priority list that includes those things we give our time to and that which bring us pleasure. Christians are far too ready to sacrifice to others, activities, and pleasure, the kind of time, devotion, and resources that only God deserves.

Day 36 | The Divine Principle of Generosity

February 5—Read Leviticus 19-22

The core of Christian generosity is love for God and neighbor. Knowing that many are physically and spiritually impoverished and that God is able to meet every need and plant more seed so it can multiply—we give to Him cheerfully and generously. Leviticus 19:9-10

God gave Israel some unusual instructions while they were in the wilderness, laws that they were to put into practice once inside the Promised Land. One of those edicts had to do with the way they gleaned or harvested their fields. He specifically told them not to harvest the edges of their fields or pick up grain that was dropped by the harvesters. The same was true for the grapes. If a bunch of grapes was dropped, they were to be left for the poor or disenfranchised. Ruth was later a beneficiary of this law.

The law God set in place was designed as a way for God's people to give to the poor. They were to trust God to meet their needs even though they intentionally left a crop to be given to others. This was not just a Jewish principle but a divine principle. As the people of God learn to give some of what God has given to them back to Him and then to others, He promises to provide them with more seed to plant and to meet their every need.

Day 37 | Anxiously Awaiting the Eighth Day

February 6—Read Leviticus 23-25

The "Feast of Booths"—Israel would dwell in crudely made booths for seven days, as a reminder of their temporary status as slaves and sojourners. On the eighth day they would emerge to celebrate their new freedom. We will one day shed our temporary tabernacles as well. Leviticus 23:33-44

Israel kept many feasts that were fulfilled in Christ, and speaks to the privileges of the New Covenant. The Feast of Booths (Tabernacles) saw the Israelite nation dwelling for a week in crude, temporary structures that served to remind them that they had once been slaves and later sojourners in the wilderness, seeking a country of their own. On the eighth day, they would emerge to enjoy and celebrate their new freedom and status as the people of God. This feast pointed to both their previous condition and their new position as God's people.

We still live in temporary structures, dwelling in earthly tabernacles that will one day be destroyed. They remind us that we are not our own and that we were bought with a price. They also serve to stir in us hearts of gratitude for the salvation we have known in Christ. We await patiently the eighth day when we will burst forth from these temporary and often tattered earthly tabernacles, and don the new and glorified bodies fashioned in the likeness of Christ, who will come to gather us and bring us back to Him.

Day 38 | The Requirements of God's Blessing

February 7—Read Leviticus 26-27

To assume that grace living means living as we want, despising and rejecting God's Word and still enjoying His blessing, is a foolish assumption of epic proportion. God told Israel, IF you walk in my statues, observe and do them, then you will be blessed. Leviticus 26:3-4

God loved His people and had gone to great lengths to redeem them, but the love and grace He had bestowed on them was not a license to live oblivious to His commands. Their history had been one of short term obedience followed by a slow but significant drift in disobedience that always led to spiritual backsliding. Now that He had brought them out of Egypt, He reminded them that their blessing was intricately tied to their obedience. They could not continue to disobey and expect to live blessed. That has not changed.

As we live under the grace of God, some foolishly assume that our lives, actions, and behaviors have little or nothing to do with our blessing. This is simply not true. We are still, though God's New Covenant people, expected to walk in obedience to His Word. We are to walk (that is live daily) in His commandments, observe (that is meditate upon) them, and do (obey) them. This is the necessary key to lives of blessing.

Day 39 | No Longer an Outsider

February 8—Read Numbers 1-3

It was the responsibility of Aaron and his sons to tend to the presence of God—any outsider that drew near would be put to death. At Calvary, Jesus became sin—the ultimate outsider, and was put to death that through His death we, formerly outsiders, might draw near. Numbers 3:10

The presence of God in the Old Testament was guarded heavily by the family of Aaron, the priestly people. To come near to the place where the Divine presence dwelt, without first being cleansed, was to ensure great peril to the trespasser and invite judgment for the community of God's people. Any outsider was forbidden to come near the Tent of Meeting and if they dared try, they were to be put to death.

Jesus, for the sake of all of humanity, became an outsider for us. He bore the sin of us all and endured the wrath of God and the complete abandonment of His Father. This he did so that through His sacrifice, shame, and ultimate rejection, He could provide a way that we, though previously strangers and foreigners, might draw near to the Holy presence of God.

Day 40 | The Blessing

February 9—*Read Numbers 4-6*

As Aaron spoke over God's people the priestly blessing that promised the richness of God's abiding presence, favor, protection, and peace, so One greater than Aaron has by His own Word, given us all we need and marked us forever by His name. Numbers 6:22-27

The words that Aaron was instructed to speak over the people of Israel in the form of the priestly blessing, or what we often call the "priestly benediction," dripped with powerful significance as the covenant name Yahweh was invoked over the recipient. To be blessed with the favor of Yahweh's countenance was something that every Jew longed for and sought after. This benediction was a crucial covenant contribution to the life and worship of the chosen people of God.

We now have a greater and perfect High Priest, not after the Levitical order, but like unto Melchizedek, and this One is the Son of God. As we place our faith in Him we step INTO Him and bear His name, and as we receive His Word into our lives, we experience His blessing. Our lives should be marked by that blessing and bear the profound character of His holy name and righteous life.

Day 41 | Our Very Best

February 10—Read Numbers 7-8

When the tabernacle was complete, the people brought offerings—offerings of great wealth, deep sacrifice and passionate generosity. No one seemed reluctant, and it was clear that though offerings differed in value, each represented the best the worshipper could bring. Numbers 7

The celebration that followed the completion of the tabernacle included a parade of offerings brought by each tribe to furnish the services of the tabernacle. Each worshipper was represented by their tribal leader who brought an offering. The offerings were not all the same but each represented the best they could bring. No one gave reluctantly, and no one cut corners. It was an honor to give, and they all brought their very best. Short-cutting the sacrifice could lead to serious consequences.

This is how God calls us to give. We will not all give the same amount, but we can all share the same passion, be marked by biblical generosity, and make sure that the gift we bring is our very best. Our best may not be measured by dollars and cents, but is instead measured by the attitude with which we give. Our gifts are to be in response to God's generosity and when given with an expression of joy and gratitude for His goodness, we will receive the smile of His provision. We can generously give our very best when we know the God to whom we give, and we trust His character. When we give generously and hold back nothing, He will reward.

Day 42 | The Danger of Ingratitude

February 11—Read Numbers 9-12

There may be nothing more repulsive than ingratitude. Redeemed from slavery, led by the divine presence, and miraculously provided for, still the Israelites longed for a revised past of demeaning bondage. In everything give thanks and be grateful for your daily bread. Numbers 11:4-6

As happened too frequently, the people of Israel complained in the wilderness as they longed for food better than the manna that God was faithful to provide. Their ungrateful hearts desired to have the luxuries of Egypt, the food that they remembered as "costing them nothing." While the price for their food was free, they had already forgotten that they had lived their lives as slaves of a brutal dictator. The food of Egypt came with a great price tag indeed, for in their ingratitude, they longed for a revised version of their bondage.

Many Christians today do the same. They have become bored with the bread of life found in the Word and have allowed their once grateful hearts to become corrupted by the culture that tells them they should have the things of the world. When we abandon the spirit of gratitude, we can become like the Israelites and long for the things of the world. Not only is this an ungodly response to the great grace of God, it is one that comes with the grave danger of being again enslaved by the world from which we were rescued.

Day 43 | Never Shrink Back

February 12—Read Numbers 13-16

When the people of God allow fear to trump faith, prefer comfort over struggle, and listen to critical naysayers instead of God's Word, they tragically forfeit their spiritual inheritance and sadly slow the advance of the Kingdom work to which they were called. Numbers 13-14

These two chapters mark the critical and tragic turning point for Israel. Concerned that the promised land of Canaan might not be as easily attainable as Moses had led them to believe, the people chose to send spies who would provide much desired perspective for their venture, one that God intended to be of faith. When the report of the spies revealed the formidable enemy that awaited them, they allowed fear to grip them and chose to disobey God rather than follow on by faith. That fateful decision led to their tragic death in the wilderness and the squandering of God's rich promise.

Many today repeat the ancient mistake of Israel in the wilderness. Rather than taking God at His Word and proceeding by faith, they shrink in fear and forfeit the inheritance promised them by God. Far too many Christians and, sadly, many churches have allowed the destructive influence of the faithless naysayer to lead to their devastating loss. God has called us to take Him at His Word and refuse to shrink from the grand promise He offers.

Day 44 | Fruit that Establishes Leadership

February 13—Read Numbers 17-19

Aaron had been faithful to what God had called him to do—not perfect—but faithful. When his staff was placed before God's presence, it blossomed and bore fruit. When we live our lives faithfully before Him, staying connected to the vine, we too will bear much fruit. Numbers 17

Many in the camp of Israel despised the leadership of Moses and Aaron and felt like the priestly role and leadership authority should be spread out. To seed all the authority to Aaron was something against which many of the people rebelled. God, however, would not allow their rebellion to stand. He ordered the rods of each tribe to be marked and placed inside the tabernacle of God's presence, and the one that budded would be the one to whom authority would be given. It was Aaron's rod that budded, and it was God's Word that prevailed.

God will establish the life and ministry of His chosen leaders by ensuring that their lives bear fruit. The key to fruit-bearing is to remain, like Aaron's rod, close to the presence of God. This was the truth that Jesus was getting at in John 15 when He taught that we must abide in the vine (Jesus) to bear fruit, and if we do abide in Him, we will bear much fruit—fruit that remains and that establishes us as chosen and appointed leaders.

Day 45 | Responses of Holiness

February 14—Read Numbers 20-22

When memories of past conflict and frustrations of present strife shape our actions instead of God's holiness an angry response may lead us to forfeit God's best (1-13). When we trust God and deal kindly with an enemy, even if they resist, God makes a way (14-21). Numbers 20:1-21

Two important and unrelated events are found in this brief section of Scripture, each highlighting heart attitudes that affect the outcomes of life and the trajectory of the spiritual journey for Moses and Israel. First, when frustrated by the people's continual failure to trust God and obey, Moses, in a moment of anger, struck the rock twice instead of speaking to it as he was instructed to do. Next, when the people of Edom refused to grant safe passage to the Israelites, instead of mounting a military offensive, they kindly submitted, and in so doing, God made a way for them.

Two great lessons stand out. We must guard against the tendency to allow the stress of life or frustration with the rebellious actions of others drive us to foolish expression. If we allow it to cause us to sin, we can miss God's best for us. Likewise, if we deal kindly with our adversaries and refuse to lash out, God will bless us and give us opportunities we would have never expected.

Day 46 | The Enemy Cannot Curse Us

February 15—Read Numbers 23-25

Scripture is clear about what brings the blessing of God—abstaining from ungodly associations and delighting in the Word (Psalm 1), trusting in the Lord (Jeremiah 1:17), and fearing God (Psalm 112). Those whom God has blessed; the enemy may not curse. Number 23:8

Balaam had been hired by the Moabite king, Balak, to prophetically curse the nation of Israel. His hope was that they would be weakened and become easy prey for him and his military forces. Though Balaam had repeatedly refused, the bribe money became greater, and finally he caved to the temptation the bribe afforded. But when he tried to curse Israel, God would not allow the words to come from his lips. Instead, he spoke words of prophetic blessing over the people of God. His conclusion? No enemy can curse what God has blessed.

This Old Testament story provides us great hope and encouragement as we wrestle with the enemy of our souls who wants to curse us and render us incapable of hopeful victory and spiritual fruitfulness. God's Word provides us many assurances and means by which we can secure His blessing. When we do that through His Word, developing trust and learning to fear Him, our lives become fortified against the fiery darts of the enemy that seek to destroy us.

Day 47 | A Heart That Will Not Be Bitter

February 16—Read Numbers 26-29

Instead of being occupied by his own regrets, Moses thinks only of the people he was called to lead—if they were well cared for, he was content. If the work was done, who got credit made no difference. This selflessness should be the aim of all who lead. Number 27:15-17

After Moses struck the rock twice in anger and disobedience, he disqualified himself from entering Canaan. He would have to be content with looking into the land of promise from the mountaintop and entering later at the Transfiguration. Instead of becoming bitter over his loss and dwelling on his past failure, he pleaded with God to find a leader that could do what he could not do—bring the people he loved and cared for into their promise. His selflessness shined, and his pastoral heart was honored by the Lord by choosing Joshua.

How easy it is for us to live in our regrets and allow them to make us bitter. When we do that we cut ourselves off from ministry and from interceding for those around us. If we are not careful, we can despise the blessing of others because we have disqualified ourselves from blessing because of our failure. But a heart after God refuses to be self-centered and instead of wishing the same fate for others, it longs to see others succeed and soar.

Day 48 | The Worth of God's Promises

February 17—Read Numbers 30-32

Possessing information about the promises and provisions of God without appreciating their worth will lead to regrettable choices, spiritual apathy, and ultimately a forfeiture of God's greatest blessings. Numbers 32:1-5

As Israel moved into Canaan and began settling the land God had promised to them, the tribes of Gad and Reuben sought exemption from the settlement. Both tribes, rich in livestock, saw the land of Gilead east of the Jordan and asked Moses if they could settle there instead of taking land by conquest. Though allowed to settle there, they first had to allow the other tribes to settle and ultimately, they never entered the land God had promised.

The experience of the tribes of Gad and Reuben provides us with a somber reminder. Like the other ten tribes, they knew that God had promised them Canaan and wanted them to inhabit the land. But their knowledge alone of God's promises was sadly no guarantee that they would inhabit this land. Instead, they devalued God's provision and never enjoyed all He intended. We must guard carefully against the tendency to treat carelessly or lightly God's promises and provision and, in doing so, miss out on His plan.

Day 49 | No Shortcut to Holiness

February 18—Read Numbers 33-36

As they entered Canaan Israel was to thoroughly drive out the inhabitants, destroy their images that demanded their spiritual attention, and completely demolish their high places where other gods were worshipped. There is no short cut or compromise to holiness. Numbers 33:50-56

The divine instructions were clear for Israel. No stone was to be left unturned as they were commanded to drive out the Canaanite inhabitants and methodically rid the land of anything that might vie for the spiritual attention of the people. People, images, and high places were all to be destroyed so that they could become a nation, wholly surrendered to the One True God who had rescued and redeemed them.

The price Jesus paid for our redemption is worthy of our full devotion and deepest spiritual attention. Too often we seem to compromise and take shortcuts in our spiritual journey, and it always leaves us short of being who God has called us to be. We are to take seriously the instructions God gave to the Israelites and do the same. Anything that seeks to take our attention or any possession, activity, or relationship that looks to replace God must be brought to an end. Our minds must be renewed as we give ourselves wholly to Him.

Day 50 | Obeying the Father Who Leads Us

February 19—Read Deuteronomy 1-3

They were carried like a father carries his own, by a God who fought for them, went before them, prepared and lit their path, and still, Israel did not believe. GREAT was their loss. We must not fail to trust and obey the God who for us has done the same. Deuteronomy 1:30-33

As Moses stood on the mountain and addressed the children of Israel before they entered Canaan, he rehearsed the faithfulness of God to them as they came out of Egypt and began to sojourn in the wilderness. He used the metaphor of a Father carrying his young and helpless son, providing safe passage past the wilderness threats, and carried to safety. Sadly, even after all of that, the people of God failed to trust God and rebelled against Him. Such a tragedy that Moses disclosed to them on that day—the sad picture of a people who failed to trust their good Father.

We must not allow this to be our testimony. Our good Father has rescued us from the kingdom of darkness and translated us into the Kingdom of the Son He loves. He has given us safe passage, delivers us from every enemy, provides a way of escape through every temptation, and promises to one day present us faultless before His glorious throne. We must bow humbly before Him and give Him our deepest trust and fullest surrender.

Day 51 | Priority of God's Presence

February 20—Read Deuteronomy 4-7

Though we possess remarkable access to God and have been given the Word of God and His Spirit to lead us, if we fail to keep ourselves near to Him, neglect rehearsing His goodness, and abandon the transmission of faith to our children, it is all for naught. Deuteronomy 4:7-10

As Moses called the children of Israel together for the last time before he was separated from them and they entered Canaan, he reminded them of the goodness of God. He told them how blessed they were, far above all other nations, and encouraged them to draw on the resources of the Law to guide their steps. His words were embedded, as well, in a serious warning, calling them to stay near to God, rehearse often God's faithfulness, and make the transmission of their faith to the next generation their highest aim.

These words speak powerfully to us. The access we have to God in the new covenant is beyond comparison. Because of the work of Christ at Calvary, the way to the Father's presence is wide open, and we have the provision of His Word and the power of His Spirit. Even with all of these benefits, failure to appropriate them is far too common. It must be our deepest desire to stay near to Him always, immerse ourselves in the rehearsing of His grand story, and pass on to our children the priority of His presence.

Day 52 | Beware of the Blessing

February 21—Deuteronomy 8-10

There may be no more dangerous state for the people of God than to be experiencing His rich blessings, for it is then that we are tempted to forget the source of those blessings, choose pleasure over devotion, and abandon our God-dependency. Deuteronomy 8:11-12

As Israel prepared to enter Canaan, Moses gave bold instructions as to how they were to conduct themselves once inside the land of promise. These directives recorded in Deuteronomy were words of life and death, guidance that would determine their fate inside Canaan. If they would diligently acknowledge and honor God as the source of their blessing and prosperity, they would enjoy long life, settled peace, and even more prosperity. If they forgot the God who had blessed them, they could not escape the sorest judgment.

The warning Moses provided God's people should be carefully heeded today by those who say they are Christ-followers. When we live our lives thankfully with Him always in mind, we experience ongoing blessing and divine favor. When, however, we forget the God who has blessed us and begin doing our own thing—struggle, loss, and divine discipline await us. We must determine to never forget the giver of our gifts and never cease to depend upon Him solely for all that we have and all that we do.

Day 53 | Embracing His Law

February 22—Read Deuteronomy 11-14

One cannot read and reflect honestly upon Moses' words without sensing a profound and swelling confidence that a life immersed in God's Word, committed to doing what the Word says, and passionate about transmitting it to the next generation will be a truly blessed life. Deuteronomy 11:18-25

The final words of Moses to the children of Israel on the mountain before he left them and they moved on into Canaan, came with a powerful emphasis on the Law of the Lord. This theme is woven through the entirety of his last will and testament recorded in Deuteronomy, but no place was it more powerfully articulated than here. Moses speaks with great boldness and calls the people to immerse themselves in the Law of the Lord, and if they do, they will know and experience the fullness of God's richest blessing.

As we read these words, we too are struck with the profound sense of the ability of God's Word to strengthen, embolden, and secure His people, and how surrendering to that Word ensures the greatest and sweetest of God's blessing. As we commit ourselves to the commandments of God's Word and to a deepening obedience and greater understanding, His promises become clear and His blessing sweeter.

Day 54 | Never Forget

February 23—Read Deuteronomy 15-17

Israel was instructed to keep the Passover so that they might remember God's work. As people who are prone to wander, easily influenced by the world, and quick to forget what God has done, we should intentionally remind ourselves of His grace that redeemed us. Deuteronomy 16:1

The celebration of the Passover was a uniquely significant event for every Israelite. Hurried life would slow, and great intentionality was given to prepare for this memorial feast. The meal itself was reflective to capture the depth of meaning for each aspect of the events they celebrated. At the heart of the celebrative feast was the call to remember and reflect upon God's miraculous work of redemption. He brought His people out of bondage and into the land of promise via a miracle, marked by great bloodshed in Egypt as God passed over the homes of all who had the blood on their doorpost. The blood was their salvation.

This kind of reflective memory is sadly missing from most of the Church today. We do not live our lives often in the shadow of the cross, but rather in our busy-ness we pass by and seemingly forget all that God has done on our behalf. God calls us to remember, to ponder His great love, to embrace the truth of redemption, and to live lives of deep gratitude for the shed blood of Jesus and the redemption it has provided.

Day 55 | High Priest and Victor

February 24—Read Deuteronomy 18-20

Before battle, Israel would be reminded by the priest that the battle belonged to the Lord, and they would be encouraged. Our Great High Priest, who defeated the last enemy, death, and has passed through the heavens, reminds us that the battle was His and HE WON. Deuteronomy 20:1-4

Moses delivered directions to Israel about how to approach their enemy in battle as they entered the land of promise. Even if they seemed to be greatly outnumbered or apparently overpowered, the priest was to gather the people and assure them that God had given them this land, that He would be with them in battle, and that He would see to it that they overcame. Fear was unnecessary!

We have a priest far greater than the Aaronic priesthood. No matter what we face or no matter how overwhelming the enemy before us may appear, Jesus stands before us to lead us into victory. He is our Great High Priest, and He has descended into Hell, taken from Satan the keys to death, Hell, and the grave, defeated death which is the last enemy, and then passed through the Heavens and entered the heavenly throne room, where He now sits at the Father's right hand. There He intercedes for us, there He dispenses all the hosts of Heaven on our behalf, and there He reigns as the righteous Victor over every enemy.

Day 56 | Being a Holy Neighbor

February 25—Read Deuteronomy 21-23

The second of two great commandments Jesus affirmed: "You shall love your neighbor as yourself." Loving your neighbor is to bear their burden when they struggle like you. It is to ensure that no one struggles alone. It is to live, yes indeed, love like Jesus. Deuteronomy 22:1-4

As Moses recapitulates the law to the people of Israel before his death, he turns his attention to how they are to care for one another. In this 22nd chapter of Deuteronomy, he underscores the need to look out for one's neighbor in the practical ways—if you see your neighbor's livestock wander away, return it to them, or if it is collapsed along the way, help your neighbor get it back on its feet. These commands are old covenant examples of what Jesus said was the second of the two great commandments: "love your neighbor as yourself."

Loving our neighbor as Jesus commanded is not a mere tolerance of their behavior or giving lip service to that which requires action. It is to intentionally lean into the life of another, to find those who are alone and share with them the burden they bear, and to help them shoulder their load and navigate the struggles. Our neighbor, when truly understood, is not a matter of locale—it is all those whom God places in our path and all those who need and long for an advocate. This is the call of Christian holiness.

Day 57 | The Virtue of Integrity

February 26—Read Deuteronomy 24-26

Godless culture is comfortable with dishonesty, expecting leaders to lie. The terms "fake news," "alternative truths," and "fact checking" all point to this reality. But HE who IS TRUTH deals harshly with lying and demands His own to be people of integrity. Deuteronomy 25:13-16

Among the laws that God gave to the Israelites were instructions describing the scales to be used by merchants as they weighed both items for buying and selling and precious metals used to pay for those items. Unjust merchants would carry unbalanced scales so they could cheat their customers. This was forbidden by the Torah, because a life of righteous integrity was demanded of those who gave their allegiance to Yahweh.

It is a sad reality that our culture has become increasingly comfortable with dishonesty, even among our leaders. Even more disturbing is that many Christians have no issue with lies of convenience or situational godliness: that when truth is convenient, we can be honest, but when it might bring consequences that are unfavorable, integrity is less important. This cannot be the position of the child of God. The One we serve is Himself truth, and He calls us to be people of truth. To become comfortable with dishonesty is to put at risk our witness, turn people away from the cause of Christ, and risk eternal judgment.

Day 58 | Our Responsibility to the Spiritually Blind

February 27—Read Deuteronomy 27-28

Among the curses Israel was called to consider was one which came to any who caused a blind person to wander off the road. It was an unconscionable act. So it is with those, who, because they seek relevance over truth, lead the spiritually blind to eternal loss. Deuteronomy 27:18

As part of Moses' recapitulation of the law to the generation raised in the wilderness and ready to occupy the land of promise, he had them repeat the blessings that followed obedience and curses that would come as a result of their disobedience to the Torah. The litany of curses was many, and among them was the seemingly odd penalty that would come to those who caused a blind person to wander off the path. Leading well those who could not see was imperative, and failure to do so would bring God's judgment.

How crucially important it is for us to realize the spiritual implications. Scripture teaches that those who are lost are spiritually blind. Many who are ungodly are willing to offer advice and the world's wisdom is plentiful but will ultimately lead the blind to eternal damnation. It is incumbent upon those who claim to know the truth that we lead the blind, not to death, but to life.

Day 59 | The Secret Things of the Lord

February 28—Read Deuteronomy 29-34

Truth that God has revealed to us in His Word is a gift of beauty to all generations. But there are secret things that are too great for our minds to conceive that belong to God alone. Still we worship Him for His awesome greatness and complete trustworthiness. Deuteronomy 29:29

There is so much about God, His person, and His ways that eludes the finite human mind. This is what was meant by Moses when he said, *"The secret things belong to the Lord our God..."* These are things that we dare not question, things we must only trust. As Moses noted when he spoke to the children of Israel, there are other things about God that we can know. *"...but the things that are revealed belong to us and to our children forever, that we may do all the words of this law."*

This principle is powerful and a crucial truth that we must embrace. While certain things about the divine character are indeed unknowable, God has revealed Himself in many unavoidable and clear ways through His Word. That Word has been given to us and must be obeyed; its truth is for us, for our children, and for every generation, that we might know and worship the one, true God.

Day 60 | Meditation that Transform

March 1—Read Joshua 1-3

While studying Scripture is essential, biblical meditation is also integral to spiritual development. It is not an attempt to expunge the mind of all desires to achieve a mystical experience, but a continual pondering and repetition of the text so that it takes root. Joshua 1:6-9

As Joshua prepared to take over the reins of leadership for the people of Israel after the death of Moses, God provided clear admonitions that, if seriously considered, would ensure his success. Among the admonitions was a clear call to be devoted to the Book of the Law. It was to be his guide, his compass, and his rule of faith. Knowledge of its content would be commendable, but the higher call was to allow it to become a part of him through constant meditation upon its truth.

This is the call we have been given, as well, as it pertains to God's Word. While the secular world loves to tout the benefits of its meditation, an ancient and mystical practice which has as its goal the clearing of the mind, biblical meditation has a different goal. It is to saturate the mind and heart, through constant rehearsing of scriptural truth, so that the mind becomes transformed by its power, and one's life becomes aligned to its principles.

Day 61 | Maintaining Our Memories

March 2—Read Joshua 4-7

When comfort, ease, and therefore complacency set in, God's people quit SEIZING new promises, quit STEPPING into the waters by faith, quit SEEING miraculous provision, and quit SETTING up memorials. THEN— the next generation is lost. Never stop SEEKING God's presence. Joshua 4

Much of what Joshua led Israel to do, as they claimed Canaan for their own, was intended to provide motivation for spiritual piety for future generations. As they stepped into the Jordan by faith, and the waters receded, a testimony was birthed. As they erected memorials where God had met them, they provided places of remembrance where they could point their children to so that God's faithfulness was lauded. God knew, and Joshua understood that if His greatness was not passed on, the next generation would fall away from Yahweh. Sadly, despite the efforts of Joshua, the falling away happened anyway.

We must be careful that we do not allow blessing to lead to complacency and abundance to cause us to stop trusting God for everything and living by faith. This danger lurks for all of God's people. When we quit trusting God for miraculous provision, the miraculous dries up. When the miraculous ceases, the testimony becomes extinct, and where there is no witness, people drift from God. Let us ensure that this does not happen to the next generation but instead, erect memorials to God's faithfulness so that our children can know.

Day 62 | A Return to Surrender

March 3—Read Joshua 8-12

Following the victory at Ai, Joshua led the people to Mt. Ebal to renew the covenant and to worship their rescuer. Victories that God secures on our behalf cannot be sustained unless we place ourselves regularly under the rule of the rescuer. Joshua 8:30-35

Because of Achan's sin, the first attempt at defeating Ai had led to tragic disaster, and the band of Israelites that had sought to take the city was forced to flee. That sin had been reckoned with, and a second attack yielded great victory. Now Joshua led the people to Ebal to secure that victory and future campaigns through a renewal of the covenant. He did not want the failure of Achan to be repeated, and he knew that the people must surrender their lives again to the God who had called them to their inheritance.

We must be wholly sensitive to our human tendency to forget God and convince ourselves that our victories and our blessings are self-perpetuated. They are not. Without Him, we can do nothing. To guard against such a fatal and devastating mistake, we must often return to our moments of calling and surrender ourselves afresh to His will.

Day 63 | Thriving in a Pessimistic Environment

March 4—Read Joshua 13-16

Caleb both survived and thrived in a culture of complaining, failure, diminished strength, and rampant negativity because he knew well the God who had promised him the mountain, and he kept the mountain, not the obstacles along the way, the focus of his attention and the object of his energy. Joshua 14:6-15

The cultural context of Caleb's day was one of overwhelming complaining, epidemic pessimism, spiritual doubt, and rebellion against leadership. Those attributes led to the four decades of wilderness wandering and the loss of thousands to the land of promise. But Caleb rose above it and was able to wait out the rebellion and claim the mountain that God had promised. He survived and thrived by knowing the God of promise and keeping his heart focused on the hope that was set before him.

It is sadly too often the case in Christian circles that the atmosphere is one of grumbling, complaining, and criticizing. When we fall prey to that, we can become sidetracked by its destructive nature. Those who hope to lay hold of God's promises must, like Caleb, refuse to join in with the pessimism and instead, lay their spiritual eyes on the prize of the promise ahead. When that is the commitment, one can thrive in an otherwise challenging environment.

Day 64 | No Shortcuts to Blessing

March 5—Read Joshua 7-20

The tribes of Manasseh and Ephraim both sought the path of least resistance, wanting the greatest blessing for the least effort. The Kingdom works differently— in sowing much we reap much—in suffering we know glory—in surrendering our all, we experience His fullness. Joshua 17:12-18

The narrative of the possession of Canaan by the tribes of Israel comes with many interesting twists and turns. One of the most telling accounts is the dialogue between Joshua and the tribes of Ephraim and Manasseh. Though they were unhappy with the allotment of land given to them, they did not want to have to possess land that would require physical labor or forcefully driving out their enemy. They wanted the way of ease.

This is often the manner in which believers proceed in their spiritual journey, wanting to find the easiest road and avoid great conflict. It may seem to be the wise path and will, in the short term, make life easier, but in the end it leaves one falling short of their potential. The Kingdom does not flourish through ease and following the path of least resistance. The Kingdom, Jesus taught, will be gained by those who take it by force, and transformative glory comes through suffering. To know God's best comes only to the fully surrendered.

Day 65 | Rest On Every Side

March 6—*Read Joshua 21-22*

"And the Lord gave them rest on every side." Not forever—there were enemies to conquer, lands to more fully possess. But weary, He gave them rest. He still offers that—a reprieve from the battle and quietness though the peril. In Jesus there is rest on every side. Joshua 21:44

As the Joshua narrative closes with Israel's occupation of Canaan, the author notes that God gave them a season of rest. For a time, they had no more battles to fight, enemies to drive out, or territory to conquer. God knew the frame of their humanity and that they could only handle so much. He slowed their pace, defeated their enemies, and gave them rest.

We too get weary from the spiritual conflict. There are days that we simply cannot bear the thought of yet another battle, the possibility of another lurking enemy, or the emotional exhaustion of navigating the terrain of spiritual growth. When we find ourselves there, we hear the sweet words of Jesus, "Come unto me all ye that labor and are heaven laden, and I will give you rest" (Matthew 11:28). That rest will not be found in activities of the world but in intimate fellowship with Jesus.

Day 66 | Choose Today

Joshua called Israel to whole-hearted service and obedience to the Lord, something woefully lacking in contemporary evangelicalism today. Instead of clinging to the idols of OUR pain, wounds, sacrifices, and even failures, we are called to lay them all down to serve GOD. Joshua 24

As Joshua came to the end of his life and prepared to hand over the reins of leadership to others, he issued a final challenge to the people of Israel. His call was to wholehearted devotion and a complete recanting of the idols and gods of the Canaanites. He spoke for his house and invited every tribe to stand with him. In the moment, they all joined with him and promised the same devotion of which he spoke. Sadly, however, it would not be long before Israel would turn away and follow the gods of their own choosing, doing what was right in their own eyes.

God is calling us today to this kind of full surrender and deep devotion. It is unfortunate but true, that while contemporary believers are not tempted by the gods and idols of the Canaanites, we have our own. Many erect idols of past hurt or past wounds and others worship at the shrine of their own failures. God has called us to lay all of these down and give our all to Him. Choose today whom you will serve, surrender the entirety of your being to Him, and never look back!

Day 67 | Confession that Requires Action

March 8—Read Judges 1-3

As decisive as the Israelite's commitment to serve God was, it could not overcome their passive failure of allowing their enemies to co-inhabit the land with them. A bold confession un-enforced by godly action, will have no staying influence. Judges 1

As Joshua's life ended, he called Israel to make a decision. Would they serve God and walk in obedience to His commands, or would they seek after other gods and turn their back on Yahweh? Joshua directed the people to choose whom they would serve and then noted, "but as for me and my house, we will serve the Lord." Though the people promised that they would follow Joshua in his bold allegiance to Yahweh, when they entered Canaan, they failed to drive out the inhabitants and their gods. Soon their failure led to their downfall.

We can make bold confessions and declare our allegiance to God when things are emotionally heightened. However, unless that confession is translated into sincere obedience and perpetual surrender to God's leading, the confession will be powerless. We have been called, not only to confession but action, and with every confession must come a corresponding action that seals that commitment.

Day 68 | Refusing to Promote Self

March 9—Read Judges 4-5

Deborah was God's instrument bringing Israel deliverance from the Canaanite king, Jabin. Though used by God before through prophesy and inspired judgments, she understood that self-promotion would not bring lasting fruit to the work of the Kingdom. She trusted God's plan. Judges 4

The book of Judges chronicles one of the worst times in Israel's history—a time when everyone did what was right in their own eyes. God raised up judges to deliver Israel occasionally and Deborah was one such judge. She told Barak that God would use him to free Israel from the hand of Jabin and the evil Sisera but Barak's fear paralyzed him. Deborah then prophesied that by the hand of a woman, deliverance would come. Though one would think Deborah would be that woman, that was not God's plan.

We too often presume upon the plan of God and seek to promote ourselves to positions that we desire and pursue. That would have been easy for Deborah, especially since God had used her before and she seemed to be the natural choice. But that was not God's plan and so she trusted God and deliverance was accomplished for Israel. It is far better to humble oneself and enjoy victory than to self-promote and miss out on God's blessing.

Day 69 | Guarding Against Compromise

March 10—Read Judges 6-8

The life of Gideon after his great victory was a life wasted. Though he turned down the opportunity to be made king, he chose to live entitled like he was a king and thus squandered his chance to turn Israel to God. When leaders lack integrity, the people of God suffer. Judges 8

The great victory of Gideon over the Midianites highlights the power of God to overcome our fears and weaknesses and the potential to accomplish great exploits when we trust God, despite our own lack. Sadly, the story of Gideon ends tragically. Instead of downplaying his own role in the victory, he allowed pride to take over and undo so much of what God had accomplished through him. His victory was a victory wasted, and the repercussions of his downfall rippled throughout the people of God.

We must always be careful not to assume that our victories give us a pass on continued obedience. A single victory in the spiritual realm does not safeguard us from Satan's temptations or our own tendency toward compromise. Gideon took no precautions, and it led to his downfall. The nation paid a price. We cannot escape the same outcome if we allow pride to gain a foothold.

Day 70 | Grace is Free

March 11—Read Judges 9-12

Though this text is hard to understand, and the story is so foreign to our contemporary minds, a powerful truth emerges. Grace does not provide space for bargaining for God's blessing; in fact, when we foolishly presume that we can, devastation often results. Judges 11

The story of Jephthah is a difficult one to grasp. God promised him victory, and God's Spirit empowered him to overcome the Ammonites who were effectively discomfiting God's people. The author does not tell us why, but Jephthah felt the need to make a vow and promised that if God would give him victory, he would sacrifice the first thing that came from his house to meet him when he returned home. When he came home, his daughter came to greet him. While we do not know if he actually sacrificed her or forced her to remain a virgin for life, we can be certain that the unnecessary vow cost him and his daughter greatly.

Grace is free. It cannot be bought; neither should we try to bargain with God to improve our position before Him. The foolishness of such an attempt will only bring unexpected pain and unnecessary devastation. When God assures us of our victory and standing before Him, we should accept that and rejoice in His provision.

Day 71 | Serve Him While You Can

March 12—Read Judges 13-16

After a life of reckless frivolity and shameful living, which led to the forfeiture of his divine gift and calling, Samson came to his senses. Recognizing God as the true source of his power, he called on Him, received grace, and won his greatest battle. God grants do-overs to the sincere in heart. Judges 16:28-30

The life of Samson was one of tragic consequences though blessed with enormous and unusual potential. Samson had great strength that was to be used to rescue Israel from enemy hands, but he perverted that strength and used it for his own fleshly appetites. It cost him God's blessing, and instead of enjoying his destiny, his life ended tragically, eyes gouged out, and his own death necessary to win a final battle. God granted him a second chance because of his sincerity, but there were still grave consequences he had to accept.

So often, we waste away our potential and never enjoy all that God intends for us. It is a sad story that is too frequently repeated among believers. Many, like Samson, fritter away the best days of their lives, and though they turn to God later, they never enjoy all that God intends. Two reminders will serve us well. One, God does forgive us when we turn to Him no matter how deeply we have failed. He will give us new opportunities. Two, it is best to serve God young and faithfully when we have strength to enjoy and accomplish great things for Him.

Day 72 | The Need to be Shocked Again

March 13—Read Judges 17-19

This chapter uncovers the almost unimaginable and sinful depths to which humanity apart from God can fall. It may be that the only thing that will revive a nation is when the people of God are once again shocked by sin and call out for God to bring restoration. Judges 19

Reading this chapter, one can find themselves shocked by the deep perversion and the utter chaos that ensues when moral leadership is absent. That was the case with Israel in Judges 19. They had no king, but everyone was doing right in their own eyes. No prophet was calling them out, and no judge stood to call them back to God. The utter horror of the rape, murder, hatred, and lack of godly hospitality is shocking. In fact, as the chapter ends, the people of God say, "What are we going to do? Who's going to speak up?"

America may well be at this same place. After millions of babies being slaughtered in the last fifty years, sexual perversion of all sorts is now not only tolerated but applauded, and people have run God out of every context, sadly often even the Church, it is time to wake up and be shocked. We must answer the question posed by the people of Judges 19 and say "WE will speak up!" "We will call out to God in repentance and ask Him to heal our land!" May the shock of godlessness stir us up to call on Him again and seek Him for revival!

Day 73 | The Folly of Covering Your Sin

March 14—Read Judges 20-21

Nothing complicates and heightens the consequences of our sin and foolishness more than making more sinful and foolish choices in an attempt to mitigate the consequences instead of humbly repenting and seeking restoration. Judges 21

This narrative of Judges underscores two key truths. One, it reminds us of the sordid fallenness of humanity without God and just how sinful and foolish it is when we choose our own way rather than obey Him. Two, it unveils the human tendency to cover our folly with even greater missteps and demonstrates to us that it is always better to come clean than to try to cover our sin. Cover-ups always make things worse and lead to more devastating consequences.

We will make poor choices in life, and there will be times when our sin will lead to great and hurtful repercussions. We must learn to be humble and acknowledge our failure, seeking God for forgiveness rather than trying to cover our failure with even more foolishness that will lead to further devastation.

Day 74 | Safe with Jesus

March 15—Read Ruth 1-4

"You might be harassed in other fields, but you will be safe with Him." These words of Naomi to Ruth about the integrity of Boaz are powerful. The world may beat at us, the enemy may harass us, and circumstances may threaten to destroy us, but we are safe with Christ. Ruth 2:2

When Naomi sent Ruth off to glean in the fields of Bethlehem, she warned her that many would not accept her and would harass or, at the very least, look suspiciously on her. She was warned about the potential dangers that might befall her but assured her that in the field of Boaz, her ultimate redeemer, she would be safe. It was there that she found protection and safe passage.

This story underscores a powerful truth for us. The world in which we live is full of danger. There are places we can go and relationships that we can make that seek to destroy us and take from us, leaving us empty and broken. But with Jesus, we are always safe—in His presence there is unending provision and fullness of joy. No matter what circumstances confront us, when we run to Him, we can rest in the assurance that He will keep us secure!

Day 75 | Only Sincerity Will Do

March 16—Read 1 Samuel 1-4

It is a tragic mistake, leading to devastating ruin, to assume that an often repeated spiritual ritual or an obligatory invitation of God's presence could ever replace the necessary holiness of heart and contrition of spirit demanded of those who call Jesus "Lord." 1 Samuel 4:1-11

This passage of Scripture is one of the saddest in the Old Testament. The people of God were living lives of wretched ungodliness; Eli the priest, though pious, could not keep his own house in order as his sons violated the priesthood with their selfish immorality. As a result of their sin, Israel was defeated by the Philistines. Thinking that their only problem was that the ark of the covenant had not been brought into battle, they went again against the Philistines—this time with the ark, only to be sorely defeated and have the ark of God's presence stolen.

We make a grave mistake when we think that our spiritual routines or traditions can save us. Many think they can live how they want, recklessly and unholy, yet still curry God's favor with their spiritual and meaningless formulas. But as the apostle Paul said, God will not be mocked. If our lives lack sincere holiness and are void of heart purity, no spiritual activity can save us. Only approaching God with a repentant heart will do.

Day 76 | A Decisive Moment

March 17—Read 1 Samuel 5-7

Standing between a storied past and a hopeful future; the enemy attacked Israel. There they raised their Ebeneezer, confessing, "hitherto has the Lord helped us." As we face our future, feeling the heat of enemy pursuit, be assured—God HAS BEEN and WILL BE faithful. 1 Samuel 7:2-12

The people of God, profoundly aware of their failure, stood prepared to take responsibility for their failed past, longing for the ark to return. Samuel told them what they must do—repent and call on God. As they readied themselves, the Philistines marched toward them. Israel was afraid. Samuel erected the Ebenezer stone and reminded the people that as God had been before, He would be again. The Philistines were subdued as the people trusted God.

That moment for Israel was a decisive moment as they committed to releasing their past and pursuing God's destiny for them as a people. We, too, have decisive moments and if we hope to experience God's best for us, we must establish our Ebenezer stones and declare the faithfulness of God in our situation.

Day 77 | Ordered Steps Not Wasted Steps

March 18—Read 1 Samuel 8-10

Saul's journey with his servant to locate his father's lost donkeys was apparently going to be fruitless—but God had other plans. It is easy to become discouraged and think that what feels like aimless wandering is serving no purpose, but God does not waste our steps. 1 Samuel 9

Israel was crying out for a king, and God had one picked out. His name was Saul, the son of Kish. When Kish's donkeys came up missing, he sent Saul and his servant to search for them. Their search was coming up empty, and when they made one last effort to secure help, they came upon Samuel who had been sent to anoint Saul as king. What seemed to be a worthless trip turned out to be the ordered steps of God fulfilled. From frustrated sojourner to anointed king, Saul found out that God does not waste our steps—He orders them.

It is easy to become frustrated and feel as if we are going in circles. God, however, has a plan. He is not wasting our steps, but He is ordering them, and in due season, we will encounter the plan He has prepared for us. Never look with disdain at the path God has you on. His path will lead to your purpose if you patiently trust Him.

Day 78 | A Patient Confidence

March 19—Read 1 Samuel 11-15

Jonathan had full confidence in God's power and embraced his own responsibility, but he never presumed upon God. He acted on faith in God's power, but submitted his actions to the all-knowing and wise God. God is able—perhaps God will—either way I will trust Him. 1 Samuel 14:6

For most of the Samuel narrative, Jonathan is second-fiddle, a backseat player that most often emerges as an extra in the grand story of Israel's second and greatest king, David. Here, however, he is the lead player as he, along with his armor bearer, made his way to the Philistine garrison where he hoped to infiltrate and inflict serious damage on the archenemy of Israel. Confident of God's power, he still submitted himself to God's plan and instructed his armor bearer that they would wait until God had made their way plain.

Great instructive wisdom proceeds from this account. It is not a lack of faith to wait patiently for what you know God ultimately wants to do. On the contrary, it is wise and patient submission to the One who is both all-powerful and all-wise. It is the truly mature who will make themselves ready, walk in assurance of God's plan, and yet still patiently wait for that plan to fully unfold.

Day 79 | Work on the Heart

March 20—*Read 1 Samuel 16-17*

When God calls and anoints one for His service, the qualifications have nothing in common with human standards—His view is one's heart. May we have eyes to see as God does, not the charisma and gifting as judged by men, but the character as known by God. 1 Samuel 16:1-7

When Samuel set out toward Jesse's house to anoint the next king, he was not expecting what he would find. He was certain that, like Saul, the next one to occupy Israel's throne would be a grand specimen of a man, strong and handsome, with great wisdom and experience. But instead, God called him to anoint a slight and ruddy shepherd—David was his name. He had no military victories under his belt, and his frame could not handle a man's armor, but God looked at his heart and knew that his faithful piety could be shaped into a great leader and king.

Sadly, we spend too much time cultivating the qualities that impress the world and recruiting allies. We focus our attention on the outward appearance, the worldly gifts, and what scripture calls sensual wisdom. That is not what God is looking for in His own. He is turned toward the heart that worships Him, the mind that longs to be renewed, and the spirit that is contrite.

Day 80 | Let this Mind be in You—Humility

March 21—Read 1 Samuel 18-21

Though David typifies Christ as King, Jonathan pictures beautifully the humility of Christ. Though he was heir to the throne, he chose not to grasp that honor, but instead humbled himself, willing to give his own life to serve and save David. Let us have the same mind. 1 Samuel 20

It is a well-known fact and established theological maxim that David stands as a type of Christ, and his royal monarchy serves to facilitate the emergence of the Messiah-King, Jesus Christ of Nazareth. At so many points in the historical narrative, the life of David provides powerful pictures and types of the coming King. The life of David is rich in imagery, and his longing after the heart of God is one of the great portraits of Jesus, who lived only to please His Father.

David's loyal friend, Jonathan, however, also provides a picture of Jesus from the pages of the Old Testament. The picture that he so powerfully represents is of humility. Jonathan, the son of Saul, was heir to his father's throne, but because of his father's sin and failure, he would lose that seat to his great friend, David. Like Jonathan, Jesus demonstrated great humility. Though divine, in His humility, He laid aside the use of that divinity for a season so that He might, as a man, die for man. This mind of Christ is our calling.

Day 81 | Transformed by Our Enemies

March 22—Read 1 Samuel 22-24

God may allow people or circumstances in our lives to develop our character and godliness, and we must submit. It is not our responsibility to avenge the hurt inflicted by others, but entrust that hurt and them to God while we allow the pain to shape us. 1 Samuel 24:11-12

The story of David's treatment of King Saul speaks powerfully to how we are to allow God to avenge our enemies and shape us by those who stand against us. Repeatedly, Saul sought to kill David and even drove him from his home and into hiding. He was merciless in his pursuit of the young king-to-be, but David, even when he had the opportunity, refused to lay a hand on the king; he understood that to do so would be to wrongly touch God's anointed and would cancel out the work that God was wanting to do in him.

This attitude of David, though challenging to duplicate, must be lived out by us. It is not our responsibility to fight our enemies or bring judgment on them. Even when those enemies are in places of authority, we are to submit to them rather than judging or seeking to avenge them. For it is through the pain they inflict on us that we are better taught to follow Christ and made to be more like Him.

Day 82 | Reverent Confrontation

March 23—Read 1 Samuel 25-28

Abigail's soft answer and reverent respect for authority averted horrific bloodshed and spared David from sinning through the abuse of his power. Christians should challenge authority in a godly and respectful manner and promote peace whenever possible. God will honor that posture. 1 Samuel 25

This narrative is one of the more interesting and instructive texts of David's life story, but it's often overlooked. Nabal, in his wicked folly, had mistreated David and his men. David's intention was to avenge that treatment with a bloody military campaign. Abigail, the wife of Nabal, sought out David, and though she was harshly treated by her husband, she pleaded with David to call off the raid. She knew that it would lead to great bloodshed. David conceded, and afterwards God judged Nabal and he died, but innocent life was spared. It was Abigail's peaceful intercession that saved the day.

Abigail was not afraid to confront David, even though he was in a position of great authority. She did it reverently and with grace. Had she not, innocent life would have been taken. It is this kind of approach that Christians should take amidst our culture of godless and immoral leadership. We must take a bold stand but do it with godly reverence and respect. God will honor that, and our opportunities for meaningful intercession will expand.

Day 83 | From Prominence to Homelessness

March 24—Read 1 Samuel 29-31

As difficult as it may seem to stand against the pressure and lead with godly boldness, doing the right thing in every circumstance will have positive lasting implications. Even if the immediate is uncomfortable, the virtue of integrity will be honored. 1 Samuel 30:23-35

This Old Testament narrative provides powerful lessons. David and his men had come across a horrific pummeling of their own people in Negev and Ziklag by the Amalekites. The cities had been destroyed by fire, the people taken captive, and their goods ransacked and stolen. David had 600 men, but 200 of them had no energy to go with the others to avenge the wrong. When David and his men won the battle and regained their spoils, the 400 with David wanted to hoard the spoils and keep it from the 200 who stayed behind. David would not hear of that. They were all brothers and they would all enjoy the victory.

David stood against strong opposition, and he did the right thing. There are times when we are faced with similar opposition and doing what is selfish and that which lacks integrity is the easy way out. This is when God calls us to overcome our selfish tendencies and live lives of sincere integrity. He will, just as He did with David, reward us for our sincere faithfulness.

Day 84 | The Peril of Resisting Truth

March 25—Read 2 Samuel 1-4

To know the truth and to fight against it brings needless pain, untold frustration, and many unnecessary casualties. Submitting to the truth brings increased effectiveness and the blessing of God. 2 Samuel 2

Abner, the commander of the army under the late King Saul, knew that the kingdom had been given to David by Yahweh, but his godless loyalty to Saul blinded him to the potential damage that his reckless rebellion might bring about. To resist David's rule, he anointed Ishbosheth, the son of Saul, to be king and then stubbornly refused to let go of his devastating pride. His stubborn folly led to great and devastating bloodshed and death.

Abner knew the truth but would not submit to it. It cost him and others dearly. We have a responsibility to not only know truth, but, even more importantly, submit to it. Often, because we do not like the implications of truth and know that it requires a change of direction for us, we resist it and fail to obey. While in the moment, this may maintain our sense of autonomy, in the end, to resist truth is to bring upon ourselves the chastening of God.

Day 85 | Blessed to Bless

March 26—Read 2 Samuel 5-7

David could not fathom God's great promises. We must learn that God does all He does, not because we are deserving, but for the glory of His name. With Augustine we say, "You have made us for yourself, O Lord, and our heart is restless until it rests in you!" 2 Samuel 7:18-29

When Nathan prophesied to David and told him that he would not be able to build a house for God, but that his son, Solomon, would instead, and that his throne would be an everlasting throne, David was overwhelmed. David knew his own weaknesses and the humanity that plagued him often, and to think that the Messiah would proceed from his line was more than his mind could conceive. He came to understand that the promises he so cherished were not meant to make him great, but instead were to provide a platform for the name of Yahweh to be exalted and for every people, tribe, and tongue to know Him.

When God blesses us and performs His promises on our behalf, it is not meant for us to consume the blessing with our own lust and pride. Rather, God blesses us to bless, fulfills His Word in us that we might proclaim His name abroad, and exalts us that we might reveal the glory of His grace to others. We were made for Him, His glory is to be seen through us, and His purpose is to be revealed by a demonstration of His glory resident in us.

Day 86 | A Seat at the King's Table

March 27—Read 2 Samuel 8:10

Grace takes a broken cripple from a failed family and sits them at the king's table, where their brokenness is covered by the king's royal tablecloth. The Son of God invites children of Adam to abide with Him so He can cover their brokenness with His unending grace. 2 Samuel 9:13

One of the great Old Testament narratives, bursting with great pathos, is found in the ninth chapter of 2 Samuel. It was the tradition of monarchies to rid the kingdom of relatives of the previous regime, but David did not do that when Saul died and he ascended to the throne. Mephibosheth, the son of Jonathan and the grandson of Saul, had been crippled since he was dropped as a child by a nurse fleeing from the enemy intruder. Rather than killing him, David gave the young castaway a permanent seat at his own table. There, at the table of the king, his crippled legs were not seen, but rather covered by the king's tablecloth.

What an apt and glorious portrait of One greater than David, our King—Jesus. In an act of stunning grace and remarkable love, He invites us to sit at His table and fellowship with Him. There we sit, even with our flaws, failures, and sinful past, underneath the glory of His grace; and there we find fellowship with the One who is our substitute, Savior, and King.

Day 87 | He's Speaking to Us

March 28—Read 2 Samuel 11-12

As Nathan confronted King David about his sin with Bathsheba, he used a parable to point out his error. Though intended to show David that he was the one who had sinned, he missed the point. Sadly, we can read the Word and miss the fact that God is speaking to us. 2 Samuel 12

In obedience to the Lord, Nathan came to David's palace to confront him about his sin with Bathsheba. The prophet told a parable about a wealthy man who had many sheep, and who took the one and only sheep from the poor man. This was to point out how David, as king, had dishonored Uriah, the common man, by taking his wife. David was furious that a wealthy man would treat the commoner so poorly. Then Nathan said to David, "Thou ART the man."

It is sadly true that we are rarely different. We hear the Word preached and read the Word in our devotions, and we see the failures and sins of others and are quick to point them out. Rarely, however, do we recognize that the Holy Spirit, like the prophet Nathan, is pointing at us. We are the ones who have sinned, and we are the ones being called to repentance. May we not look for ways to apply God's Word to others, but be quick to hear what God is saying to us.

Day 88 | So that No One will be an Outcast

March 29—Read 2 Samuel 13-15

All of Scripture reveals a God who reconciles broken relationships, removes the obstacles that separate, and restores wholeness. Love devised a means by which we could be reconciled to Him, and His heart calls upon us to do the same with one another while time allows. 2 Samuel 14:14

As is so often the case, wonderful and glorious lessons can be learned, though the imperfection of the Old Testament saints and the wonder of God's grace is easily visible. Here David, longing for reconciliation with his son, Absalom but too proud to take the first step, is approached by a widow from Tekoa, whose story was designed to soften the king's heart. She had been hired by Joab to encourage reconciliation, but David saw through the ploy. In the midst of her appeal, one profound truth was made clear. "God will not take away life, and he devises means so that the banished one will not remain an outcast."

The truth is simple and universally applicable. God wants all to be forgiven and wants all to know the experience of genuine reconciliation and relationship with others. It is the broken He longs to heal. Those who have the heart of God must embrace and share this same passion, and allow God to use them to affect such healing.

Day 89 | It Takes More Than We Have

March 30—Read 2 Samuel 16-18

Despite deep love for Absalom, David found he could not overcome his own parenting failures, nor could he effect reconciliation with his son himself. Let this remind us that only in Christ can our failures be redeemed, and by Him alone can our relationships be healed. 2 Samuel 18

One of the most tragic realities of the Old Testament is the failure of David with many of his own children. No failure of this sort was more grievous than David's estrangement from Absalom, that led to his son's usurping of his throne and ultimately his untimely death. David's love was deep for Absalom, but no matter how deeply he loved, and no matter how hard he tried, no reconciliation was ever realized. It was not a failure that he could ever overcome.

We often try hard to make up for our own failures and missteps. We can beg, manipulate, cry, and devote huge resources to overcome our weaknesses, addictions, and losses. But, our greatest efforts can never make up for the consequences of our sin and selfishness. Only the blood of Jesus applied to a heart that is broken and contrite can wholly restore and fully heal. It is the surrender of our will and the relinquishing of our rights and pride that will often pave the way for a true miracle of healing.

Day 90 | Grace Without Limit

March 31—Read 2 Samuel 19-21

The ancient text unveils without gloss, the great depth of human depravity, the unfathomable nature of God's holiness, the divine necessity of justice, the grave consequences of sin, and the hopeful expectation of a substitutionary atonement fulfilled in Christ. 2 Samuel 21:1-14

The Old Testament often jolts us by the deep evil that so pervaded ancient cultures. The inspired authors did nothing to gloss over the depravity and sin that existed. Certainly, there are no heroes in the inspired text—the only hero is God. This narrative reveals pride, hate, jealousy, revenge, and the selfish works of the flesh. There seems to be nothing redeemable. Only as the Old Covenant closes and the New emerges does hope come.

We should not approach the Old Testament with great hope of finding positive examples of human progress and praiseworthy behaviors. Instead, we should be reminded of the depth of human awfulness without God and the surpassing grace that is able to overcome even the vilest offense. The songwriter said it so well, *"His love has no limit, His grace has no measure. His pow'r has no boundary known unto men. For out of His infinite riches in Jesus, He giveth, and giveth, and giveth again."*

Day 91 | Guarding our Hearts from Pride

April 1—Read 2 Samuel 22-24

While we so often strive to legalistically "keep the law," we fail to be aware of the fact that the greatest and most devastating of sins are those of the heart. A census did not violate the Torah, but pride stood as an affront to a holy God. We must guard our hearts. 2 Samuel 24

The text before us reads strangely to contemporary ears. David, wanting to know the size of his kingdom, ordered a census. On the surface, this would appear to be a benign action. But his motivation was pride. He wanted to know how great he had become and how wide his domain had expanded. That pride became his downfall, and though no law forbade a king from taking a census, one after God's heart should not have been seeking his own glory, but the glory of the One he worshipped. David paid a great price for his pride.

So much effort can be given to law-keeping or in the contemporary church, seeking to stay away from the "big" and noticeable sins that can bring public shame. God, however, is looking for hearts of sincere integrity, cleansed from destructive pride, and willing to decrease so that the One they serve may increase in their own lives and, thus, be made famous to a world in need of His love and bountiful grace.

Day 92 | Without His Presence We Are Nothing

April 2—Read 1 Kings 1-2

The rule of the law can establish kingdoms, secure national peace, and mandate submission to earthly leaders, but only the mitigating presence of Christ, still anticipated in the Old Covenant, can reconcile relationships, transform hearts, and bring lasting peace. 1 Kings 2

The second chapter of Kings highlights the final words of David to his son Solomon as the time of his death drew near. He reminded him of God's covenant and warned of all that would need to be done and the threats that would pose themselves as he ascended to the throne. The rest of the chapter outlines Solomon's steps in asserting his rule and establishing peace in the kingdom. His structure, power, and authority allowed him to rule with a strong hand and maintain peace, but without the presence of God, this peace was only superficial.

There is only so much that our efforts, creative systems, and hierarchical arrangements can do for the work of the Kingdom. We can build systems that will attract and maintain the allegiance of people and arrange personalities so they work well together. We can work diligently to provide excellence that will make people proud to belong. None of these, however, can change a man or woman's heart or bring them closer to the holiness that Scripture demands. For that we must have and experience the divine presence of God.

Day 93 | This Rock is Jesus

April 3—Read 1 Kings 3-5

When Solomon sought stones that would be used for the foundation of the temple, he cut no corners and spared no expense. Only the largest and strongest would be used for the temple's foundation. We must never look for shortcuts in laying a foundation for the work of God. 1 Kings 5:17

The narrative describing the erecting of the temple is full of inspirational encouragement and great teaching moments; this is one of them. Solomon sent out a requisition for materials to build the temple's foundation, and he asked for the biggest and strongest stones. The temple would be magnificent in beauty and overwhelming in grandeur, but if its foundation was not secure and steady, it would not last.

What a powerful lesson for us, both individually and corporately. We are as individuals a temple wherein the Spirit of God dwells, and as a people we are to be the temple of God declaring His greatness and majesty. We must be intent on building lives and churches that stay strong and steady regardless of what comes. That is impossible unless we invest well in the foundation of our lives and churches. Jesus is that foundation, and there is no other. Unless we are firmly rooted and grounded in Him, we will not flourish.

Day 94 | Quiet Submission to the Spirit

April 4—Read 1 Kings 6-8

All of the stone used for Solomon's temple was to be prepared offsite so that there would be no noise at the temple site. As living stones and His temple, His shaping of us should come with less drama and noise and be more sacredly and gratefully received. 1 Kings 6:7

Of the many obscure texts of Scripture that provide great spiritual truth, none may be more informative than this nugget. In order to keep the area where worship of Yahweh was to take place holy, all stone cutting for the temple was to take place at the stone quarry so that there would be no noise at the temple site. This was to preserve the integrity of worship and to signal great reverence for the holy majesty of Yahweh.

There is a powerful lesson for us here. We are the living stones of God's holy building, His spiritual house. God, through the sanctifying work of the Holy Spirit, is shaping us to be holy and effective stones in the house of God—His Kingdom. Instead of resisting His work and loudly protesting the Spirit's activity, we are to submit to His gentle but firm purging, His purposeful and thorough cleansing, and His loving and deeply penetrating shaping of our hearts. Instead of resistance, we should gladly submit and allow His work to be complete.

Day 95 | Answers for a Wondering World

April 5—Read 1 Kings 9-11

There are moments in time and history that the world is in desperate need of answers—this is one of those times. May the people of God, who have available to them divine wisdom for the asking, rise to the occasion and answer the hard questions of our world that God may be glorified. 1 Kings 10:1-9

Solomon's wisdom was known far and wide, a wisdom that was divinely given. Many came to him seeking wisdom, but none of greater importance than the Queen of Sheba. Every question she asked him he was able to answer and her amazement at his wisdom led to her testimony. "The report was true that I heard in my own land of your words and of your wisdom, but I did not believe the reports until I came and my own eyes had seen it. And behold, the half was not told to me. Your wisdom and prosperity surpass the report that I heard."

We are living in a time when the world is looking for answers, and many complexities face this generation. The people of God have the truth—we are carriers of the truth that will set men and women free. If we walk faithfully before God and give ourselves to knowing and loving His Word, He will orchestrate opportunities for us to share that wisdom with a lost world. These opportunities expand our sphere of influence and make possible a Kingdom impact that will point people to truth and steady their anxiety in a world of chaos.

Day 96 | Hold to the Truth

April 6—Read 1 Kings 12-14

Grave consequences follow when the clear Word of God is abandoned for another "prophetic" or pseudo-inspired word. Paul warned the Galatians if he or even an angel tried to improve on the Gospel, they should be accursed. We MUST embrace and guard truth. 1 Kings 13

This Old Testament narrative, as strange as it is to read, yields powerful and relevant truth. It begins when a young prophet, a man of God, determined to speak truth and maintain his prophetic integrity, powerfully confronts the godless monarch. He refused to compromise or allow himself to be wooed by the royalty who was steeped in sinfulness. Yet later, this same prophet, with his spiritual guard down, fell prey to a new and false word from the old prophet, and it cost him his life and ministry.

So relevant is the truth that emerges from this ancient pericope. When we abandon the revealed truth of God's Word and follow after that which comes from another source, no matter how convincing or spiritual that source may seem, we recklessly place ourselves in grave danger. We must not waver, and we must not abandon the only truth that sets us free.

Day 97 | The Finish is as Important as the Start

April 7—Read 1 Kings 15-16

A strong start of godly faithfulness with pious accomplishments along the way can never make up for a finish that is weak and faithless, turning to others in fear, forgetting the faithful God who got them to this point. Finishing strong must be the passion of us all. 1 Kings 15:9-24

The story of King Asa is a story of two chapters. As he began, he was faithful to God, re-instituted the forsaken customs of worship, and guarded with passion the purity of the temple. He did away with the profane Asherah pole and burned it in the Kidron valley. Sadly, the second chapter of Asa's reign was an unraveling of the good he had done. When Baasha, the king of Israel, invaded Jerusalem, he did not go to the temple to worship or pray, but he stripped the temple of its gold and silver and gave it to the Syrian king in order to ensure his relationship with Syria and hopefully buy protection.

Asa's story ended with a dreadful foot disease. According to the chronicler, he sought help only from the doctors and not from God. His ending was sad and doubly so because of the start he had and the potential that clearly marked his rule. It is not enough to start well in the Kingdom. We must finish strong and bear the marks of the holiness that pleases God.

Day 98 | Overcoming Our Forgetfulness

April 8—Read 1 Kings 17-19

When her son died, the widow from Zarephath forgot the faithful provision of God that had made little much, but when her son came bouncing down the stairs, her faith was enlivened. Let us never consider a crisis too great for the faithfulness of God. 1 Kings 17:8-24

When Elijah first appeared to the widow from Zarephath, he was hungry and the famine in Israel was great. He tested the widow's faith by asking her to give him her last scrap of food, and when she gave her all to the man of God—the miracle happened. The flour and the oil never dried up in her cupboard until the famine was over. The miracle was great, but when her son died, she immediately forgot the provision of God just a short time before. God restored her son's life, and her hopeful expectation returned.

We must guard against the spiritual amnesia that too often overtakes us in difficult days. It is easy to forget the goodness and faithfulness of God when the skies are darkened and the future looks bleak. But the promises of God are not subject to the shifting seasons, our emotional whims, or enemy tactics. We have a living hope rooted in the resurrected Christ, and the character of the living Christ is unchangeable.

Day 99 | God of the Valleys Too

April 9—Read 1 Kings 20-22

We must resist and adamantly refuse to entertain Satan's lie that there are limitations to the work of God. Neither the mountain nor the valley pose a threat to His sovereign power and likewise, there is no difficulty of ours that He cannot save us from. 1 Kings 20:23-30

Benhadad, the arrogant king of the Syrians, attempted to attack the Israelites but was sorely routed when he fought the people of God in the hills. The servants of the Syrian king counseled him that the reason for their loss was that the God of Israel was a God, only effective in the hills, and that a battle in the valley would lead the Syrians to overcoming victory. They were wrong. Yahweh helped the Israelites, and the Syrians lost again.

Sometimes, very foolishly, we assume that God is only faithful to us or His power efficacious only when we are soaring in the spiritual heights or living on the mountaintop. This is an anemic faith that discounts the whole of God's deep love and overcoming power. God certainly can and does bring us victory when we are living in the heavenly places that He has called us to, but His power has no limits and His grace is not relegated to our faithfulness. Even in the valleys of failure, disappointment, and pain, the God of all grace whom we serve, stands ready to defend us against our enemy and establish our victory.

Day 100 | Tragic Rebellion

April 10—Read 2 Kings 1-3

Privy to Yahweh's power over Baal (1 Kings 18), still Ahaziah lived as if there was no God in Israel—it was his destruction. To have known the power of the true God and yet live as if He does not exist is the epitome of foolishness and a prescription for complete loss. 2 Kings 1

Ahaziah was the son of Israel's wicked King Ahab and Queen Jezebel. He grew up in a home that was determined to resist Yahweh and serve Baal instead. He likely was with his father on Mt. Carmel when Elijah called fire down from Heaven and watched as Yahweh consumed the water-soaked altar prepared by the prophet. He knew the true God and His power, but his stubborn rebellion would not allow him to surrender. When he needed God's healing touch, he turned to Baal instead of Yahweh and died without divine intervention.

 How sad it is to watch people who know God, who have experienced His presence and known His touch, refuse to submit to His hand. So often the pride of the stubborn heart will not allow one to acknowledge the goodness and unique power of God, but it is always at the cost of personal loss. It is indeed the epitome of foolishness to deny the power of a God once known, and will, without question, place the final nail in the coffin of eternal loss.

Day 101 | Eyes to See the Victory

April 11—Read 2 Kings 4-7

Through the eyes of flesh, trained by negative, critical, and doubting voices of the world, a vision of despair emerges—fueling fear. Through the eyes of faith, trained by the Word and the still small voice of God, a vision of assurance emerges—fueling victory. 2 Kings 6:15-17

This text is one of the epic stories of the Old Testament. The prophet Elisha's trail of miraculous activity followed him, but he and his servant found themselves in a troublesome dilemma. Surrounded by the Syrian army, muscled by chariots and horses, Elisha's servant felt they had no recourse but surrender. Elisha prayed that God would open the eyes of his servant and when he did, the servant saw that the armies of God actually stood around the Syrians and no weapon had any chance of getting near to them.

It is a sad fact that contemporary Christians draw their conclusions and foster their fears by the reports of the world, the cynical, the skeptical, and the fear-mongering agenda of the enemy. Our eyes must be trained by the study of God's Word and anointed by the power of God's Spirit to see that we are hedged in by God's presence, and stand certain that no weapon formed against us will be able to prosper.

Day 102 | Learning to Trust

April 12—Read 2 Kings 8-10

At times God may call us to great and radical acts of faith that demand immediate action. Our response to those moments sets the stage for divine blessing later. Unless we cultivate a relationship with God now, we may fail to hear Him later and miss our great opportunity. 2 Kings 8

Famine struck the land of Israel, so Elisha told the woman, whose son he had previously brought back to life, to leave everything and go somewhere else to settle. She went immediately and settled in Philistia for seven years. It was a radical move and one that forced her to trust the Word of the Lord. Seven years later, by divine appointment, she was in the presence of the king, who because of her faithfulness, saw to it that everything she had lost was restored.

This miracle of restoration is beautiful and powerful. However, had the woman not seen the hand of God in the healing of her son, she may not have capitulated to the word of the prophet and would have missed out on the great experience of restoration. We never know what our obedience may set us up for or what great miracle may later come our way. How important it is to be obedient to God the first time He calls us. With each encounter our faith is deepened, and with every new work of God our witness is expanded. Know God now so that you can fully trust Him later when He calls.

Day 103 | The Danger of a Proud Heart

April 13—Read 2 Kings 11-14

Amaziah's pride was his downfall and brought tragic ruin to Judah. God hates pride and will resist the proud. Success can fan the seeds of pride, but it must be guarded against. Humility, on the other hand, will lead to all the benefits that pride will prevent. 2 Kings 14:7-14

Amaziah's routing of the Edomites led him to believe that he was invincible and to assume that with his military strength and strategy, he could defeat the people of Israel as well. Jehoash, Israel's king, warned him that the people of Edom were not to be compared with the might of the Israelites, and that his best course of action would be to enjoy the Edomite victory and stay home. His pride would not allow that, and Amaziah charged into battle only to be sorely defeated, he and the people of Judah, by the armies of Israel.

Pride is frequently the downfall of humanity, and the people of God are not exempt. Even when we accomplish victory in our spiritual battles, a heart of pride can set us up for defeat. When we begin to think that our superior strength, rather than the goodness and faithfulness of God is the reason for our success, we are on dangerous ground. God does indeed resist the heart lifted up in pride, but will look to the humble and contrite heart and grant His grace.

Day 104 | You Cannot Serve Two Gods

April 14—Read 2 Kings 15-17

"And though they worshiped the Lord, they continued to follow their own gods…" This describes the new citizens of Samaria, placed there by the Assyrian king. How sad to think that one can worship God and still hold on to relationships with the gods of this world. 2 Kings 17:33

The ancient Assyrian battle strategy was to overcome a land and then re-populate that land with a mix of natives, as well as transplanted aliens from other countries. The hope was that the mix of faiths would water down the native people, and their religion would become extinct. That is precisely what happened, and why the Samaritans and the Jews were at such odds. Here, the sad state of religious pluralism, powerless as it is, is clearly seen.

We live today among many who are not citizens of Heaven and do not know Christ. While they may give a nod to the God of Scripture and tolerate the practice of our faith, but at the same time, the want to continue to worship their gods of pleasure, wealth, lust, and entertainment. If their compromised piety infects the people of God, we ultimately lose our spiritual power and effectiveness. Jesus was clear… "you cannot serve two gods."

Day 105 | God's Plan Will not be Defeated

April 15—Read 2 Kings 18-19

The pompous predictions of powerlessness and doom leveled by the enemy must never be the definitive word for the people of God. Our trust lies in the One who takes offense at words spoken against His own and who long ago devised the plan that He will carry out. 2 Kings 19:20-26

When Rabshakek from Lachish and Sennacherib of Assyria came together and formed an alliance to take on King Hezekiah and the people of Judah, their threats were great. They sent word to Hezekiah that they planned to attack and spoke blasphemously against Yahweh, the God of Judah. Playing on Hezekiah's past failures, they sought to discourage him to the point of retreat and surrender, and their assessment of his God was one of weakness and ineptitude. But Hezekiah prayed, and God assured him that the words of his enemies had been heard, and they would be forced to flee.

The enemy of our soul seeks to disparage our faith and undermine our confidence in God. Often our past weakness and faith failures become targets for enemy attack and can leave us feeling weak and defenseless. Like Hezekiah, the Spirit of the Lord calls us to trust Him, forget our past failures, and rest in the assurance that our enemies will be defeated as God fulfills His plan in us.

Day 106 | Regarding the Law of the Lord

April 16—Read 2 Kings 20-22

A generation that discarded the Word of the Lord led to one that buried it. That generation led to one that disobeyed it in ignorance. God's judgment followed. We must be diligent, for the sake of those who follow, to re-introduce them to the Word of the Lord. 2 Kings 22

When Josiah ascended to Judah's throne, he was just eight years old. He was the grandson of Manasseh who, though he seemingly turned to God toward the end of his reign after much bloodshed and evil, reigned over Judah at a time when the Law of the Lord was being disregarded. When he died, his son Amon reigned. His time on the throne was a period of doing evil in the sight of God, and the Law that had been discarded during his father's rule was buried. Josiah found the Law buried in the house of the Lord when he took over.

Today we find ourselves in the precarious position of being a generation that is seeing the Word of the Lord fully disregarded. Its place of prominence in culture is no longer valued by most, and its veracity is being challenged by the secular and academic. It seems that the goal is not only to disregard its truth, but to bury it altogether. The Church must uphold that Truth and safeguard the very Word that is in fact the protector and preserver of civil society—if not, the judgment of God will for certain be experienced.

Day 107 | Deep Change

April 17—Read 2 Kings 23-25

A generation that discarded the Word of the Lord led to one that buried it. That generation led to one that disobeyed it in ignorance. God's judgment followed. We must be diligent, for the sake of those who follow, to re-introduce them to the Word of the Lord. 2 Kings 23:26-27

Despite Josiah's godly leadership the change that took place in Judah was superficial. After his death God fiercely judged them. Unless our hearts are changed, no superficial adjustment, verbal commitment, or physical act will appease the righteousness of God.

One of the few bright spots of the final years of Judah's existence was the reign of Josiah. He was just eight when he ascended the throne once occupied by David and made marked changes in the southern kingdom. He called the people to a return to the Law, restored the temple worship in its original purity, and made an end to the rampant idolatry in the land. Despite the sweeping reforms, the hearts of the people were not changed and after his death they returned to their ungodly ways.

Spiritual superficiality may be the greatest cancer of the modern church. Enthusiastic and energetic singing that moves human emotions has replaced holy worship, therapeutic sermons that soothe the soul have replaced Spirit-anointed proclamation of God's Word, and the embracing of our humanity and the acceptance of our flaws as "how we are" has replaced deep conviction and repentance. All is superficial transformation and all leaves us woefully short of the glory of God.

Day 108 | The Glory of the Last Adam

April 18—Read 1 Chronicles 1-4

In Adam, it all began—we all descended from him. In Adam, we are just a name, another sin-stained mortal destined to flourish and then be cut down as the grass. In Christ, the "last Adam," we are born again to eternal life, having become the righteousness of God. 1 Chronicles 1:1

Rarely do we pause to reflect on the truths that may be hidden within the many genealogies of Scripture. Instead, we tend to rush through and assume there is no lasting meaning or eternal significance that we might glean. Failure to do so here is to miss one of the glorious revelations of God's Word, that is, in Christ our fortunes have been reversed and He has made us His own.

The chronicler's genealogy begins with Adam. His name stands at the front of the human journey to remind us that we are all of him. Each of us from the earth, created in the image of God, but fallen and incapable of self-redemption, sinful and void of hope, we must acknowledge our utter futility. Here humanity stood until the "last Adam" came—His name is Jesus, and if born again into Him, we receive restored righteousness, revitalized hope, and a renewed future. From darkness to light, from Hell and Heaven, from death to life, we have come and been freed from the bondage of decay and set free to life eternal.

Day 109 | The Greatest Weapon is Trust

April 19—Read 1 Chronicles 5-6

Trusting God goes beyond confidence in His power. It is yielding to His wise plan whether He does what we think is best or not. The greatest and most satisfying of all victories come to those who truly trust Him. 1 Chronicles 5:19-20

The tribes of Reuben and Gad, as well at the half tribe of Manasseh, had to do battle with some formidable military opponents who challenged them for the territory that God had promised to them. While the chronicler notes the heavy weaponry and large armies that God's people were able to muster, he notes that their ability to prevail was found in the fact that they trusted Yahweh. That trust led to the defeat of their enemies, and the Hagrites who had opposed them became their servants. God was powerful, and their military was strong, but without trust, they would not have been able to achieve victory.

There is a rich lesson here for us. The power of God is unlimited, and there is no enemy that He cannot defeat. In addition, we are instructed to prepare, to work hard, and to use wisdom so that we can withstand our enemies. However, if we do that, the victory is not ensured unless we sincerely trust the God who has called us.

Day 110 | Wisdom of the Ages

April 20—Read 1 Chronicles 7-9

Biblical genealogies reminded God's people that they had a history to learn from and to honor and a cloud of witnesses to which they would one day belong. Healthy is the church that honors its past leaders and understands its place as PART of the people of God. 1 Chronicles 7-8

There may be no more mundane reading than the seemingly endless genealogies that appear in 1st Chronicles. To the casual and modern reader there seems to be no clear importance, and the thought of Spirit direction to record such matters is hard to grasp with human reasoning. Yet, both Old and New Testaments of Scripture seem to give some real credence to their value. There must be some significance for us, since genealogies are often found in inspired Scripture.

In a world that seems to always be looking for the new and novel and disregarding the wisdom of the past, the genealogies serve to remind us that we have a shared history, and that the work of God is ongoing from generation to generation. Those who have gone before us form the cloud of witnesses that await us, and as we, the people of God, learn to remind ourselves of their history, glean from their lives and strive to follow in their footsteps, we will grow healthier and navigate the issues of this world more effectively!

Day 111 | He Sees the Small Things

April 21—Read 1 Chronicles 10-12

King Saul's epitaph— "he died because he was unfaithful to the Lord...he failed to obey." Small decisions may seem unimportant—one lie, one incomplete obedience, one failure to follow a command. Not such a big deal? Small decisions—in the end—write our story. 1 Chronicles 10:13

Saul's rule began in a promising fashion. Called by God, gifted with prophetic ability, and possessing a commanding appearance and charisma, everything seemed to be in favor of a fruitful tenure as Israel's first king. Yet, with all things leaning in his favor, his failure to heed the voice of God through the prophet Samuel and his poor decision-making led to a disastrous end. It wasn't one colossal failure that led to his downfall, but a series of unwise and ungodly decisions.

Too often we downplay the importance of our decisions about the "little things." Surely a simple act of disobedience, a small indiscretion, a dishonest but advantageous transaction, or a rumor spread won't make a great difference. But it is precisely these decisions that mark our lives and end up defining our path. Guard carefully your decision-making and live as those who know they serve a God who sees.

Day 112 | Never Take God's Presence for Granted

April 22—Read 1 Chronicles 13-16

The improper handling of the ark of the covenant dealt lethal consequences to Israel. As carriers of God's presence, there is no substitute for faith working itself out in informed obedience. No enthusiasm or zeal can ever make up for this lack. 1 Chronicles 13:1-14; 15:1-15

The text before us is both captivating and frightening. After having been without the ark of God's presence in Jerusalem for two decades, David rightly desired to bring it back to Jerusalem. With great fanfare and demonstrative praise, the people joined David in returning the ark to Zion. Sadly, however, despite clear instruction from the Law of Moses, David failed to transport the ark properly and disaster struck—Uzzah was killed. Three months later, and with careful observance of the law, the ark found its way back home to the holy city, but not before a great price was paid.

The contemporary Church has become quite casual in our approach to the presence of God. We often busy ourselves with other things, grumble if the conditions for worship do not suit us or the atmosphere is not conducive to our stylistic preferences, or approach God as if He is not wholly other and immersed in divine holiness. While we may not be struck dead in the moment, wise is the one who duly notes the holiness of God's presence, approaches Him humbly and in a holy manner, and never takes for granted the God who invites us to draw near.

Day 113 | The Importance of Extending Grace

April 23—Read 1 Chronicles 17-20

Because the Ammonites wrongly assumed David meant evil toward them and grossly misunderstood his intentions, great bloodshed ensued. "A gentle answer deflects wrath but harsh words make tempers flare" (Proverbs 15:1). We must pause, pray, and think before acting or speaking. 1 Chronicles 19

This ancient story provides us with great wisdom. When Nahash, the Ammonite king, died, and his son, Hanun, was crowned in his stead, David sought to honor him and extended an offering of friendship and goodwill. Because he was distrusting of David, Hanun rejected David's offer, thinking him to be cunning and possibly planning to destroy the Ammonites. What ensued was an unnecessary loss of life of both the Ammonites and the Syrians.

There is a great lesson to learn here: failing to think the best of others and assuming evil intentions can lead to devastating loss. Instead of returning a suspect response to the overtures of others, we should learn to trust and think well of them, knowing that God will honor and keep safe those who reflect His character. Churches often lose their credibility, and believers push away those who don't know Christ when we live suspiciously or fail to extend grace.

Day 114| Focused Energy and Devoted Resources

April 24—Read 1 Chronicles 21-24

David's directive to Israel's leaders speaks to us today. Our priorities should still be to intentionally seek the Lord, to give ourselves wholly to humbly serving God's Kingdom, and to do all we can to ensure His presence is both welcome and honored among us. 1 Chronicles 22:19

David's days as king of Israel were numbered, and he was checking off his list all that needed to be accomplished before he gave way to his son Solomon. He charged Solomon with the building of the temple, and then he brought the leaders of the nation together and gave them this charge: *"Now set your mind and heart to seek the Lord your God. Arise and build the sanctuary of the Lord God..."*

It seems that there is no advice more relevant than these words from the one whose heart was after God. He knew there could be no greater devotion and no better use of resources and energy than to spend them on seeking God and building His Kingdom. So much could be accomplished that would honor the Lord if God's people would follow that advice. The world needs the people of God to be so focused, and the harvest of souls depends upon it.

Day 115 | The Necessity of a Friend

April 25—Read 1 Chronicles 25-27

After naming David's chief counselor (Jonathan), the teacher of his children (Jehiel), and his royal adviser (Ahithiphel), the text simply says, "Hushai the Arkite was the king's friend." While we all need various people in our lives, everyone needs a friend. 1 Chronicles 27:32-33

While there are some magnificent narratives to be found in both 1st and 2nd Chronicles, much of the material is relegated to the reporting of matters pertaining to the king's court. This text—case in point. Earlier, both military and tribal leaders are noted, and then the author focuses on the people closest to David—those in charge of his children and his own counselor. As almost a postscript comment, Hushai is then described as David's friend.

This underscores a very important principle that is unalterable. No matter how important we may think we have become, and no matter what professional teams may surround us, everyone needs a friend. A friend will challenge us when we think too highly of ourselves, listen when we need a sounding board, give us grace when we are at our worst, and encourage us when we are low. *He is your friend, who pushes you nearer to God*—Abraham Kuyper.

Day 116 | Christian Givers

April 26—Read 1 Chronicles 28-29

When we come to terms with where we were before Christ redeemed us, realize that we own nothing and it all belongs to Him, and embrace the truth that giving to the Kingdom is not an act of reluctant obligation but a humbling privilege, we become CHRISTIAN givers. 1 Chronicles 29:14

This chapter highlights the extraordinary and sacrificial giving of God's people in order to build and furnish the temple that would be built by Solomon. As King David stood before the people who had brought their gifts, he commended them for their great generosity, and though he himself would not build the temple, he rejoiced with them. In the presence of the entire assembly of Israel, he offered praise to God and led the people in prayer.

The prayer of David reminded the people that all things belong to God, that His majesty alone was worthy of worship, that only through Him were they able to prosper, and that even the ability and privilege to give was a gift that God had afforded to them. This is the heart of Christian giving—we OWN nothing that He didn't give us, we ARE nothing without Him, and if not for God, we could never even have the privilege of giving. This is the heart of Christian giving.

Day 117 | A Manifestation of His Glory

April 27—Read 2 Chronicles 1-3

The skill, wisdom, and patience required to build the earthly temple, along with the divine fashioning together of the skilled laborers into a team, is an apt picture of the Spirit's work in gathering, gifting, and empowering the Body of Christ to build the Kingdom. 2 Chronicles 2

It is a fascinating and telling description of how God works through humanity to achieve His purposes that is unveiled in the opening sections of 2nd Chronicles. Thousands of individuals, many supernaturally gifted to perform certain tasks, along with the amassed provisions shared by the people of God is what made possible the building of the temple to house the manifestation of God's presence. It took shared sacrifice, surrendered gifts, and supernatural empowering to carry out the plan of God to display His glory among the nations.

What a glorious picture of the Body of Christ, God's chosen vessel to declare His name and glory to the world. It is not the gift of one, the sacrifice of a few, or the great talent of a handful that demonstrates God's power to a lost world. Instead, it is the Body of Christ, ALL surrendered and ALL willing to sacrifice, that makes His glory known to a lost world.

Day 118 | His Majestic and Knowable Presence

April 28—Read 2 Chronicles 4-7

A marvelous revelation of God's nature is unpacked in Solomon's dedicatory prayer. Though God's holiness and majesty transcend human nature's capacity to know and receive, His immense grace, forgiveness, and power are available to the contrite and repentant heart. 2 Chronicles 6

The majestic reverence that flowed from the lips of young King Solomon as he stood on the temple's threshold and breathed the dedicatory prayer to the temple, still capture our imaginations today. The prayer is dripping with powerful theological implications and deep revelations of the nature and character of God. His tender mercies stand together with His unapproachable glory and leave the worshipper with a sense of mysterious awe that drives their passion to know the high and exalted One even better.

It is indeed impossible for us to ever know fully the nature of an incomprehensible God. That truth, however, should not discourage us from seeking Him, but rather stir in us a passion to know Him better. This was the catalyst of Paul's prayer in Philippians, *"that I may know Him!"* As we come before Him with a heart of curious and reverent wonder, He longs to reveal Himself to us and flood us with His glorious presence.

Day 119 | Lasting Impressions on Inquiring Souls

April 29—Read 2 Chronicles 8-10

Though Solomon later drifted away from God, his wisdom, stature, organization, and generosity, marks of God on his life, made a deep impression on the inquiring soul of the Queen of Sheba. May Christ in us make lasting impressions on inquiring souls around us. 2 Chronicles 9:5-12

The later years of Solomon's life went sadly awry as he followed after the idols of the many foreign wives he had taken, contrary to the command of the Lord. Yet, early in his rule, the great gifts and wisdom that he had been blessed to enjoy made a great impact on many lives, Israelites and foreigners alike. None more so than the Queen of Sheba, whose heart was deeply impacted by the wisdom and Spirit-anointed leadership that he exhibited.

Many around us are yearning for answers, diligently pursuing a depth, a revelation, or a person who can bring satisfaction and peace to their restless souls. May we be people, like Solomon, who make a lasting impression on the hungry hearts that long for peace and inquire to find meaning in their lives.

Day 120 | Prepared to Seek the Lord

April 30—Read 2 Chronicles 11-13

"And he did evil, because he did not prepare his heart to seek the Lord." This, said of Rehoboam, pinpoints the origin of our failures, struggles, and fruitless efforts to impact the world for Christ. There is no substitute for a heart prepared to seek the Lord. 2 Chronicles 12:14

Rehoboam, though given ample opportunity to succeed and lead the unified nation of Israel as an heir to the throne of his grandfather David, failed miserably and saw the kingdom divided. The origin of his failure was his insistence on moving forward without divine direction. Human counsel betrayed him, and God was not sought. Instead of marking the annals of history with great stories of national victories, his is a name noted for folly and failure.

Those who hope to make great Kingdom impact must first learn the discipline of seeking the Lord. To embark upon a vision that requires supernatural aid without preparing one's heart to seek the source of that divine empowerment is the behavior of the foolish and leads to consequences that not only fall short of God's best, but often leads to unnecessary pain and heartache. The wise will prepare their hearts to know God's heart, fine tune their spiritual ears to hear His voice, and seek His face to be encouraged by His presence.

Day 121 | Staying True in the Hard Times

May 1—Read 2 Chronicles 14-16

When we turn to man in times of struggle or seek to be buoyed by worldly resources, personal gifting, or godless ingenuity, we will surely falter. But when we rest in One who seeks for those who depend on Him, we will weather any storm and conquer every mountain. 2 Chronicles 16:9

The chronicler records what was a sad chapter in the reign of Asa as king over Judah. The majority of his reign was godly and prosperous as he worked to rid the nation of the false gods that had spotted the landscape of Judah, and he demolished the shrines where many kinds of sensual evil had taken place. Asa was proactive in ridding the nation of evil, and he sought to do what was right in the eyes of God. But sadly, at the end of his reign, Asa, fearing the alliance that had formed against him, turned to ungodly allies and failed to trust God. This became his downfall.

We must avoid the temptation to go the way of Asa. It is easy to serve God and be faithful as long as things are going well. But when times are tough and things begin to press in on us, we often are too quick to compromise. We must hold steady in these times and stay true to God's Word. He is faithful and will bring us through to victory if we will trust Him.

Day 122 | Our Eyes Are Upon You

May 2—Read 2 Chronicles 17-20

A heart fully dependent upon God is far better poised for spiritual victory than one that is presumptuously capable and confident in its own wisdom. 2 Chronicles 20:12

Jehoshaphat was faced with devastating news that struck a chord of fear in his heart. Enemies from the Syrian region had formed an alliance designed to take out the young king and the kingdom of Judah. The people of Judah were looking to Jehoshaphat for guidance, but he had never known such a crisis. He set himself to seek the Lord, proclaimed a fast, and called the families together to pray. His prayer was simple: "*We have no power against this great multitude that is coming against us; nor do we know what to do, but our eyes are upon You.*"

As the people prayed and the worshippers praised, the enemy became confused and ended up destroying one another. The honest humility of Jehoshaphat and the praise of God's people brought the resounding victory. Acknowledging our weakness and declaring our dependence upon God is the means to true and a lasting spiritual victory.

Day 123 | A Kingdom of Life

May 3—Read 2 Chronicles 21-23

Many are they, who like Athaliah, seek to stifle and stamp out the voice and work of God. As the people of God, we should be like Jehosheba, willing to risk life and reputation to seek out, protect, and nurture even the tiniest and seemingly insignificant seeds of Kingdom hope. 2 Chronicles 22:10-12

Athaliah was the wicked and godless mother of Ahaziah, king of Judah, who was the son of Jehoram. Athaliah was also the daughter of wicked King Ahab and his wife Jezebel, who ruled previously over Israel. She did all she could to counsel her son in the godless ways of her heritage, and when he died, she snuffed out the entire royal line of Judah, that is, with one exception. Jehosheba, who was the daughter of the slain king and wife of Jehoida the priest, managed to steal away with the youngest member of the royal family, Joash, who later became king. He, too, ruled in wickedness, but the royal family line was preserved.

The world and godless culture is seeking to stamp out the work of the Kingdom and any spiritual vitality that can be found. Even the horrific sin of abortion seeks to destroy seed that God would otherwise use for His work. We must be committed to the value of every life, the purpose of all who are marked by the *imago dei*, and the eternal hope of the Kingdom.

Day 124 | With A Whole Heart

May 4—Read 2 Chronicles 24-26

"And he did what was right in the sight of the Lord, but not with his whole heart." Amaziah's reign was hard and ended poorly. He knew what was right but questioned and rebelled against God's Word. Partial surrender is no surrender—a divided heart will not stand. 2 Chronicles 25:2

This text is hard to read. Amaziah was a young king, just 25 when he began his reign, and was full of potential. As he did things according to the Law, he pleased God. But while his actions were seemingly obedient, his heart lacked full devotion. He was not wholly loyal to God, and while outwardly it seemed he was aligning himself with the Law's obligations, inwardly he questioned and rebelled against God. His rebellion led to idolatry, and his spiritual infidelity led to a tragic end.

Without wholehearted devotion, we are in a vulnerable spiritual position. To outwardly observe the expectations of God, but live inwardly in a manner that fulfills one's own desires and lusts, is to place one's spiritual condition in great jeopardy. God calls us to complete devotion, full surrender, and passionate submission to His Spirit that works within us to develop lives that are consecrated for His service and to His name.

Day 125 | True Greatness

May 5—Read 2 Chronicles 27-28

The way to greatness is not by political maneuvering, pursuing power, or carving out a name for oneself by impressive feats. Rather, it comes as we order our ways before the Lord, approach His presence in a reverent manner, and refuse the world's enticements. 2 Chronicles 26:6

Jotham was just twenty-five when he ascended to the throne of Judah, replacing his father, Uzziah. Uzziah had been a good king, but he brought peril to the throne when he foolishly entered the temple to offer incense. The priests tried to restrain him, but in his pride, he became angry and God, in that moment, brought judgment through the disease of leprosy. Jotham would not be so presumptuous. He honored God in all that he did, stayed in his kingly role, and though the nation backslid, he remained devoted as God made him great.

Greatness today is sought through many means. People push their way to the top, and some, like Jotham's father, Uzziah, presume that the rules do not apply to them, and they try to achieve status by their own frenetic activity. When we humble ourselves before God, remain in the place He calls us to, and refuse to manipulate our way to the top, He will make us prosperous and bless us with His glory.

Day 126 | The High Priority of Soul Cleansing

May 6—Read 2 Chronicles 29-31

Ahaz allowed the temple to become a storage barn—filthy, cluttered, and in disrepair. Hezekiah cleansed it, restored worship, and told the priests to not be "negligent." We cannot neglect the temple of our hearts. They must be cleansed, de-cluttered, and sanctified. 2 Chronicles 29

The history of Judah's kings was a hodge-podge of good and bad, godly and wicked, effective and disastrous. Ahaz was an ungodly king who failed to seek after God and do what was right in His eyes. He sacrificed to idols, sought alliances with godless kings, and dismantled the furnishings of the temple, turning it into a glorified junk barn. The very thought of such behavior makes those committed to the holiness of Yahweh and reverence in worship, heartbroken. Hezekiah, the son of Ahaz, who reigned in his stead when he died, made the temple's restoration and temple worship a priority.

Paul was clear that we are all the temple of the Holy Spirit in the new covenant. Our souls must be regularly de-cluttered and made fit through the sanctifying work of the Spirit and the washing of the Word for God's presence. We must not take this task lightly, and we cannot neglect this priority. Our lives are what the lost world sees of Jesus, and unless our souls have been inhabited by the Spirit of God, they cannot adequately reflect Christ's glory. Like Hezekiah, this work of cleansing must be our greatest and highest pursuit.

Day 127 | A Humble and Obedient Heart

May 7—Read 2 Chronicles 32-34

It is the humble heart, not a perfect or self-righteous one, that God hears and responds to with His favor. A humble heart is broken by the Word of God, offers no excuse and provides no self-vindication—it simply repents and obeys.
2 Chronicles 34:17

Josiah was but eight years old when he ascended to the throne of Judah, succeeding his father, Amon, and his grandfather Manasseh (both wicked). He refused to do as they had done. When the Law was located during temple renovations, he called the people to repentance and obedience to God's Word. God honored him and allowed him to live in peace.

God rejects self-righteousness and yet, knows our frame and imperfections. Josiah was not perfect, but he was humble and did not seek to gain the favor of God in his own goodness. God honored that and his honest brokenness as he stood before the Law of the Lord. This is the heart God seeks and honors today—one that is humble and willing to obey.

Day 128 | The Final Words

May 8—Read 2 Chronicles 35-36

The final chapter of 2 Chronicles states two things. One—repeated failure to obey the Holy Spirit and give up spiritual idols will reap serious consequences. Two—rebellion leading to those consequences need not be the final word. Grace to restore is still available. 2 Chronicles 36

The author of Chronicles makes use of the final chapter of his second volume by summarizing the final years of the southern kingdom of Judah and their ultimate downfall at the hands of the Babylonians. He notes the fall of the final kings, their deportation, and the 70 years of exile in Babylon. All of this happened because of their ongoing refusal to hear the Word of the Lord and turn back to Yahweh. In the closing verses of 2 Chronicles, the writer tells us that when Cyrus reigned as king in Persia, succeeding the Babylonian reign, he decreed that the people of Judah could go home.

This final chapter of the chronicler has powerful relevance to us today. We, too, must be reminded that a continued denial of God's authority in our lives and a rebellion against His Word will ultimately bring dire consequences. But we also must remember that God's ear is turned toward the repentant cry and will respond quickly to restore those who call out to Him with His grace.

Day 129 | Generations of Praise

May 9—Read Ezra 1-3

The moment was holy. The temple foundation was laid. Young men, excited for the future, shouted with joy. Older men, grateful for God's goodness despite their failures, wept. Perfectly holy—generations worshipping God in unique ways. This is how it should be. Ezra 3:10-13

This is one of the most dramatic Old Testament texts and the scene is rich with powerful pathos. The people of God were back in their homeland with a chance to restore the pride of their national heritage and the hope of their spiritual future. The foundation of the temple was being laid, and as the people rejoiced, two groups stood out. The young men, excited about progress and teeming with hope, shouted with exuberant praise. The old men, holding closely to the memory of former days, wept as the hopes, once thought destroyed, were rekindled. Young and old, together with hearts of grateful praise.

This is a glorious picture of what the church should look like today. Too often generations are pitted against one another and worship styles and dress codes create unfortunate barriers. This ought not to be. Instead, young and old, all saved by grace and washed in the blood of Christ, should lift their hearts and voices in a concert of praise, giving thanks for all that God has done.

Day 130 | The Favor of the Lord

May 10—Read Ezra 4-6

These chapters underscore powerfully the truth of divine favor. When God's people align themselves with His purpose, humble themselves under His hand, and present themselves in repentance TO His service, the magnitude of the task becomes a non-factor—HE will make a way. Ezra 5-6

This narrative is one of the most fascinating pericopes of the Old Testament and testifies powerfully to the protection and provision of Yahweh in arming His people and His house. When questioned by adversarial neighbors about their building of the temple, the elders of Israel laid claim to the decree of King Cyrus made 25 years before. When the new Persian king, Darius, checked the records, he found the decree. He then called for the neighbors to help with the temple's completion and provide anything needed by the Jews.

This was a period of time that God's people had determined to hear the Word of the Lord and obey. This obedience led to their diligence in completing the temple and curried the favor of the Lord. When we walk in obedience, God honors that and resists the overwhelming circumstances or insurmountable obstacles. God provides and makes a way and He will go to great lengths to ensure that His name and His house are honored.

Day 131 | We Are Responsible

May 11—Read Ezra 7-10

Most believers acknowledge that our nation's drift from biblical principles has greatly contributed to a compromised moral stability. Have we acknowledged our own culpability in failing to reverence God's Word as we have chased after fashionable church trends? Ezra 9:3-15

Ezra, along with Nehemiah, is largely responsible for the spiritual reforms and deep repentance of God's people after their return from exile. As Ezra led the people in acts of repentance, he made no attempt to gloss over their culpability. They were to blame. It was their compromise, their self-confidence, and their bend toward the novel and new that led them into bondage.

In the church we pass blame and point fingers at societal compromise and cultural immorality when we see the backslidden nature of our nation, but we must accept responsibility ourselves. As believers we have become bored with the Word and sought experience instead, and we have preferred the new and edgy over the tried and true—all while watching the decline of both church and culture.

Day 132 | Enduring the Resistance

May 12—Read Nehemiah 1-4

When we embrace God's commission to us, the spiritual resistance will be great, and opportunities for retreat will present themselves. Rather than retreat, we must remind ourselves of His call, stand firm against our enemy, and lean into the faithful One who has promised victory. Nehemiah 4

Nehemiah lived out a call that had been crystal clear. He was to leave his comfortable role in Persia and return to Jerusalem to rebuild the broken down walls of Jerusalem. The task was vital to the plan of God and the future of God's people. To leave the Holy City in disarray would be to acknowledge defeat and allow the enemies to claim what belonged to God. This call was greatly opposed by enemies of Judah, but Nehemiah stood firm, trusting in the Lord who had called Him.

God has called us to rebuild the broken and to restore that which has been burned over and forgotten. Lives hang in the balance and await this generation's Nehemiahs to step up and fulfill God's call. All who answer the call will experience enemy resistance, but can overcome when by faith they stand on His Word, depend on His Spirit, and rehearse His promises.

Day 133 | The Keys of Kingdom Effectiveness

May 13—Read Nehemiah 5-7

After just fifty-two days of unintimidated, focused effort and preserved unity among the people, the walls were rebuilt, and Judah's enemies were afraid. The greatest threat to the efforts and strategies of Satan is a focused, unafraid, diligent, and unified people of God. Nehemiah 6:15-16

The rebuilding of Jerusalem's walls under the leadership of Nehemiah was one of the great feats of the post-exile return by the remnant of God's people. They were successful because Nehemiah would not cower to Judah's enemies or allow them to intimidate him. Instead, he led with strength, kept the people focused on their work, and insisted they work together and deal with any conflict that arose. He knew the great danger that division could cause, and he made certain it was not ever nurtured if it sprung up.

Herein lies the secret to the church's effectiveness today—the enemy will do all he can to get us to lose our focus. Threats of peril or accusation will always surround the people of God committed to growth and Kingdom impact. Division will be exploited by Satan every chance he gets. We must deal with conflict when it occurs, forgive fully and readily, and commit to a unified effort in carrying out God's call on our lives.

Day 134 | The Word—Living and Powerful

May 14—Read Nehemiah 8-10

Ezra read the Law to a generation who had not heard, and they responded in repentance and worship. Instead of changing His Word to fit our culture or dismissing it for fear of offending, we must declare truth to a generation yet to hear and expect the same results. Nehemiah 8

The people who Ezra addressed were the exiled generation, and during the exile, the Law had not been propagated. They had not before heard the Word of the Lord or been subject to its authority. Ezra determined not to water it down, leave anything out, or interpret it contextually. He read it and explained it as truth. The people responded in repentance and worship.

Our generation is ignorant of God's Word. Scripture has, in most sectors of society, been silenced, and our culture is biblically illiterate. Many have chosen to reject it as truth, scoff at its claims, and deny its authority. God's people, however, believe it to be alive and powerful, and when it is proclaimed in its fullest truth, with all of its holy demands, a generation will repent and draw near to God in worship.

Day 135 | No Room for Compromise

May 15—Read Nehemiah 11-13

A close tie between the priest and an enemy of God resulted in the deterioration of Judah's obedience, impure worship, and a drift from God's covenant. We must take great care to not leave room in our lives for the habits, people, or forces that drive us from God. Nehemiah 13

When Nehemiah left Jerusalem to return to Persia after having rebuilt the walls and the temple, he did so with a sense of certainty that the people were in good hands under the leadership of Eliashab, the priest. But when he made a return visit to Judah, he found that the room where the offerings for sacrifice were to be kept in the temple had been rented to Tobiah, the Samaritan who had stood in opposition to the rebuilding. Nehemiah, angered by the compromise, drove Tobiah out with all of his belongings and ordered that the offerings be replenished and the worship of God's people be restored.

There is a grave danger when the people of God, especially those in leadership, become too tightly allied with those who may tout political power, but whose character stands in opposition to the Gospel. The Church must not become a political action committee, tempted to sell out the truth of the Gospel for notoriety or prestige. Instead, they must remain true to the principles of sound doctrine and holy living.

Day 136 | We Must Not Be Silent

May 16—Read Esther 1-4

A generation must arise that understands that to remain silent is to be complicit with the enemy of man's eternal souls and that what is called for in this day is a people who will lay aside self-preservation and selfish desires and fight for the lost to be saved. Esther 4:13-17

Mordecai pleaded with Esther to go before the king and ask him to save the Jewish people. The edict had been signed, and the death sentence was waiting to be executed. At first, afraid she had fallen out of the good graces of the king who had not invited her to see him for a month, Esther feared for her own life and pushed back on the request of her older cousin. After realizing her silence would most certainly mean the extermination of the Jewish people, she laid down her personal fears focused on self-preservation, and consented to visit the king.

It is easy today to shun personal responsibility and assume that someone else will do the work for us. However, a generation is being destroyed—spiritually lost for eternity without God. Despite the cost and the potential pain, we must embrace the sacrifice and refuse to be silent. The world must have a witness, and that is our responsibility.

Day 137 | God Is Watching

May 17—Read Esther 5-7

In a culture consumed by instant gratification, addicted to social media, and driven by a 24-hour news cycle, we can forget that the eyes of God watch all, that the wicked and deceptive will ultimately be judged, and the righteous, though often unnoticed, will be rewarded. Esther 6

In this text, it appears that Haman has the upper hand. Mordecai has been overlooked for his kindness, and the Jews will be ruthlessly exterminated. The plan of Haman seems to have worked, and the plight of God's people was dire. But ultimately, though the name of God never technically appears in the book of Esther, His activity is seen. Mordecai's kindness comes to light, and the sin of Haman is exposed. Justice prevails, and the people of God are spared.

We often feel as if no one notices what we have done, the effort toward holiness that we have exerted, or the evil that goes unchecked. Will there ever be equity and justice? God IS watching, and though His works are not confined to our cultural demands and instant gratification pursuits, He misses nothing and will bring everyone into account for what they have done, good or bad.

Day 138 | Sharing God's Faithfulness with the Next Generation

May 18—Read Esther 8-10

It is imperative that, as God's people, we do better at passing on to the next generation the assurance of God's faithfulness and celebrate often God's certain deliverance as a reminder that the fruit of victory cannot be enjoyed without the process of struggle. Esther 9:20-28

The story of Esther is one of the great narratives of the Old Testament, and the providential deliverance of God's people from the wicked plans of Haman is a beautiful reminder of God's care and faithfulness to His people and to His plan. The narrative is exciting and engaging and unveils how God works behind the scenes, even when we wonder if He is at work at all. As a testimony to God's faithfulness, the Jews established the Feast of Purim to remind every generation how God preserved them, and that feast continues today.

The Jews were committed to passing on God's goodness to those generations that followed. The establishment of feasts and celebrations was common for the ancient Jews who were determined, for their children, to know their God. This depth of commitment is sorely lacking in our culture today. In a society where making sure our kids are on the best sports teams, have the fanciest clothes, and are pulled away from worship every weekend to be on a field, court, or dance floor, the passing on of our faith has been lost as a parental priority and will, if not corrected, reap disastrous results.

Day 139 | The Good Purpose of God

May 19—Read Job 1-3

Job's assessment of the reality of life, even for the one who places their trust in God, is airtight theology. In this fallen world, we will receive and must accept both the good and bad and still know that both are under the watchful and caring hand of our God. Job 2:10

"You speak as one of the foolish women speaks. Shall we indeed accept good from God, and shall we not accept adversity?" These were the words of Job to his wife who had counseled him to curse God and die. All that belonged to Job had been taken. His family had been decimated by tragedy, and his own body was now covered with painful boils that left him reeling in pain. His wife, lacking his faith and piety, suggested that he seek escape from the pain and disregard any notion of faith. Job, however, knew that the character of God must not be reduced to the analysis of humanity based on any particular season of life.

This is such a rich and needed lesson that we must all learn. We do God great injustice and sell ourselves short when we judge God's character by our present circumstances. Both good times and bad times meted out to us by God serve a divine and always good purpose.

Day 140 | The Friend We Need

May 20—Read Job 4-7

Job's friends showed themselves wholly inadequate, inconsistent, and disappointing—the classic "fair-weather friends." Godly friendships, though sadly rare, are anchored in unwavering loyalty and yield dependable encouragement and reliable grace. Job 6:14-21

For those who are students of Scripture, it is commonly noted that Job's friends were at their best when they were saying nothing. When they began to speak, their words dripped with hurtful critique, and their friendship with Job was further injured. In this text, Job finally shares his thoughts about the counsel of his "friends," and his words help shape for contemporary readers what friends should and should not do or be.

Loyalty is a sadly lost quality in most relationships today. People seem far too eager to move on to the next and best, trading friendships, jobs, and marriages like they do cell phones, always looking for an upgrade. This is not the sort of friendship modeled for us by the One, who though He is our Savior and Lord, is also willing to call us His friend. His example of friendship calls us to demonstrate loyalty no matter what the circumstances, be unwavering in our care and support even during the most challenging of times, and when a word of correction is needed, to do so with grace that aims to heal and restore.

Day 141 | The One Who Has Gone Between

May 21—Read Job 8-10

Suffering helps us grasp God's plan. Job, in his pained cry, laid a foundation for the revelation of Jesus, who came to feel what we feel and resolve forever the longing of the human heart to bridge the gulf between our sinful brokenness and His majestic holiness. Job 9:33

"If only there were a mediator between us, someone who could bring us together." These were the words of Job in the midst of his pain. His words reveal the dilemma that is as ancient as Adam and Eve. Humanity is broken and lives in the depths of pain and confusion. At the same time, God is beyond our reach. What has always been needed is a go-between, one who can bridge that gap. Job's pain elicited this cry, words that perfectly describe humanity's plight, and point to the Redeemer who was to come.

We no longer have to cry out for an arbiter or one to fill the void. Jesus fulfilled the longing cry of Job. He, perfect Son of Man and yet Eternal God, would bring the Divine into our human pain. He made Himself of no reputation and took upon Himself the form of man so that He might experience what we do, so that He might sustain us when we struggle. He was and He IS the go-between, the One who brings God and man together, even in pain.

Day 142 | Yet Will I Serve Him

May 22—Read Job 11-14

Unaware of the battle raging in the heavenlies that targeted his soul, Job, subjected to the theologically impoverished doctrinal critique of his friends, grieving the tragic loss of his family, and discouraged by his wife's lack of support, still knew it best to trust God. Job 13:15

"Though He slay me, yet will I trust Him. Even so, I will defend my own ways before Him." This was the godly sentiment of Job when everyone else was questioning his integrity and accusing him of wrongdoing that had led to his misfortune. Job had no idea that Satan had bargained with God for the right to pursue his soul and undermine his integrity. He did know that although he could not explain Him, the God that he knew and served was trustworthy.

We too often forget that what is visible to the naked eye is not the end of the story. There is, as Craddock said, *"something going on behind what is going on."* This is when the child of God must choose to trust. Others may encourage us to give up or posit reasons for our struggle, but those who have placed their trust in God can rest in the assurance that He is still worthy of our trust and fully capable to keep us through it all.

Day 143 | Without Excuse

May 23—Read Job 15-17

Without the written Word or the indwelling Spirit, Job was able, despite devastating trials, incalculable pain, and his friends' betrayal, to soar in faith, trust God's sovereign integrity, and boldly confess that his heavenly advocate was for him. We are without excuse. Job 16:19

"Even now, behold my witness is in Heaven." These were the confident words of Job, even after the excruciating trials he endured, the pain that accompanied those trials, and the utter failure of his friends who offered no comfort—only ridicule, accusation, and blame. He was not shaken by the struggle, but only grew stronger and confessed confidently that God would defend him before the heavenly tribunal.

The strength of Job is both curious and impressive. His great faith was sustained without the weapons that we have been blessed to know and utilize. There was no written Word, which is the source of our faith, and he lived before the indwelling Spirit was available, and the Holy Spirit is the force that empowers us to stand when the struggle is great. Still, Job stood to face his enemies and to rebuke his friends, so that even under overwhelming pressure, he stood firm. We have been given all we need to stand, so we are without excuse.

Day 144 | Our Ready Redeemer

May 24—Read Job 18-21

Faced with his friends' accusations and living in great despair, Job longed for a record of his life to vindicate him. But by faith, he knew a Redeemer would one day appear. Our confidence is not in the witness of our own life, but in the advocacy of our Redeemer. Job 19:23-25

The story of Job is pregnant with portraits of a longing heart. Though Job likely preceded Abraham and had no understanding of a Messiah, his heart longed, like every human heart, for One to redeem him. His friends showed no mercy for his plight, and instead accused him as one deserving of all he had experienced. They spoke evil of him and suggested it was his own sin that led to his awful circumstances. Job cried out in faith for One that would appear and become his advocate. While himself unaware, Job was longing for the Christ.

We often find ourselves under the attack and accusation of the enemy of our soul. He often tells us that we deserve the pain we experience and that it is our own failure that has led to our untimely suffering. By faith we can join the chorus of Job and cry out for One to plead our cause. On this side of the cross, we know to whom we cry. Our Redeemer lives, and His name is Jesus. He stands ready to come to our defense and emerges to set straight the accusations of the evil one.

Day 145 | Tried in the Fire

May 25—Read Job 22-26

The furnace of Job's suffering did not come to fruition because God was neglectful or because Job had transgressed. Though Job struggled to fully comprehend, the heat was divinely permitted to intensify, so that through suffering Job might be refined and his faith might deepen. Job 23:10

It would have been easy, and frankly natural, for Job to have felt that God was punishing him as he experienced the great loss of family and wealth, betrayal of friends, and physical trial. But he knew that the heat of the furnace would produce the purity of gold and that his faith, being refined, would more fully please God in the end.

Too often we consider the trials we face or the fire we must endure as acts of divine disapproval or personal rebuke. Instead, God may be allowing the heat of the furnace to purify our hearts, grow our faith, and ready us for Kingdom victory. God's work in our lives is not focused only on our present happiness or personal ease of existence. He is at work to make us like Him, to produce in us His character, and to work through us in a manner that both brings Him glory and draws others in need of hope and restoration to the cross.

Day 146 | Humble Certainty

May 26—Read Job 27-30

The truly wise acknowledge their limitations, allow their questions to be embedded in the certainty of God's just workings, they approach the holiness of God with a sense of deep awe, quietly trusting in a good God, and live with worshipful expectation that God will make Himself known. Job 28:28

Throughout the book bearing his name, Job wrestles with his plight, wondering at the peril that had befallen him. Yet, he understands that the counsel of God lies beyond human comprehension. Though he questions and challenges God, his proclamation is unwavering— *"Behold the fear of the Lord, that is wisdom, and to turn away from evil is understanding."* He knew the source of wisdom and, though it was often untraceable, he knew the reverent fear of Yahweh was his answer.

Many questions fill our minds as we navigate an often ruthlessly evil and desperately broken world. Our inability to plumb the depths of the mind of God, coupled with our sinful frailties, leave us with a sense of frustrated helplessness. This is where we must submit to the wise counsel of Job and know that as we root our confidence in wisdom we do not fully understand and worship the One from whom all wisdom flows, we can know the steadfastness of divine security.

Day 147 | In Him We Live, Move, and Breathe

May 27—Read Job 31-34

Though the source is questionable (Job's "friend"), he states truth. "...the breath of the Almighty gives us life." This should humble us, for if we have breath, God has a purpose for us. With words and deeds, "let everything that has breath praise the Lord." Job 33:4

Job's friends were terrible. Instead of supporting him, they mocked him. Instead of standing with him in his pain, they heaped criticism and speculative judgment on all that he experienced. In their attempt to philosophize, they set themselves up as seers who knew God and His ways, yet they showed no compassion to the one they claimed as their friend. Surprisingly, in the midst of their misguided criticism, Elihu managed to speak one nugget of truth— *"it is the breath of the Almighty that gives us life."*

This truth, even from the lips of a wrong-thinking critic, should be embraced. It reminds us that we are not our own, that we do not control our own destiny, and it is in Him, that we find breath and life. When we embrace this reality, it will change the way we live, serve, and worship. Our breath emerges from Him and as stewards of that breath and all that He gives to us, we must use His blessings, not to heap upon ourselves personal benefits, but instead to make certain that our lives reflect the glory that He, as our Lord, deserves!

Day 148 | A Word that Matters

May 28—Read Job 35-38

The resounding truth of Job 38 doesn't answer the nagging question of humanity, "why do pain and evil exist?" It does FAR better. It assures us that though all that IS—God made from nothing, nothing was made without a plan, and it all continues to be under His watchful care. Job 38

The story of Job has historically been what theologians call a "theodicy," an attempt to answer the question about the existence of pain and evil in a world created by a good God. The narrative begins with Job, described in the text as "perfect," losing all that he owns and cherished and experiencing the depth of physical pain and misery with no relief. The rest of the narrative is spent with Job and his three "friends," and then one other spectator musing about the reason for Job's misfortune.

As the story ends, no answer has emerged that satisfies the longing heart. What the story, all of the back and forth dialoging, and all of the critiques and challenges of God does is leave the reader frustrated and wondering why bad things happen to good people. Then God speaks and brings a word to Job. The word does not come in the form of an answer—instead it is a word of assurance. That assurance was simply this—nothing gets past Him, He always has a plan, and every hurt and every pain is felt and shouldered by a loving God.

Day 149 | Words That Declare What Eyes Have Seen

May 29—Read Job 39-42

When I read Job's final words, I wonder if we might speak less about what we really don't understand, and trust more the God who has our times in His hands, if instead of just hearing and talking about God, we could really see Him? Job 42:1-6

So much of the book of Job is filled with speculative humanity positing their theological theories about life and God. Each one seems to try to one-up the next in an ongoing cycle of philosophical pandering and harsh critique. Even Job, who took the brunt of the criticism, finds himself making assumptions about God and His dealings with humanity. It is not until Job concludes the matter with these words that the folly stops. "I had heard of you by the hearing of the ear, but now my eye sees you." Job 42:5

This, it seems, may be the antidote to the endless and most often words of fallen humanity when it comes to the working of God. So often we try to explain Him and only end up making matters worse for those who seek understanding. Maybe we have heard enough, but we need to see more. Maybe what we need is not another uninformed speech that seeks to frame the ways and workings of God. Maybe what we really need is someone who has ascended to the hill of the Lord and can speak of what they have seen! This is the word that will heal.

Day 150 | He is Our Shield and Protector

May 30—Read Psalm 1-8

It is neither the witness of our enemies nor the frustrations of our own souls that determine our spiritual position. It is the DECLARED TRUTH of God's Word. He IS the shield that protects us and secures our ultimate victory. He WILL keep our heads from bowing in shame. Psalm 3:1-3

David, though called and anointed by God, was always under attack from his enemies. Saul tried to take David's life on many occasions, and David's own son, Absalom sought to murder his father. David was often on the run, and the third Psalm was written from a cave where he and his servants were seeking refuge from those who wished them harm. The enemies of David were firing insults at the king and telling him that God had forgotten and forsaken him. David, however, knew that it was not their witness that determined his destiny. It was the Word of the Lord that would be final.

What a powerful lesson this is for us to learn! It is not what the enemy says of us or the whispering of Satan telling us that our failures have disqualified us from Kingdom service that carries ultimate weight. It is the truth of God's Word, and it reminds us that He will protect us, immerse us in His glory, and lift our head above the shame of our sin and failure.

Day 151 | The Certain Promises of God

May 31—Read Psalm 9-13

Though godly statesmen and leaders with integrity are fast disappearing from our secular culture, and truth is now a scorned value, "the Lord's promises are pure, like silver refined in a furnace, purified seven times over." Psalm 12

It is the lament of the psalmist that the *"godly man ceases."* Though we hate to acknowledge this observation, to deny the fact that godliness in our culture is fading is to bury one's head in the sand. Many there are who speak boastfully and who make grandiose claims, but few are those who know the Lord who is holy and who anchor their lives to His indestructible truth.

Despite the rarity of such godly people, we should set our minds to resist our godless culture and root ourselves in the holiness of God and the veracity of His Word. The promises of boastful men and the rhetoric of the carnal will one day come crashing down, but those who have made His holiness their aim and have staked their present peace and future hope in His tried and certain promise will be preserved in the safety of His presence and flourish in the world that is to come.

Day 152 | He Journeys with Us

June 1—Read Psalm 14-18

We may journey through dark valleys, but His presence will light our way; we may encounter formidable enemies, but His power will overcome their threats; and we may navigate slippery terrain, but His promise is to keep our feet steady and free from slipping. Psalm 18:28-36

The words of the psalmist in Psalm 18 reflect the heart of one who has known the keeping power of God, even in the difficult moments and challenges of life. There are days when we awaken to the weight of darkness and wonder how we will ever rise above it. At times the enemy stares us down and tries to paralyze us in fear. Still other moments scream danger as we attempt to navigate the most challenging, sensitive, and dangerous of journeys.

Through it all, the psalmist found God to be faithful. This unchanging and merciful God stands ready to aid us in our moments of darkness, empower us in times of enemy attack, and steady us in days of danger. God is faithful, and He is always near!

Day 153 | His Revelation Overcomes Doubt

June 2—Read Psalm 19-22

Men can speculate, criticize, philosophize, and argue against the existence of God, but nothing can shield them from the glory and handiwork of God's creation and the resounding declaration of His majesty and power! Psalm 19:1-6

Here the psalmist David, blessed with the luxury of spending countless dark nights under the moon and the stars and awakening on the hillside to the brilliance of the Jerusalem sunrise, announces with passionate fervor the glory of God declared by the heavens and the handiwork of the Creator. No foolish theory or human philosophy would ever persuade him that the magnificence of creation emerged save the Word of God. Doubters could run, said David, but the glory of God's creation would find them wherever they would retreat.

Today many seek to undermine the bedrock truth of God as Creator and, in so doing succeed in casting doubt on human value and worth as the crown jewel of His creation. Believers need not cower in fear or be intimidated by the folly of those who profess themselves to be wise. Wherever we turn and wherever we go, *"The heavens proclaim the glory of God. The skies display His craftsmanship"* (Psalm 19:1, NLT).

Day 154 | The Shepherd He Is

June 3—Read Psalm 23-29

There are times when my fears, anxious worries, and present stress make rest a challenge— "He makes me to lie down." There are moments when the noise of busy-ness deafens. — "He leads me beside still waters." There are days my heart is cold and my emotions are spent— "He restores my soul." Psalm 23

No psalm is more often repeated or more frequently turned to than the psalm of the shepherd—the 23rd. It was penned by a young man who had been promised the throne and anointed to be king, yet forced to wait until the day the throne was vacated before he could ascend to his majestic destiny. In the meantime, he waited under the stars at night, tending to the sheep of his father, Jesse, and exploring, reflecting upon, and learning to know the great God who had called him, the One he knew to be his shepherd. David's words provide hope for us in every situation of life.

There are times when rest and relaxation eludes us and in those moments we find rest in Him for our weary souls. At other times, we can't find a moment to clear our heads from the thundering voices that vie for our attention and demand we take notice. He leads us beside still waters that provide only the sound of peace and tranquility. When we are spent and emptied from years of giving and have no more to give, He restores our souls.

Day 155 | The Light of His Presence

June 4—Read Psalm 30-36

"In Your light we see light." Because Jesus is the light, and in Him there is no darkness at all, it is THROUGH HIM we see light and beauty, and BY HIM we see clearly the Father of lights in whom there is no shadow of turning. Then we are able to see what is true and pure. Psalm 36:9

This psalm is one of the great poetic works of David, and this statement is truly profound. David knew God to be light, and that in His presence, gloom, despair, and heavy darkness would be dispelled. It is through the presence of the Father of lights that clarity chases out confusion, hopelessness gives way to anticipation, and night succumbs to day.

It is still the case for us today—in the presence of God, the light of His glory is experienced. Not only does the brilliant light of Christ and His Word open up the way for us to more confidently navigate life's journey, it is through Him that we see more intensely the character of God the Father. Without the light of Jesus, our world remains dark, our ordained paths continue to elude us, and our revelation of God is minimized and skewed. In His light, the fog is cleared away, and certain faith and spiritual insight become our reality.

Day 156 | The Way of the Blameless and the Transgressor

June 5—Read Psalm 37-41

Here the psalmist reminds us that a life committed to peacemaking, honesty, and a determined focus on what really matters, leads to a future of peaceful calm. The contentious and rebellious find their way to be hard and their future is bleak. Psalm 37:37-38

The 37ᵗʰ psalm is well known for its call to trust both the plan and provision of God in our lives. In this psalm, we are reminded that God orders our steps, never allows the righteous to beg, and that when we delight ourselves in Him, He blesses us with the desires of our hearts. The two verses that highlight this devotion are less known, but still drive home the same truth of God's provision and care for His own. There are so many rich lessons for us here.

When we commit our lives to integrity and use the resources we have to bless people and lead them to Christ—God blesses us with peace and wholeness. This is the way of *shalom* and its dividends are both present and eternal. When we, on the other hand, use people to gain resources and lack integrity in the way we live, the way before us is hard in the present, and dark and hopeless in eternity.

Day 157 | Inspiring the Next Generation

June 6—Read Psalm 42-48

Unless we take time to experience and reflect upon the greatness of God, we will have nothing to pass to the next generation. God has called us to know well His presence, to seek and tell of His majestic greatness, and to inspire those who follow to faithfulness. Psalm 48:12-15

This is a psalm of invitation. The worshipper is invited to walk around Zion, behold its beauty and glory, see its vast magnificence, and wonder at the glory of God. Having seen it, the sojourner would have something to share, something to declare and shout, a message to pass to the generations that would follow. *"We have beheld God's majesty and you are invited to come and share this as well."* This would be the hope of the next generation.

We have today a generation emerging that knows little about God or His greatness. Not unlike the days of the judges, a generation has been born that does not know God or the works of His hands. This must be remedied. The answer is found in us, the people of God. We must reflect often upon His greatness, we must tell of His wonderful works, and we must speak of His power to perform. Only then will our children and grandchildren know our God, and only then will they taste and see of His goodness.

Day 158 | The Lord our Defender

June 7—Read Psalm 49-54

The practice of David would serve us all well when we are faced with enemies and opposition. Instead of seeking others to take our side or working to undermine those who may oppose us, we should take our conflict to the Lord, trusting Him to be our Helper and Defender. Psalm 54

This psalm is penned by David while he is fleeing for his life and hiding in the wilderness of Ziph. Saul, enraged by the growing popularity of David and embittered by having lost the anointing of Yahweh because of his disobedience, wanted to have David killed. Like a madman, he journeyed from village to village with the express intent of taking David's life. David, however, trusted the God that had promised him the throne and who had met him with His presence time and time again. His psalm indicates that he was not anxious, and he did not seek vengeance. He simply trusted the God who had called and anointed him.

David did not try to get others to side with him; he knew he needed only the Lord. How much better off we would be if, when faced with trials, enemies, and opposition, we sought the presence of the Lord as diligently as we have sought the help of others.

Day 159 | The Rock of New Perspective

June 8—Read Psalm 55-61

David sensed a lurking enemy, imposed high expectations, and knew his own weakness. Let his prayer be ours. "Lead me to a high rock for new perspective, let me rest in the shelter of Your presence, and preserve me with your steadfast love and the truth of Your Word." Psalm 61

This psalm chronicles the life of David in one of the many instances in which he was forced to flee and hide. The psalm presumes an enemy that is after the king, and likely his own son who had usurped his throne and sought to take David's life. But when pressed to the limit and backed into a corner, the cry of David was for new perspective, a shelter in which to rest, and a high place upon which to stand so that he could see what was really going on. His prayer was *"lead me to a rock that is higher than I!"*

Enemies seek to discourage us and keep us out of the game. If Satan can sideline us or cause us to cower in discouragement or defeat, he has accomplished his task. When we feel pressed, confused, or afraid, our prayer should echo the prayer of David, and we should seek a rock upon which to stand to gain new perspective and shelter in His presence from the onslaught of the enemy.

Day 160 | Make His Praise Glorious

June 9—Read Psalm 62-67

Great the mystery and profound the truth that God, whose enemies cringe before Him, who rules by might forever, and whose eyes watch over the nations, has tested us, found us wanting yet does not reject our prayer or remove His steadfast love from us. He is to be praised. Psalm 66

The 66th psalm provides the worshipper a powerful and elaborate revelation of the greatness and majesty of God in His dealings with His own. As we ponder its truth and meditate in its glorious wonder, our spiritual roots grow more deeply secure, and the fruit of our lives richer. God, we come to understand, not only superintends over the nations in mysterious transcendence, He also stoops to us, confronting our enemies, and preparing our paths.

Most profound and so wonderfully full of grace is the reality that His majestic greatness, which crushes our enemies and renders us unworthy to approach Him, is yet crowned by His steadfast love, which chooses to hear our cry and to bring us near to Him. This is a God whose praise should be proclaimed and whose name should be extolled.

Day 161 | Every Burden He Carries

June 10—Read Psalm 68-72

Here the psalmist unveils the marvelous majesty of God, the ascended One whose chariots are without number, and in whose presence the earth quakes—HE daily stoops down to us, to bear our load. This is the One who invites us to cast our care on Him. Psalm 68:19

The opening of this psalm serves to catalogue the greatness of God. His very presence creates such a sense of awe that His enemies melt like wax and flee His presence. The righteous are called to sing His praise and are readied to tell of His care for the widow and the fatherless and His manner of revealing His lovingkindness to all of humanity. The extent of His provision is summed up with this word of praise, *"Blessed be the Lord, who daily bears us up…"* (ESV).

While some translate Psalm 68:19 as the One who *"daily loads us with benefits"* (a truism as well), the better translation says *"who daily bears us up."* This portrays the One whose presence consumes the enemy as kneeling down beside we who have fallen along the way and picking up the burden we can no longer carry—carrying them for us. As Simon of Cyrene carried His cross, Jesus carries our burdens. The One who invites us to cast our care on Him, carries our load for us, even when we have no strength to transfer that load to Him.

Day 162 | God's Presence is my Good

June 11—Read Psalm 73-76

"But as for me, God's presence is my good." Profoundly true are the words of the psalmist. Many things vie for our attention, perplexing circumstances seek to distract us, and the propensity for self-indulgence always looms near, but God's presence is my good. Psalm 73:28

The psalmist in Psalm 73 pondered the seeming inequity that the world displays. The wicked are allowed to prosper in life without penalty despite their evil behavior while the righteous fight and struggle along the way. The author even admits that this injustice pushes him to the brink of nearly stumbling. His answer, however, is found when he moves into the house of God and is able to see from a divine perspective. The final curtain has not yet been drawn, and by and by, it will all make sense.

At the end, the psalmist lands where we must all land. He realizes that what is good for him is to stay near to God—to abide in His presence. How beautifully true that still is today. When all else swirls chaotically around us and questions abound, there is a place of refuge and safety to which we can always turn—His presence. While the world challenges us, distracts us, and causes us pain, with the psalmist we say, *"God's presence is my good."*

Day 163 | The Way of the Sea

June 12—Read Psalm 77-79

God does not often remove the seas and storms that face us, but most frequently leads us THROUGH them. His plan is often challenging to comprehend— "His footprints are unseen." Yet His character leading us through our storms is impeccable and His reputation unmatched. Psalm 77:19

This psalm addresses the response of God when we call out to Him in our distress. He always hears, and He always responds. Here, however, the psalmist lays out the theology of deliverance. God does not always remove the storms that confront His people. He did not remove the fiery furnace of Nebuchadnezzar, but instead joined the three Hebrew boys in the fire. He did not keep Daniel out of the den, but instead shut the lion's mouth. This is the way of God's faithful deliverance.

We must learn God's way of dealing with us in trials. As often His way may be *"in the sea,"* or His path may be *"in the great waters."* This way of deliverance is forgotten or discounted as we assume the only way He will work is to remove the storm. When we make that assumption, we fail to see the activity of God on our behalf, and our faith is often challenged. His character through the storm cannot be matched, and His track record is perfect.

Day 164 | Longing for a Steadied Heart

June 13—Read Psalm 80-86

"Teach me your way, O Lord, that I may walk in your truth; unite my heart to fear your name." May God's truth be so clear that we walk IN it every day, and may our confused hearts be whole by understanding that the fear of the Lord is the beginning of all wisdom. Psalm 86:11

This was the simple prayer of David, who makes this psalm unique by the seven time use of the Hebrew word for Lord: Adonai. It means master. He understood that God was His master and as Master, His truth was both absolute and universal. He longed for that truth to become crystal clear and for his heart, so often conflicted by the fear that plagues humanity, to become whole and unwavering in the midst of trial and confusion.

This too should be our heart cry. So many times we find ourselves perplexed by the competing ideologies of a postmodern world and challenged in our commitment to truth. The world and its pursuit of selfish toys does all that it can to permeate the Christ-follower and contaminate our devotion and surrender. Easily our hearts can become confused. But God, when approached as Master, delights in revealing His truth and steady growth of our restless hearts.

Day 165 | Our Shield and Buckler

June 14—Read Psalm 87-91

The truth of God's Word is the restraining and protecting force for Christ-followers. In a world so infatuated with lies and ideologies that not only fail to satisfy, but actually destroy, we have the truth in which to stand and by which we are preserved and kept safe. Psalm 91:4

From one of the great psalms of the Old Testament canon comes one of the most powerful and pristine characterizations of God's truth—His Word! It is our "shield and buckler." The shield was the large, barely mobile, and body-sized protection that would defend one from the frontal attack of their enemy. The buckler was a smaller and much more mobile shield, carried in the hand and always ready to fend off any unexpected and close range assault.

Satan, the enemy of our soul, longs to destroy us. Many times his efforts come through crushing circumstances or full frontal attack of our faith. The shield of faith which remains strong through the Word is ready to repel those evil attempts at sabotaging our faith. Often Satan is subtler, weaving his lies and doubts into our minds, hoping to form just a small crack of fear or unsettling anxiety. Again, truth is our buckler, the very Word of God is able to quench those fiery darts and leave us whole and victorious.

Day 166 | The Lord Reigns

June 15—Read Psalm 92-99

Instead of joining the worldly refrain of fear, defeat, and pessimism, the redeemed should join heavenly voices with praise continually on our lips—His greatness boldly declared, and His loving majesty stirring in us the sweetest of worship and the deepest of devotion. Psalm 96

"Sing unto the Lord a New Song!" "Declare His glory among the nations!" "Worship the Lord in the Beauty of His Holiness!" These are just three of the exclamatory declarations of the psalmist, extolling the greatness of the One who has established the earth and created the heavens. This majestic God, praised by the author of this great psalm, is the One who will also return and judge the earth. *"The Lord Reigns"* is the majestic refrain repeated often through all the psalms and viewed by many as the organizing center of the book.

It is easy to become caught up in the slow dribble of bad news, the endless cycle of pessimism, and the profoundly overwhelming sense of hopelessness that is being propagated by an angry culture of godlessness. This must not be the lot for those redeemed by the work of Jesus at the cross. We instead should join the song of the psalmist, collaborate with the angelic choir, and happily blend our voices with those who have already overcome and declare *"The Lord Reigns!"*

Day 167 | The Renewing Spirit of God

June 16—Read Psalm 100-104

In creation the Spirit hovered over the waters, God spoke, and all that is came to be. Even now, in the seasons and with fresh grace, the Spirit renews the face of the earth. Today all that is worn, tired, weary, broken, or defaced can be renewed by God's Spirit. Psalm 104:30

In Psalm 104, the psalmist provides grand insight into the creative work of the triune God. The Father spoke the Word, the Word created all that is, and the Spirit, the very breath of the Father, was sent forth as the agent of creative power of the divine Godhead. Nothing that exists today does so without having been initiated by God and sustained by the power of His Word. The same Spirit active in creation is described by the psalmist as the One who "renews the face of the earth."

How thankful we should be to know that our Creator God, by His Spirit, is both Creator and Sustainer and also renews the broken and heals those in need of repair. It is deeply crucial that we, as followers of Christ, cultivate with great intention a relationship with the Spirit of God that humbly acknowledges our deep dependence of His ongoing renewal.

Day 168 | Remember

In a culture perpetually attached to and enamored by "the moment," it is easy to think that most recent history is one's destiny. The people of God are called to live differently. We are called to remember our faithful God and know that His faithfulness never ends. Psalm 105

This psalm traces the faithfulness of God from Abraham to Isaac to Jacob and to all of Israel. The evidence is clear—God has never failed His people, and He has been on time and fully present from the beginning. The psalmist calls on the reader to sing to Him, give thanks to Him, call on His name, and remember His faithfulness. If one is faithful to do this, they too may be brought out of bondage, as was Israel, and brought into a life of joy and abundance.

It is easy to become overwhelmed by the reminders of our broken world. They are everywhere, and the news and social media are unrelenting in their reports. Humanity is broken, and the reminders of that devastation can quickly turn to a sense of hopelessness. But God has better things for us. He has invited us to recall and confess His faithfulness, rejoice in the assurance that He is a covenant-keeping God, and remember that He will never abandon His own.

Day 169 | Come to Him with Confidence

June 18—Read Psalm 107-110

With a faith rooted in historical FACT—Christ's death, resurrection, and ascension, we face our enemy confidently. The ascended Christ, victor over death, reigns sovereignly over our lives, knows NO anxiety in battle, and awaits the bowing of every knee to His Lordship. Psalm 110

This is one of the Messianic psalms that, though written hundreds of years before Christ, it was pointing readers to ONE DAY when Christ would appear. Here the psalmist unveils the ultimate sovereignty of the Christ who would come, and who, after engaging His enemies, would sit down at the Father's right hand as conquering Savior and rule and reign in full majesty.

This is the throne we now approach—one occupied by the Christ who defeated all of His foes through the cross, the resurrection, and His ascension to the Father's right hand. While we may fret and be riddled by anxious moments, He is not. As the conquering warrior who has time to take a cool drink from the brook in the heat of battle, He sits enthroned with no worry or care. We can come boldly to this throne and this King!

Day 170 | Light in the Darkness

June 19—Read Psalm 111-118

Whether it's through renewed strength that overcomes a besetting sin, victorious escape from serious trial, the Son of Righteousness rising with healing in His wings, or the Shepherd of our souls leading us through death's dark valley, "Light dawns in the darkness for the upright." Psalm 112:4

Few psalms bring more comfort than this psalm in which the poet articulates the blessing of the upright and righteous. The one who fears God and delights in His law, and the nature of that man. The psalmist notes that by nature that man is not moved to fear by bad news, but is steadfast. He gives generously to the poor, and he handles his own business with utmost integrity. His blessings include material prosperity, a rich and lasting heritage, and the beautiful promise of light dawning in his darkness.

This is a promise most striking and most helpful, for we all walk through dark times. It may be our own struggle with sin, the pesky and fiery trial that will not relent, the sickness that won't subside, or the pain of loss that comes with the passing of one we love. That darkness, for the man or woman of God, is not navigated alone. For in many forms and in perfect time, the light of God's glory will mark the path of every darkness we are asked to endure.

Day 171 | The Sum of Your Word

June 20—Read Psalm 119

A culture of irony insists on the relativity of truth and then obsesses about "fake news" and "disinformation." As believers surrendered to the sufficiency of Scripture, we say confidently with the psalmist, "the sum of Your Word is truth!" Psalm 119:160

It is normal postmodern thinking to deny the existence of absolute truth. Those who claim to be great thinkers hold to the notion of relative truth—your truth is yours and mine is mine. This worldly conviction, however, is impotent as it seeks to reject themes that the world wants to deny and call untrue. For if one denies the existence of truth, then untruth cannot exist either. The godless are then faced with an irreconcilable dilemma.

For those who follow Christ and believe in the authority and inspiration of Holy Scripture, there is no dilemma. The psalmist said, *"the sum of Your Word is truth,"* so with confident and steadfast hearts, we embrace His Word as absolute and confess that while all else will one-day pass away, His Word will not. He who IS TRUTH has spoken TRUTH that will never fade or pass away.

Day 172 | My Help Comes from the Lord

June 21—Read Psalm 120-131

There is no better way to start your day than to turn your eyes toward the One who made all that has been made, Who watches over you without growing weary, Who catches you if you slip, Who protects you from the enemy, and Who guards your going out and coming in—HE is your help! Psalm 121

There may be no sweeter psalm and no more encouraging declaration from inspired Scripture than this celebrative song, most often rehearsed by the sojourners as they traveled toward Jerusalem for an annual feast and season of worship in the temple. As they traveled together, the expectant worshippers would sing of God's attentive faithfulness, His undying commitment to their well-being, His watchful care and provision, and His majestic protection that would keep them safe. This was the stuff of which the people of God were made—trust in a faithful God.

This psalm provides the perfect statement of faith for us today, and its repetition serves well our faith development. The enemy of our souls works tirelessly to cast before us the notion of doubt and fear, but this psalm provides the confession that will cancel out the enemy's devices. *"My help,"* we sing with the psalmist, *"comes from the Lord who made heaven and earth"* and can keep all who are His!

Day 173 | The Church is Gathering

June 22—Read Psalm 132-138

Modernity's emphasis— "the Church is not a building" has fostered a disregard for the GATHERING of believers. The Church isn't a building—it isn't the individual either. It is the collective gathering of His people where His presence is manifest—for THIS we should long. Psalm 132

Those critical of the institutional church love to point out that the New Testament portrait of the Church is not a brick and mortar building donning pristine stained glass windows and steeples. While the point they make is valid, the motivation is suspicious. Too often such statements are made with a smug sense of spiritual pride that seems to suggest that they do not need others and their relationship with God is all that matters. The reality is that this notion of the Church is no more accurate than the one with stain glass and steeples.

The Church, as seen by Jesus and New Testament authors, is not possible in a hideaway of individualized worship. It is instead a gathering of people together with the purpose of welcoming His presence, worshipping Him for His worthiness, and witnessing His manifest glory. Within this context we must encourage, challenge, and serve one another and set aside our personal and selfish pursuits for the cause of Christ and His Kingdom.

Day 174 | Help From the Cave

June 23—Read Psalm 139-142

From a lonely cave, far removed from the throne for which he had been anointed, David learned that there is no cave so deep and dark that out of it he could not cry to God and be heard. Even in disappointment and pain, the Lord was his portion and victory was assured. Psalm 142

David found himself running from his enemies and hiding out in a dark, cold, and lonely cave. There is no question that he wondered how he ended up there. He was king and had been especially chosen and anointed by the prophet and judge Samuel to rule over Israel. He had won great battles, inspired Israelite masses to bravery, and modeled a life of worship. But now he has been reduced to a weary vagrant, questioning if ever again he would sit on the throne. Then he prayed. Then he lifted his voice in worship and song. Then he yielded his doubt and questions to the God who had promised to be his refuge—his heart was lifted, his emotions calmed, and his spirit soared.

You may feel like you are in a cave and falling short of where you know God has called you to be. It may seem like your enemy is nipping at your heels and your destiny is in question. The darkness of your cave may threaten to quell your hope and crush your peace. Like David, it is time to call out to Him. Call on the One who is your refuge and fortress. Stand in the certain assurance that He sees you in your pain and, in His time, will lift you out of your disappointment.

Day 175 | Declaring His Great Praise to the Next Generation

June 24—Read Psalm 143-147

It is the express responsibility of each generation to ensure that the next knows of God's greatness. The transmission of His greatness is not merely a teaching of facts, but an expression of praise for who God is and what He has done. Failure here is devastating. Psalm 145:4

These words of the psalmist are some of the greatest and most significant words ever penned by an inspired author. The importance lies in the responsibility set out for each generation to pass on the goodness and greatness of God to the next. When this is faithfully discharged, there can be great hope, but when neglected, great tragedy occurs. The psalmist speaks not only of the passing on of doctrinal truth, but also giving praise and expressing gratitude to God within the hearing of the young who watch and follow.

This ancient principle has never been more important. Today's young generation is being deeply influenced by the things of the world, and the noise of a godless world is deafening. The enemy seeks to arouse the level of worldly lust and glamorize a meaningless life that is void of hope. We must rise to the occasion and declare boldly the truth of God's Word, insist on sound doctrine, and even more importantly, declare the praise of God in their hearing so they may know that God is indeed good and faithful!

Day 176 | Let the Redeemed of the Lord Say So!

June 25—Read Psalm 148-150

Robed in the glorious splendor and majestic beauty invoked "in the beginning" by the divine fiat, the heavens declare the praise of their Creator. Clothed in the righteousness of Christ, let the redeemed pinnacle of His handwork shine like stars in highest praise. Psalm 148

This psalm captures the magnificent scene of all creation joining together in robust praise to declare the majesty of their Creator. There is no lack of unity, no prodding necessary, and no one corner of creation seeking their own acclaim. It is as if all created order understands their divine origin and fully embraces their utter dependence upon the Creator's Word to sustain their existence.

Humanity, called by God at creation "very good," stands as the apex of God's handiwork and is clothed not only in the *imago dei,* but the redeemed are fully cloaked in the perfect and glorious righteousness of Christ. How much greater should our commitment to unity be? How much more should we join in songs of high praise to the One who made and redeemed us? How much brighter should we shine in a dark universe, pointing people to the Savior, the Christ who has created, redeemed, and now sustains us?

Day 177 | A Healthy Foundation

June 26—Read Proverbs 1-3

Earthly wisdom is no wisdom at all—it is folly. True wisdom comes from God when we ask of Him. It is to FEAR (trust, reverence, surrender to) THE LORD as He leads us through experiences—joyful and painful, that will teach us how to discern and then apply knowledge. Proverbs 1:7

As Proverbs, the great compilation of wisdom sayings, opens, we are reminded of the foundation to authentic knowledge, *"The fear of the Lord is the beginning of knowledge."* It seems that the author is rushing to say, "before you run and fill your heads with knowledge and information of all sorts, start with a humble and reverent posture before the Lord." That, he notes, is the building block for all knowledge and ultimately any true wisdom.

Seeking to know more is a worthy pursuit. The journey of knowledge and learning is one that we should all embrace. To settle into mediocrity is an easy step for those who have no passion for learning or understanding. With that said, however, we must always remember that knowledge without a foundation through which to utilize that knowledge will lead to faulty and even devastating outcomes if the knowledge is wrongly applied. Modernity has certainly witnessed that very thing. The foundation is a holy and healthy fear of God.

Day 178 | Wisdom—The Principal Thing

June 27—Read Proverbs 4-5

There is no greater use of our time and energy than to get wisdom and develop good judgment. Make this the prize you pursue. Let God's Word penetrate deep into your heart and guard it—embrace and honor its truth—contently stay on this path and your life will be blessed. Proverbs 4

Sad is the reality that common sense seems to have become extinct in our culture today. Even more perilous is the fact that wisdom is rarely sought after. Many want to make their mark with great splashes of oratorical genius or intoxicating charisma. Those who follow them soon find that these qualities, when wisdom is absent, serve only to disappoint those and often produce great hurt and loss.

The writer of Proverbs calls the reader to seek after wisdom. Wasting time cultivating the polish of leadership without a heart deeply entrenched in the wisdom and counsel of God is of no value. We should run after wisdom and make its pursuit the *"principal thing."* Then our lives will be well prepared for the challenges of life, the opportunities we desire will come our way, and the people we influence will be preserved.

Day 179 | Guarding the Parental Place

June 28—Read Proverbs 6-9

Many factors contribute to our culture's chaos, but academia's undermining of parental counsel and a generation anxious to pursue deceptive agendas that flaunt a false intellect while dishonoring their parents' wisdom, may be the most damning. Proverbs 6:20-23

The wise sage was ahead of his time when he penned the words of this powerful and ever-relevant proverb. Here he hails the ongoing virtue of parental counsel and instructs the young to listen well and heed the advice of those parents who speak into their lives. The counsel of godly parents is irreplaceable and must never be discarded or relegated to uninformed, ignorant, or irrelevant thinking. It is the divine design and the plan of God for the development of godly children.

This sacred and crucial part of God's plan has been under great attack in recent years. It seems that one of the great schemes of our enemy is to undermine the teaching, principled direction, and virtuous wisdom imparted by parents to their children by the use of academia, which far too often is driven by a godless and humanistic agenda that discards the truth of God's Word and the foundational traditions that build godly character and produce holy living. This attack must be both guarded against and defeated.

Day 180 | The Wise and Correction

June 29—Read Proverbs 10-12

The wise receive instruction well, always seek to learn more, and will not resist or refuse discipline. Their lives will be full and blessed. The foolish babble their way around correction and ignore its truth. Their resistance leads to their downfall. Proverbs 10:4, 8, 17

This proverb, though ancient as a literary work, bears fascinating contemporary implications. In reality, humanity of every generation bears a universal pride and stubbornness that makes the reception of correction a challenge. In fact, as the author notes, most will go to great lengths to avoid correction and will even do their best to talk their way out of the need to receive direction. But ultimately it will be their end.

It should be the desire of us all to develop and grow spiritually. Correction is part of that process, and the wise will receive that correction gladly. Rather than taking offense when others seek to correct, we should see them as those through whom Christ may speak providing correction as part of the process that will make us more like Him. To talk around the need for correction and refuse to hear may be to miss the work of God in our lives.

Day 181 | The Truly Wise has Counselors

June 30—Read Proverbs 13-14

Pride that keeps one from seeking counsel and befriending the wise will bring the most anticipated individual to ruin. Humility that seeks advice from the wise and embraces criticism and correction can make a great leader of one who was not projected for greatness. Proverbs 13

Throughout this ancient proverb, multiple admonitions appear, calling us to seek wisdom from others. The author implies that to go it alone instead of seeking out counsel is an act of great folly. The wise person may not, notes the inspired writer, be the most inherently wise and skilled, but rather it may be instead the one who is willing to surround himself with others who provide new insight, perspective, and counsel. These will often far surpass the one who seems to possess keen wisdom.

Pride is a destructive force. It can easily lead one to lose perspective and miss potential opportunities and pitfalls. Many are gifted with the skill of perception and discerning situations, but no one is without blind spots. The wise will seek out others to provide counsel, to consider with them strategies and plans of action, and to help guard against pitfalls that can destroy forward movement. Wise is the one who knows they need others to truly walk in wisdom. It is the fool who thinks they need no one and seeks instead, to go without help.

Day 182 | At Home with the Wise

July 1—Read Proverbs 15-17

When we are defensive and refuse to receive correction that comes from one we trust, we reveal our pride and injure our spiritual growth. When we open ourselves to the reproof of a friend, we gain understanding and find ourselves among the wise. Proverbs 15:31-32

There are many groups of people we can choose to associate ourselves with, but it is a special joy to be at home with those known for their wisdom and prudent counsel. Not everyone is at home with such people. The proverbial author makes it clear that there are some who, by their defensiveness and arrogant stubbornness, and their unwillingness to receive godly correction, eliminate themselves from the company of the wise.

Humbly accepting the critique of those who have our best interest in mind and desire to see us mature and bear fruit is the path of those who will enjoy success. Theirs will be, not only the beauty and fulfillment of fruit borne, but the calming and hospitable welcome of those who are wise. True friends who will dare challenge our actions and hold us accountable in our motivations are of great value and should always be sought after.

Day 183 | Fear that Brings Blessing

July 2—Read Proverbs 18-20

Life—full and abundant, rest that is satisfying, and protection from an enemy that seeks to destroy is the promise for those who live in the fear of the Lord. Cultivating and nurturing that wholesome fear of God is crucial for those who long for peace. Proverbs 19:23

One of the great themes, indeed one might even argue the central theme or organizing center of Proverbs, is the notion of the fear of the Lord. The most well-known of biblical axioms is *"The fear of the Lord is the beginning of all wisdom."* The importance of fearing the Lord is found outside the book of Proverbs and even shows up outside the canon of the Old Testament. It is a universal truth to be embraced by the people of God in all generations. It is not the promotion of anxious panic, but reverent awe that is suggested.

In this proverb, the inspired author notes the benefits of fearing the Lord that extend beyond just the origin of wisdom. An abundant life that lives protected from the peril brought on by the enemy is also experienced by those who cultivate this holy appreciation for the divine majesty. In a world so often fraught with turmoil and chaos, the peace of God that passes our human understanding is desperately longed for and may be found when we learn to fear God.

Day 184 | The One Who Knows Our Hearts

July 3—Read Proverbs 21-22

No matter how hard we try to convince ourselves or others that we are right, the Lord is the keeper and the examiner of our hearts. He knows every motive and every thought. Our daily practice must be to submit our heart and thoughts to Him and accept His critique. Proverbs 21:2

This wisdom of the author of Proverbs is spot on! *"People may be right in their own eyes, but the Lord examines their heart."* It is a reminder that ultimately it is not mortal flesh that makes the final decision or issues the ultimate accounting. It is God who weighs all that we say, think, and do and, as One who knows perfectly the heart of man, He alone determines their integrity.

This realization should cause us to walk lightly and live cautiously. Our hearts are innately deceptive, and as Jeremiah said, *"desperately wicked."* We cannot trust our own thoughts for they must make their way through our weak flesh and are easily tainted by our pride, envy, and selfishness. Instead, we must discipline ourselves to surrender on a daily basis our hearts, thoughts, and motives to the One who is our judge and then attune our spiritual ears so that we may hear the Spirit as He whispers, convicts, and encourages us.

Day 185 | Praying for the Ungodly

July 4 —Read Proverbs 23-24

The temporary success of the wicked should never be our envy, and their failure should never be our delight. When WE fall, by God's grace we are restored, but they have no such hope. Instead of gloating, we should pray for them to know God in their weakness. Proverbs 24:1, 16-20

The wise sage who penned the wisdom of Proverbs 24 knew the danger of expending one's energy on emotional revenge and relishing in the downfall of those who mistreat us or live lives of ungodliness. This, he cautioned, would only serve to bring guilt and even divine discipline on the gloating party and would further deface the image of godliness that is to be portrayed by those who walk by faith. Rather than rejoicing when the wicked fall, we should pray.

The underlying reasons for such counsel are made clear. The righteous have the advantage of God's restoration when they fall. They may fall time and time again, but God will pick them up. This is not so with the wicked. As God's people, seeking to sojourn through a world of ungodly inequity and escalating wickedness, it is easy to rejoice in the failings of the wicked. Instead, we are called to intercede on their behalf and ask God to turn them around for Him.

Day 186 | A Guarded Spirit

July 5—*Read Proverbs 25-26*

In a culture that excels at passing blame, crying "foul," and shirking responsibility, Proverbs calls us to do better. "Whoever has no rule over his own spirit is like a city broken down without walls." Obedience to His Word by the Spirit's power conquers the flesh. Proverbs 25:28

This ancient proverb is so rich with truth and so relevant today. Here the writer calls on readers to manage their own spirit, emotions, passions, and behaviors. To fail in this endeavor is to leave oneself exposed to all the evil of the world and all of the destruction that comes to a city left unguarded. This wisdom powerfully speaks to our generation today.

Our culture loves to pass blame to others, and the notion of personal responsibility has been almost eliminated from public discourse. Everyone has someone to point the finger at or a past hurt or experience that explains away their poor actions. This is not the way of the Word or the expectation for a Christ-follower. We have the power of God's Spirit that raised Jesus from the dead residing in us, and we possess the living Word of God that is able to save, transform, and strengthen. We are without excuse. With the Word and the Spirit, we can control our actions, and our lives can be safely guarded and kept free from the demise our enemy seeks to impose.

Day 187 | Our Hearts Reflect Our Character

July 6—Read Proverbs 27-29

"As a face is reflected in water, so the heart reflects the real person." The heart easily deceives itself, so it must be carefully guarded from corrupt input, filled with God's Word, and searched daily by the Holy Spirit. Probers 27:19

As with many proverbs, this one deals with the heart. The metaphor is not difficult. Each of us has stood above a pond on a sunny day and seen the reflection of our face in the water. While the specific lines and marks of the face may not be clearly identifiable, there is no mistake that what is reflected is indeed the face that looks into the water.

What is true of the face in the water is true of the heart. That is, what emerges through our words, actions, attitudes, and lifestyle is merely a reflection of the condition of our heart. If our words are harsh, our heart is cold—if our attitude is crass, our heart is spiritually unkept. We must guard what comes into our hearts, fill it often with the truth of God's Word, and spend time daily soaking in the transforming power of God's Spirit.

Day 188 | Standard-less Humanity

July 7—Read Proverbs 30-31

Well did the ancient scribe describe this generation, one that fails to see its own wickedness and lives in haughty rebellion against God. This is a result of removing the standard of God's Word from culture and church, and the only remedy is to return that standard. Proverbs 30:12-13

The author of Proverbs describes the arrogant qualities of rebellious humanity that fail to consider the authority of God or His law. He notes that they seem to be unable to see their own folly or the consequences that their sin will ultimately bring. Instead of humble submission and honest acknowledgement of their need, they shake their fist at the thought of God, supposing that their knowledge is superior and sufficient.

These words of the proverbial author, though ancient, describe well our contemporary culture. Vast developments in technology and intellectual pursuit have created a generation that has removed from its consideration the law or directives of a transcendent God. With the removal of that standard, sinful humanity is left to anarchical behavior that, unless a standard is returned, will lead to devastating consequences.

Day 189 | He Seeks What's Been Driven Away

July 8—Read Ecclesiastes 1-6

"That which is already has been; that which is to be, already has been; and God seeks what has been driven away." These words remind us of God's sovereign rule and His power to redeem our failures of the past. Nothing escapes His power to heal and reconcile. Ecclesiastes 3:15

Many profound nuggets of truth emerge from Solomon's treatise on wisdom, known as Ecclesiastes. This statement in Ecclesiastes 3:15 is so true. At least two possibilities exist for what the first part of this verse means. Some suggest that this speaks of the cyclical nature of all things—that all things will eventually be repeated. Others see here that the events of the present, past, and future, all known by God before the foundation of the world, tie together. The second part of this statement may be the most beautiful, however.

Here the author makes it clear that those things that have been hurt, broken, or deemed hopelessly lost are not given up on by God for *"God seeks what has been driven away."* No matter what areas of your life you feel are too far gone, God seeks to restore them to health. Nothing extends beyond His ability and desire to heal and restore.

Day 190 | The Wisdom that Keeps Us

July 9—Read Ecclesiastes 7-12

Great are the truths summarized for us by Solomon. The words of the wise, though painful they may be to hear, will serve us well if heeded. Fearing God and obeying Him is both our duty and supreme privilege. One-day God will judge all and make it all plain. Ecclesiastes 12:14-16

Ecclesiastes chronicles the life, most likely of Solomon, the son of David and the third king of Israel. His was a life a deep tragedy. Though granted wisdom by God that exceeded any other human, his pursuit of happiness and meaningful existence through multiple worldly avenues always left him empty and looking for something else. Ecclesiastes tells that sordid story, and through his failure and pain, we are able to learn and apply great wisdom.

His final conclusions provide all who followed him with lasting and sustaining truth. Wisdom from those who have great life experiences should be carefully followed, and when they are, great meaning will be realized. Fearing God is not only a means of securing eternal hope but the very thing for which we were created. Finally, one day when we stand before God, His eternal wisdom will be clear as we no longer see through a dark glass, but then face to face. Then we will realize that His truth was indeed the truth that saves, keeps, and sustains.

Day 191 | His Love Pursues

July 10—Read Song of Solomon 1-8

Here—a love between a man and a woman demonstrates the powerful commitment of a godly marriage. Scripture uses the marriage metaphor to depict God's love for His people, a love driven by an active desire. For God so loved that He gave. He gave His all. Song of Solomon 7:10-13

The Song of Solomon is the grand love story of a shepherd in love with the beautiful Shulamite woman who is being pursued by King Solomon, who hopes to add yet another woman to his harem. The woman is in love with the shepherd, unimpressed with the riches of the king, but smitten by the devotion of the simple man who has won her heart. Their commitment to one another stands as a stellar portrait of godly integrity and marital faithfulness.

The New Testament unpacks the metaphor of marriage as it points to the relationship we (the bride) have with Jesus (the heavenly bridegroom). Throughout this ancient poetic book, we see the pursuit of the shepherd driven by desire for the beautiful bride and his willingness to do what it takes to have her as his own. What a powerful picture of the divine pursuit by God for those He created, loved, and has now redeemed.

Day 192 | Return to the Branch

July 11—Read Isaiah 1-4

The words of Isaiah are spoken to a people amidst national disaster and moral decay—a people JUST like us. There is hope for those who trust in the Branch (Christ). Those who trust in Him will be made holy, and find refuge in Him as they journey toward Zion. Isaiah 4:2-6

Isaiah prophesied to the people of Judah, the southern kingdom of the divided nation, during a time of great peril. Their continued moral decline and their idol worship had led them to the place where God had no choice but to allow foreign powers to threaten them in the hope they would repent and turn back to Him. The prophetic promise was of the hope available if they turned to God (the Branch) and sought again to live as His people.

The culture of Isaiah's day was much like ours. The church in America has turned to the idols of pleasure, wealth, and entertainment and, unless she turns back to God, the future looks bleak. But if the people of God will turn to the Branch, the Lord Jesus Christ, a future filled with the greatest of days and the most fulfilling of spiritual blessing will be ahead.

Day 193 | An Invitation from Jesus

July 12—Read Isaiah 5-8

When we refuse to yield to the gentle and tender prodding and prompting of God's Spirit and fail to take the gentle yoke of Jesus, we will find ourselves, instead, mastered by the brutal and destructive devices of sin and an enemy bent on our destruction. Isaiah 8:5-8

God warned His people of the coming invasion of the devastating Assyrian army led by their brutal king. He promised His help would come if they would return to spiritual fidelity and sincere worship of Yahweh alone. But they forsook the "waters of Shiloh," the familiar and trustworthy help of the God of Israel. That rejection would lead to their downfall.

God longs to help His people today. He has given us all we need through the love of Christ, His Word, and His Spirit, but unless we embrace His offer and take upon ourselves His gentle yoke, we will continue to wallow in defeat. Our enemy seeks to devour us and bring us to a devastating end, but Jesus invites us to draw near to Him and experience newfound strength. His Spirit is tender and His voice quiet when compared to the blasting rebellion of our enemy, but when we follow Him and respond to that voice, we can experience blessed safety and certain refuge.

Day 194 | Wells of Salvation

July 13—Read Isaiah 9-12

The Gospel—God's anger toward us was turned away as our sin was placed on Jesus Who knew no sin. He bore God's wrath for our sin at Calvary, becoming salvation for us—the One in whom we can trust and from whom we receive ongoing benefits of His goodness. Isaiah 12:1-3

The prophet Isaiah prophesied to the southern kingdom of Judah more than seven centuries before the incarnation of Christ. Often his words dripped in significance for his present 8th century BC context, but also spoke powerfully in a futuristic manner toward a time much later, the time of Messiah. The opening verses of chapter twelve are a case in point. Here he speaks of a day when God's anger would be deflected, His salvation would be revealed, and the wells of salvation would be released.

Without question, this points to Calvary and the glorious day toward which we turn by faith, laying claim to our eternal hope. For it was there that Jesus stood in our place and became sin for us, turning the wrath of God away from us so that He could bear it for us, and where He made possible the way of salvation and eternal life through faith in His sacrifice. In so doing, He made available the manifold benefits of being His children. It is from these wells of salvation that we are privileged to draw and in which our souls are satisfied.

Day 195 | The Plan that Cannot Be Stopped

July 14—Read Isaiah 13-16

"As I have planned, so shall it be...For the Lord of hosts has purposed, and who will annul it?" This was God's word to Assyria when she tried to destroy Israel, to death when it sought to defeat Jesus, and to Satan when he tries to thwart God's plan in our lives. Isaiah 14:24-27

Despite their rebellion and their disobedience, God would not forsake His own forever. He allowed the Assyrians to bring down the northern tribes of Israel, but even as they were invading the northern territories, God warned the Assyrian superpower that they would not forever prevail for He would ultimately rise and defend His children. His plan was to make a great nation of His people, and His plan would ultimately prevail. Despite the reality that there would be times of national backsliding, no power, nation, or enemy would be able to thwart His plan.

The certainty of God's plan is not relegated to His promise to make a great nation of Israel. It extends as well to His victory over death and the future He has planned for us. Though Satan thought he had stopped Jesus at Calvary, the empty tomb announced a different story, and though the enemy of our souls will at times get us off track, God will ultimately fulfill His purpose in us and bring His promise to its full fruition.

Day 196 | Never Give Up

July 15—Read Isaiah17-20

Here we are reminded that we are to love the lost, even those many despise, that the kingdoms of this world WILL belong to the Lord, that global revival is coming, and that we must diligently work and generously give until every knee bows and all confess Christ as Lord. Isaiah 19

This unusual and rarely noted prophecy speaks of the day that Israel's archenemy, the kingdom of Egypt, will turn to the God of Israel and find their way into the land of God's people. Surely it speaks of the eschatological kingdom, but it underscores the truth that even those opposed to Yahweh are loved by Him and are not beyond His reach. It foretells of the day that people of every nation, tribe, kindred and tongue will gather around God's throne.

The implications of this truth ring clear. There is no one beyond the reach of God's love, and to write off someone as hopeless is to doubt the heart, plan, and power of the God who so loved the world that He gave His Son for the sake of lost humanity. The message is unmistakable. We are called to work diligently to share the Gospel and never give up.

Day 197 | Repentant and Trusting Hearts

July 16—Read Isaiah 21-24

The Church should learn from Judah's failure instead of human strategy and carnal ingenuity; God invites His people to seek and revere HIM again. Likewise, rather than folly disguised as cutting edge relevance, a spirit of repentance should mark the people of God. Isaiah 22:10-14

In this prophetic announcement of Isaiah, he notes the attempts that Judah had made to ensure their own prosperous way. They had built homes, dug reservoirs, fortified walls, and built their arsenal of weaponry. Sadly, however, they had not consulted Yahweh, the only One who could guarantee their success. The tragic outcome of a people who had forgotten their need of God was devastating and despite their attempt to secure themselves, they fell at the hands of the enemy.

It is imperative that the people of God today learn from the failure of Judah. Our ingenuity, strategies, and most elaborate plans and attempts at accomplishment will always fall short when we do not include God in those efforts. Without God's direct help and leading, we can never accomplish His intoned destiny for us; neither can we effectively advance Kingdom activity. We must trust the Lord for all of our plans and lean on Him to accomplish His will.

Day 198 | Perfect Shalom

July 17—*Read Isaiah 25-27*

Perfect Peace (Shalom Shalom) is promised to those whose minds are stayed on the Lord. I can't come to Him occasionally and know this peace. I can't stay my mind on obstacles or looming trials and know this peace. When I stay my mind on Him—perfect peace covers me. Isaiah 26:3-4

Here Isaiah prophesied of a day that was coming—a day when the captive Jews, exiled in Babylon, would return home to Jerusalem and enjoy the land of promise again. God had promised to destroy Judah's enemies and build them into a strong city again. Shalom, perfect Shalom, would be theirs if they would maintain their focus on Yahweh and not turn away from Him again.

This promise is still real for the people of God. Peace for so many is elusive in a world filled with fear and dread, where the promise of the next day seems to be uncertain. Even amidst the constant turmoil and tumultuous times, there is a peace, unlike what the world offers, that Jesus can provide. It is available to all who learn to rest in Him, dwell in His presence, and abide in His Word. This peace is enduring and wholly complete. It is *perfect Shalom*!

Day 199 | In Quietness and Trust

July 18—Read Isaiah 28-30

When life is hectic, challenges are great, and the unexpected piles on, human default is to be anxious, work harder, and push more fervently. God says, "be calm, submit to My plan and timing, and rest in Me" for "in quietness and trust is your strength." Isaiah 30:15

Isaiah prophesied to the people of Judah and tried to show them the way back to God. The remnant that longed to be right with God and turn from evil had found themselves struggling to find the way. They had attempted to impress God with great sacrifices, earn His favor with their offerings, and catch His attention by their frenzied overtures. But these were not the way back—instead God wanted them to simply obey, rest in His presence, and submit to His plan. It would be in that posture that they would find renewed relationship with Yahweh.

Today we try to impress God with our efforts, energy, and fervent drive to get His attention. There is no need. Like the people of God who heard from Isaiah, the answer is in quiet trust, calm submission, and steady obedience to His plan and leading. This will be our strength and certain assurance.

Day 200 | The Quiet Assurance of His Righteous Reign

July 19—Read Isaiah 31-35

This righteousness will bring peace. Yes, it will bring quietness and confidence forever." Though not wholly fulfilled until Christ returns and humanity's capacity for righteousness is unlimited—godliness does breed peace not vitriol, and Christ's presence brings hope. Isaiah 32:17

In the 32ⁿᵈ chapter of his prophecy, Isaiah writes with anticipation of the day when universal peace will reign through the person of Messiah; the Prince of Peace will come and establish peace that will last for eternity. The reign of the Messiah King will be a reign of righteous rule and those who have placed their faith in His righteousness will know Him and be glad. This is the grand and glorious day that we all await.

We live in a day when that anticipated hope is not yet wholly fulfilled. Yet we can stand confident in the righteousness of Christ, and He can reign in our hearts today. When He takes up residence in the throne of our hearts, even though we are limited by our humanity, we can know the byproduct of His righteous rule in our lives is His abundant and quiet peace, and the confident assurance that we are His and He holds us in His hands.

Day 201 | Spread Out Before the Lord

July 20—Read Isaiah 36-39

There is no greater response to enemy threats and no more effective means of withstanding their pressure than to "spread them before the Lord" in prayer. He will respond, and He will sustain us. Isaiah 37:14

The news was bad, the outlook was dark, and the anxiety for King Hezekiah had reached epic proportions. The king of Assyria had delivered an ominous letter via a messenger to Hezekiah, and there seemed to be no way out. The Assyrians had marched through region after region, pummeling cities and wreaking havoc among the people, and Judah was their next stop. Jerusalem would not be spared despite their hope in Yahweh. Hezekiah had nowhere to turn, so he entered the temple, anxious and distraught, and "spread it before the Lord."

God answered Hezekiah's prayer and brought great victory to His people. Hezekiah's inadequacy would not be the final word—His God was more than able to bring victory. When our enemies beat down on us and when the evil one threatens to overtake us, we, like Hezekiah, should admit our inadequacy and spread it out before the Lord.

Day 202 | Remember

July 21—Read Isaiah 40-42

Twice Isaiah questioned the faculties of God's people— "Do you not know? Have you not heard?" In question was God's sovereign and universal rule and His unending mercy toward His own. He sits over the circle of the earth, He never wearies, and He always gives us strength. Isaiah 40

"Have you not heard?" This is a popular refrain from the prophet Isaiah as he poses the question to the captive Jews, asking them if they could remember the previous work and character of God. Isaiah had wanted them to remember that, though they were in a season of judgment, they were not forgotten. The God that had allowed their discipline was the same God who had called them by His name, and His mercy would not allow them to be forgotten or forsaken.

We can take great comfort in these words. We, too, may find ourselves in the throes of divine chastening or may be experiencing much needed discipline at the hand of God. But the hands that chasten us are hands that were scarred for our salvation, and though we grow weary and feel we may not be able to continue, His strength is never exhausted and His mercy endures forever. This—we must remember!

Day 203 | All Things New

July 22—Read Isaiah 43-46

To Israel, who had lived in a cycle of obedience—disobedience leading to perennial captivities, God said, "forget your past, I'm doing a new thing!" His name is Jesus! His promise holds today. Our past can be laid down as we turn to Christ—He makes all things new! Isaiah 43:16-19

In this grand chapter, the prophet reminds the people of Judah of their history of on-again, off-again fidelity to His name. They had often failed and found themselves in enemy captivity and here, once again, they were under the strong arm of the Babylonian empire. But he had a word of hope for them. A time was coming that their fortunes would change. A Messiah would come, and their past would be put away—all things would be made new!

We live on the opposite side of the cross from the captive Jews who sat in Babylon hoping for a new day. The new day came with Christ, and when we turn to Him and His work at Calvary, we experience hope for a better future. We no longer must be bound by our past or hindered by the memories of our failures. The One who bore our sins at the cross and vacated His tomb on the first day of the week has given us a new start as well and the assurance that all things are now new!

Day 204 | Never Forgotten

July 23—Read Isaiah 47-50

May we live with calming confidence that overrides the waves of doubt—a steadfast assurance that tames the lies of the enemy. God cannot forget us, our names are etched in the palms of the hands that sustain us, and a vision of what He is making us is ever on His mind. Isaiah 49:15-16

The people of Judah had failed God repeatedly. Their sin was so grievous and their backsliding so abhorrent that they feared God had forgotten them, and their sin had made them beyond restoration. Isaiah assured them that their fears were unfounded. While highly unlikely that a nursing mother would ever forget her child, the thought of God forgetting His own was foolish. It was impossible. His people were always on His mind, and their destinies were etched on His hands.

What a powerful reminder. Our failures may make us feel as if God is distant and that He no longer cares about us or loves us. Nothing could be further from the truth. His thoughts of us are many and beautiful. We never escape the divine mind, and our names are eternally engraved in the hands of the One who allowed those same hands to be pierced for us.

Day 205 | Our Only Hope is Christ

July 24—Read Isaiah 51-53

While the world scurries about trying to make sense of culture's pervading evil, growing hopelessness, and impotent leadership, we anticipate the appearance of Christ who will triumphantly startle the nations and silence the voice of all who oppose Him. Isaiah 52:13-15

This prophecy portrays a day when the world was looking for a way out, an answer for the pervading evil that had plagued their culture. They are seen as looking all around them, seeking answers to the pain and hopelessness that seemed to have gripped humanity and relentlessly drained them of their strength. It points to the pitiful impotence and failed leadership that marked that day. Only those who looked above for an answer could find any hope of escaping the turmoil and emptiness. It was a dark day, and efforts to find a way out all seemed to be thwarted.

This prophetic word has powerful implications today. The culture is marked by a pervading evil and sense of hopelessness. The spiritual impotence of leaders is wholly evident and many, especially those who do not trust Christ, simply meander through life with cynical doubt and a disdain for spiritual answers. But, those who know Jesus also know their answer is found only in Him and in His return. This is a day that the people of God must passionately proclaim the hope of Christ and anticipate His coming that will serve to upset the kingdoms of this world and bring to an end the opposition to Christ's Kingdom.

Day 206 | No Weapon Will Prosper

July 25—Read Isaiah 54-56

"No weapon formed against you shall prosper." Glorious promise—yet, we often look at the pain and wonder, "is it true?" When, however, we look with eyes of faith toward a "city which hath foundations" and rejoice in the daily renewal of our inward man, we do not waver. Isaiah 54:17

This prophetic chapter powerfully reveals the promise of God to the people of Judah, promising their coming restoration. A divine reversal of their fortune was on the way. Because of their rebellion, God had allowed them to go into exile in Babylon. Now God was bringing them to restoration, and their enemies would be silenced. The power the enemy had exerted over them would be no more. Any weapon the enemy would try to use would be stopped, and their accusations would be silenced.

This promise is one we can still claim. As children of God and joint heirs with Christ, we lay claim to all of His inheritance. At times, it seems the enemy IS winning, and His strategies against us are effective. But God calls us to look with eyes of faith and to understand that this world is not our home, and the fulfillment of His promise will be fully realized when we arrive in the city to which we are journeying and lay hold of the promise we diligently pursue.

Day 207 | A King Who Wants to Live with Us

July 26—Read Isaiah 57-59

Despite the magnificent splendor of the thrice holy God who flung stars into space and spoke the world into being, He who inhabits eternity longs to dwell in the hearts of the humble and revive the spirits of those who draw near to Him in sincere contrition. Isaiah 57:15

The prophet Isaiah was given unique access into God's throne room. In the year of King Uzziah's death, he saw the Lord, highly exalted and arrayed in all of His brilliant glory (Isaiah 6). This vision of the high and lifted up Creator changed forever the trajectory of the son of Amoz and catapulted him into a prophetic ministry, unparalleled by any of the prophets of Judah. His uncleanness was purified, and his commission was clarified.

Despite his vision of God's transcendent splendor, Isaiah also proclaimed this majestic God as the One who longs to dwell in the hearts of those who are humble and contrite. Though possessing a holiness that caused the seraphim to shudder and a voice that caused the foundation of the temple to tremble, His immanence was attested to by the prophet as well. This is the heart of the Gospel so powerfully demonstrated in the incarnation. God, the Creator and Sustainer of the universe, dwelling in the light that is unapproachable, has come to us and desires to take up residence in the hearts of lowly and broken humanity.

Day 208 | The Word of God—Ever Seen but Never Hurried

July 27—Read Isaiah 60-62

God promises Israel she will one day be glorious, bringing the nations to Him. But this isn't happening now. Like the luminaries and the seasons, God's work can be seen, but never hurried OR stopped. We must not doubt. His timing will never diminish His blessings. Isaiah 60:19-22

This prophetic word of Isaiah promises the people of Judah that a day of great restoration is coming, a day when their eternal purpose will be fully realized. Then they will be the people who will lead other nations to know God, to turn to and worship Him. As beautiful as this promise may be in the day it was declared, it was far from being reality. Like the lights of the heavens, the work of God was real, but its effect was not known in the moment.

This is true for us today. God is extraordinarily patient with His people, and while the availability of His presence is real, and His purpose for us is clearly defined, we often fall well short of its realization. As He was with Judah, so He will be with us. He is patient, long suffering, and committed to the fulfillment of His purpose among us. Our light will shine, our testimony will go forth, and though it delays, His will shall come to pass.

Day 209 | Father, Potter, and Clay

July 28—Read Isaiah 63-64

Everything happening in my life today is part of God's master plan to shape and mold me into His image. He is the POTTER, a merciful One—my FATHER, so the pressure I feel, the squeezing I may experience, or the heat that I may endure, is HIS hand at work on me. Isaiah 64:8

Despite the fact that God had arranged it, their return from Babylonian exile had been difficult. The temple, walls, and much of the city of Jerusalem lay in ruins, and the people of God were discouraged and had lost their passion to worship. They were still under the hand of God's chastening, but here the prophet reminds them that while God does indeed discipline His people, His hand is one of a Father, and He could be trusted.

While the discipline of the Lord can often be painful, we can take comfort in knowing that when God works to correct us, He is both a potter with a glorious image in mind, and a Father who loves us and wants only the best for us. Instead of resisting His work in us, we should submit, knowing that everything He allows to happen to us is intended for our good and will work to make us what He has created us to become! He is a trustworthy Father and a mercifully skilled potter, and we are merely the clay.

Day 210 | The Place He Longs to Dwell

July 29—Read Isaiah 65-66

Glorious mystery—God who reigns from Heaven created billions of galaxies and all they contain, upholding them by the word of His power, stoops in His wondrous grace to dwell in the heart of the one who is humble, contrite, and who stands in reverent awe of His Word. Isaiah 66:1-2

This text at the end of Isaiah's prophecy is rich in meaning and speaks hopeful revelation to us who long for the presence of God to be active in our everyday lives. Here Isaiah rehearses the eternal greatness of God by describing Heaven as the place of God's throne, and the earth, controlled by His sovereignty, is but a place on which the Creator rests His feet. This underscores His vastness and His majesty. But then the prophet speaks of the kind of heart to which this magnificent God is drawn.

The understanding of this marvelous text stirs the hungry heart with gratitude and worship. To think that this great God would be pleased to reside within the heart of broken humanity is nearly too much to fathom. The truth is, however, that the character of the God we serve is so filled with grace that He longs to dwell, not in ornamented temples or angel-filled throne rooms, but in the heart of ordinary humans who have surrendered themselves to His Lordship.

Day 211 | Having Hearts that Know Him

July 30—Read Jeremiah 1-4

Jeremiah warned God's people about being what Jesus would describe as those who "honor me with their lips, but their hearts are far from me" (Matthew 15:8). Deceived by a godless world, many PROFESS Christ, yet at the same time are "wise to do evil"—failing to KNOW God. Jeremiah 4:22

The warning of Jeremiah to his people was not to be *"foolish"* like *"stupid children"* who know well how to enter into mischief and explore the depths of the ungodly, but have little heart or passion for knowing God. The prophet called out harshly those who seemed to be wise in their own eyes and were even able to fool those around them. Despite their reputation for wise and creative ways to dishonor God, they had little or no understanding about how to live for Him.

This warning speaks clearly to our generation today. We have come to be quite knowledgeable in thousands of things that don't really matter, but at the same time, woefully ignorant in that which pertains to knowing God. Many profess the name of Christ, but their hearts know nothing of Him. They speak boldly about His creation, excel in the manifest gifts that He has blessed them with, and posit theories of His grand creation, but are deaf to the still small voice that beckons them to draw near and truly know Him.

Day 212 | Unchecked Rebellion

July 31—Read Jeremiah 5-6

Though exalted as the pinnacle of God's created work, modern and secular humanity reveals itself as infinitely more foolish than the rest of the created order, which surrenders in obedience to God's commands, as we arrogantly disobey and choose our own way. Jeremiah 5:22-24

The prophet Jeremiah is clearly disillusioned by the waywardness of humanity to whom has been given the honor of being God's choice creation. Marked by the *imago dei,* privileged to be made just a little lower than the angels, and entrusted with all that exists to rule and exercise dominion over it, we are blessed, favored, and honored beyond comprehension. Still, as Jeremiah pointed out, stubborn humanity transgresses God's commands and seeks to make their own way.

Today, we not only have the supreme privilege of our created position, but we have at our fingertips and within our grasp, all the blessings of the modern world, and yet still we insist on making our own way. This rebellion is the pathway to eternal destruction, and if not addressed and reversed, will empty the world of a witness for Christ.

Day 213 | The Impotence of Emptied Law

August 1—Read Jeremiah 7-9

Jeremiah's word identified Judah's sin that led to exile, leaders by scribal pen, emptying the law of its indictment of sin, promising cheap grace. They replaced conviction with peace. This—our present danger. As like Judah, we drift AWAY from God and TOWARD captivity. Jeremiah 8:7-12

As the prophet Jeremiah prophesied to the people of Judah, he identified their primary failure that had led them to their dreadful destiny of captivity. They had not understood the times, the gravity of their sin, nor the distant relationship with God they now possessed. The blame was laid at the feet of the religious scribes who had altered the Word of the Lord so that the people would remain ignorant of God's ways.

Religious leaders today have gutted the Scripture of its spiritual power, whitewashing the notion of sin. We no longer feel the depth of conviction that should grip our souls, and we live for the next moment of pleasure. Disregarding the call of Scripture to holiness and failing to warn of the grievous nature of sin is to have encouraged the spiritual and moral drift of our day and to have sealed the fate of divine judgment for many.

Day 214 | The Steps We Order of Our Own

August 2—Read Jeremiah 10-13

Judah was in dire straits, seeking to "direct their own steps," an act Jeremiah said was impossible, for "the way of man is not in himself." We are here today. With Jeremiah we pray, "Correct us O Lord, but in justice, not in your anger, lest you bring us to nothing." Jeremiah 10:23-24

Judah had become arrogant and self-serving, feeling as if they had no need of God. They trusted their own wisdom and failed to heed the voice of the prophet Jeremiah as he sought to call them back to God. They were self-assured, boasting that their wisdom and choices had brought them to the point of national prosperity and universal acclaim. They did not know that it was all about to come crashing down—all because they depended on their own ability to chart their way.

Despite the call of Jeremiah, the people of God continued to direct their own way and correction was upon them. The prophet prayed that God's response would be strong, but not devastating. As a nation that has continually veered away from God's Word and presence, we see a future that will most certainly bring judgment. Our prayer, as those interceding for our nation, is that God will turn us without destroying us, a hope that will be determined only by our nation's willingness to fall back on Him.

Day 215 | The One True Source

August 3—Read Jeremiah 14-17

As a nation, we must acknowledge that there is but one true fountainhead—the triune God of Scripture. To seek after other gods to provide is an exercise in futility. To wait on the true God is an act of faith and the source of great strength and hope. Jeremiah 14:22

As Jeremiah tried to call the people of Judah back to Yahweh, he reminded them that there were no other gods capable of providing sustenance and rich blessing. Only the Creator could bring rain, make their crops grow, and cause their livestock to flourish. He made them, and only He could control them. Jeremiah's determination— *"we will wait for You (oh God), since You have made all of these."* Sadly, the people did not follow the advice and conviction of Jeremiah and exile was their lot.

This is a lesson we must heed and heed quickly. Slowly but consistently, this nation and even the Church has drifted from the pure worship of the triune God, the only One able to bless and meet the needs of His people. We have turned to the gods of our own ingenuity and our own lusts and have found ourselves as a nation impoverished. It is time we turn back to the source of all blessing and seek the One who alone is able to make us abound in all good things.

Day 216 | Truth at the Potter's House

August 4—Read Jeremiah 18-21

Though the truth is often repeated, it never loses its immediate relevance. God is the potter. We are the clay. The circumstances of life, like the wheel, keep us ever in the potter's hands, pressuring and shaping us into the vessel that pleases Him. Jeremiah 18:1-4

One of the most powerful lessons of Scripture is found in the 18th chapter of Jeremiah's prophecy. Here God takes the prophet to the potter's house to observe the work of the artist in his house. The clay on the wheel does not conform to the potter's plan, and so he removes it from the wheel and starts over again to make the vessel as He chooses. The message is clear. God had a plan for Judah and through pressure and pain, He would ultimately accomplish His work in them.

He is the potter. We are the clay. How profound the truth and how encouraging this sweet metaphor. Though pressure is often applied with strength which causes discomfort, it is the loving hands of the Father/Potter that causes the pain. We can know that it is in tender love that He works. Though at times His face is not visible, it only means that we are on the other side of wheel, not out of the potter's hands.

Day 217 | He Never Turns Away

August 5—Read Jeremiah 22-24

Precious is the truth that if we draw near to Him, He draws near to us and fills us with His presence. Comforting is the reality that even when shoved away, He is not absent, but rather watching and listening, ready to respond to those who will call on Him. Jeremiah 23: 23-24

Jeremiah prophesied to the people of Judah in their days of rebellion and warned them of impeding judgment and Babylonian exile. He often reminded them of God's purpose for their lives and His unending mercy. Yet His holy justice could not overlook their sin forever. But in light of the harsh and painful judgment that was coming, they would not be forgotten by their Creator. He would draw close when they called and even when they did not, He would be watching and ready to respond.

How grateful we should be that God assures us that His ears are always attuned to our cries, His grace ready to answer our repentance, His eyes always watchfully focused on us, and His mercy great enough to cover our sins. Even more comforting it is to know that even when we have turned away, He does not turn away from us. Instead, He looks on and longingly awaits our call for help.

Day 218 | Influencing Our Evil World

August 6—Read Jeremiah 25-29

Instead of lashing out at the world's evil, perhaps we should turn to the Lord and ask Him to help us bear testimony to His goodness and graciousness in troubling times. God is still in charge, His purposes will be accomplished, and His glory must be declared. Jeremiah 29:5-14

Through the words of the prophet Jeremiah, God instructed the people of Judah, who were captives in Babylon, to pray for their captors, to pray for the welfare of their city, and to ask God's blessing on them. He also told them to plant gardens, build houses, and live among the Babylonians with the hope that their spiritual influence would ultimately impact the pagan empire.

We spend too much time criticizing, rebuking, and casting judgment on the evil world in which we find ourselves. Often we spew our vitriol at their lifestyles, forgetting that a sinful world is the very reason Jesus came. God so loved them (us) that He sent His Son. Far greater impact would be made for the Kingdom if we changed our strategy and instead of pointing OUT their sin, we pointed them TO Jesus. We can be *in* the world without being *of* the world, but we cannot influence them if we withdraw. May we grow fruitful in the world in which we sojourn, and may that fruit reflect the love and beauty of Christ.

Day 219 | Nothing is Too Hard for God

August 7—Read Jeremiah 30-32

Our struggle with understanding why things happen is generally a result of limited perspective, finite ability, and self-focus. God sees the ways of ALL humanity, nothing is too hard for Him, His deeds are mighty—His purposes are GREAT—beyond our comprehension. Jeremiah 32: 17-19

Jeremiah's day was dark; his people had strayed so far from God, and he was under pressure to recant his bold prophetic words calling the people to repentance. Things looked bleak for the people of Judah, and yet God still promised that He would one day restore. Jeremiah could not reconcile the evil of the days with the glory of God's promise, but as he prayed, he wrestled through his doubts and came to the conclusion that nothing was beyond His ability, and ultimately He would accomplish His purpose in His people.

Today, the world is in a bad place, and evil dots the landscape of our culture. It seems beyond our comprehension that things could turn around, yet Scripture tells us that one day the knowledge of God's glory will, "cover the earth, as the waters cover the sea". How that will happen is a question for the ages. As we pray, we too will become convinced that His power is more than able to accomplish what He has promised to perform.

Day 220 | Call on Him

August 8—Read Jeremiah 33-36

Wise is the person who, in seasons of pain and uncertainty, chooses not to focus on the immediate, but instead calls on the God who orders every step and Who faithfully answers every call, and is shown the hope-filled future God has promised to bring to pass. Jeremiah 33:3

Jeremiah 33:3 is historically known as one of the great verses of Scripture and one of the more robust of God's promises. *"Call unto me and I will show you great and mighty things that you do not know."* So famous is this promise that some have even tagged it as *"God's telephone number."* Call and God WILL answer you. At the very core of this promise is a trusting heart that knows God is reachable and through all the pain and uncertainty, He may be found. It is the wise soul who refuses to look at their *present* circumstances and rather focuses on their *ever-present* God.

This is the way for the man or woman of faith. Trials and circumstances may threaten to suck us in, but they are fleeting—God is not. He invites us to call on Him and assures us that He will answer and reveal to us majestic and glorious hope for the future, and promises that will transcend our fondest imaginations. Whatever hopeless situation confronts you, God can enable you to overcome if you will simply call on Him!

Day 221 | The Meeting of Mercy and Truth

August 9—Read Jeremiah 37-40

The people who refused God, God refused. Those who burned incense to false gods in the temple saw their temple burned. The king who could not see had his eyes gouged out. God's goodness is long suffering, but His justice must be satisfied. It is time to turn to Him. Jeremiah 39:1-10

This text is one of the most tragic of texts in the history of God's people. After centuries of rebellion and disobedience, the judgment of God was finally meted out at the hands of the Babylonians. The temple, so beloved, was destroyed; the king, blind to his own sinful ways, was himself blinded by the servants of Nebuchadnezzar; and the people of God, so great and proud, were humbled by their captors.

It is important to be reminded that while God's mercy is long suffering, His justice must be satisfied. His holiness will not allow Him to overlook sin forever, and His righteousness cannot leave rebellion unchallenged. As culture mocks the holiness of God and exploits divine love, we are called to declare a balanced message. His love must never be diminished, but his holy nature cannot be compromised by an imbalanced message of love, void of justice. As the psalmist promised, *"mercy and truth have met together."*

Day 222 | Surviving Divine Chastening

August 10—Read Jeremiah 41-45

Divine chastening can make weary the people of God. If careless, we can faint under it and become lukewarm, complacent, and self-promoting. Instead, God calls us to trust and faithfulness, despite the circumstances, and promises to keep us and reward us. Jeremiah 45

Baruch was an assistant to Jeremiah, and while little is known of him, enough is understood to provide a great lesson for us. He had been the scribe that had copied down the prophetic words of Jeremiah, and he knew his words of judgment to Judah would come true. Though he knew it to be truth, the reality was that he felt unprotected and in his musings accused God of not protecting him in his weariness. God, who knew the thoughts of Baruch, reminded him that he would be cared for, and if his concern was faithfulness to Him rather than self-preservation, his future would be prosperous.

We may find ourselves under the hand of divine chastening. It is easy in those seasons to feel forgotten and forsaken. The truth is, however, that chastening is truly a reminder of God's fatherly love. If we remain faithful through the struggle and seek holiness in the pain, He will keep us safe and produce in us His fruit of righteousness, and give us a name that we could never claim on our own.

Day 223 | Lavish Love

August 11—Read Jeremiah 46-47

The mercy extended to Judah, even after their unthinkable disobedience, is explained by nothing less than elective love=GRACE. This is our hope and inheritance. As the apostle John said in his epistle, "See what great love the Father has lavished on us that we should be called children of God." Jeremiah 46:28

This text is one that challenges our human nature and our concept of fairness. After announcing his great judgment on those that He had beforehand used to bring discipline to His own people, God announced destruction of those very nations. God had indeed elected the people of Israel for a purpose, not just to be blessed or favored, but to carry out the purpose of making His name great to all nations. Though they acted foolishly toward God, still He would restore them and make them a great people in the end.

This truth of God's elective grace should give us great comfort. Nothing within us is deserving of that love, and yet still He has lavished His great grace on us and called us His children. If our merit was the source of our hope, we would be miserably lost and without recourse. Instead, we rest in the merciful character of a God who deals with us as His chosen and beloved children, worthy of nothing, but recipients of His lavish love.

Day 224 | Kingdom Without End

August 12—Read Jeremiah 48-50

Babylon, it seemed, in all of its grand strength, would dominate forever. But it would not—it would fall as was the case and still is for every earthly kingdom. Yet the Lord's throne never wavers. Kings and kingdoms will all pass away, but God's Kingdom stands firm. Jeremiah 50:1-5

The great power of the north seemed unstoppable. Nebuchadnezzar, in all of his furious might, had pummeled nations, carried away captives, and brought the greatest of armies to their knees. To the people of Judah, whose king was humbled at the hands of the Babylonians as he watched his offspring murdered and had his own eyes gouged out, this force against which they stood seemed overwhelming, and their hopes of freedom and prosperity were sucked out of them. With their worship harps hanging on the willows of Babylon, they were certain that this kingdom would never be undone. But they were wrong.

There was a King greater than Nebuchadnezzar and a Kingdom mightier and more forceful than the Chaldeans. That King was Christ, and the Kingdom belonged to God. Earthly powers will promise great things but fail, spew great threats but be overturned, and appear unconquerable but be humbled by God. The Kingdom of God will stand forever strong, and while others come and go, God's rule will never be stopped, and His Word will never be silenced.

Day 225 | Kings and Kingdoms

August 13—Read Jeremiah 51-52

"Babylon will sink, never again to rise"—the final word of Jeremiah. His oracle spoke specifically to the ancient kingdom but prophetically to the kingdoms and false philosophies of THIS world—all of which will one day fall and become the kingdoms of our Lord. Jeremiah 51:64

Jeremiah's prophecy to Judah was strong and direct. He warned them for years to turn away from their wickedness and idolatry and back to God. Still they continued to drift from pure worship of Yahweh and more and more to the vain philosophies of the godless Babylonians. But, though God would judge His own people, Jeremiah brought his prophecy to a close with a strong word to Babylon, *"Thus shall Babylon sink, to rise no more."*

This was a clear and direct word to the historical Babylon, made great by Nebuchadnezzar, but its implications are far more reaching. For all who would dare stand in opposition to the King of Kings and Lord of Lords, this warning is pregnant with meaning. God will share His glory with no one, and His Kingdom stands over them all. While earthly kingdoms come and go, and new powers emerge, one day every knee will bow to Christ, and every kingdom will submit to His Lordship.

Day 226 | A Warning to Spiritual Leaders

August 14—Read Lamentations 1-2

Because the spiritual leaders shunned truth, offered a compromised version of God's nature, and eliminated His holy and just demands, Judah foolishly hoped for good while falling into powerless bondage. It is this same pattern that threatens the Church today. Lamentations 2:14-15

Jeremiah was bold and clear in his accusations against the spiritual leaders of Judah. They, according to the prophet, shared a great deal of the blame for Judah's failure and ultimate captivity. Instead of pointing out the people's sin and calling them to repentance, they had overlooked their sin and instead, gave them false hope about their future. The city of Jerusalem was lying in ruins and had become a laughingstock of neighboring nations, and the people were humbled in Babylonian captivity. The leaders had failed their people.

The Church today is in dire spiritual condition. Sin has placed many in bondage, and their spiritual lives have been bankrupted. It is the call of spiritual leaders to awaken them to their sin and call them to repentance and holiness. If they do not, however, a season of spiritual bondage and deep struggle awaits them. The Word must be preached by spiritual leaders, and the sin which produces disastrous consequences must be revealed.

Day 227 | Looking to the Crucified One

August 15—Read Lamentations 3-5

"It is good that one should hope and wait quietly for the salvation of the Lord."
Waiting quietly—voicing no complaint, refusing to grumble, blame, or doubt—
silencing all second guessing and finger pointing—waiting patiently on God.
THIS—our calling...our peace. Lamentations 3:26

These were the words of Jeremiah as he walked through the city
streets of Jerusalem, inspecting the irreparable damage done to the
Jerusalem walls and temple at the hands of the brutal Babylonian
regime. Every human emotion was piqued, and every fiber of his
being wanted to be angry, cry out in despair, and question how God
could allow such destruction to His house, to the city of His splendor
and glory. Instead, he reminded himself that waiting and hoping was
what he had been called to do.

It is easy in times of pain and hardship to place blame on others,
cower in fear and despair, or expend energy critiquing the work of
God. But this will never bring the answers we hope for or the relief
for which we long. God has called us to wait quietly, to be still and
know that He is God, to watch patiently as He works in ways we
could never know and by means that transcend our imagination. In
waiting on Him, we experience true peace.

Day 228 | Humbly Before the Throne

August 16—Read Ezekiel 1-4

Ezekiel is humbly and cautiously describing his vision of God's glory— "this was the appearance of the LIKENESS of the glory of God." No grandiose claim was made—mere mortal TRYING to describe eternal majesty. God's glorious and majestic presence must never be taken lightly. Ezekiel 1:28

Great and awesome was the vision given to Ezekiel of the glory and presence of God. The majesty his eyes beheld surpassed his vocabulary, and the impact it made on him was enormous. Carefully, humbly, and with great fear and reverence, he penned his description of his encounter, specifically avoiding any claim of inerrant accuracy. He was a mere mortal groping for words to describe the immortal and the unapproachable light of God's transcendent splendor.

How cautious we should be. The presence of God is too often treated with careless activity, casual posture, and arrogant rhetoric. He is holy and wholly other. None can compare, and no one should dare draw near without understanding these realities. We are invited to come near to Him, but that invitation is not granted to us based on our deserving nature, but rather because of a great price paid by Christ to open up that way. Let us draw near with reverent pause, hearts of grateful contrition, and lips purged and cleansed by the Spirit's power, which enables us to see Him in His beauty and worship acceptably.

Day 229 | Thoughts to be Cleansed

August 17—Read Ezekiel 5-8

Marcus Aurelius said, "The soul is dyed the color of its thought." Entertained idols of our thought lives can destroy our awareness of God's presence and stunt leadership effectiveness. It's foolish to think we can hide idols of thought and desire without consequence. Ezekiel 8:12

This powerful look into the Spirit's work in the hearts of humanity is revealing. The Spirit of the Lord points out to Ezekiel that the elders of Israel, though going through the motions of spiritual piety, were entertaining idols of godless thought in dark rooms where they thought no one could see. Ezekiel was called to speak against their sin and remind them that what they thought was in the dark was in plain view of the Spirit, and unless those idols were removed and their thoughts purified, their days of spiritual leadership would come to an end.

It is the idol of our thought lives with which we most often struggle, and it is here we live most perilously. We often think that we can manage those thoughts, or that as long as no one knows, they are harmless. But in reality, they will not only stifle our spiritual growth, they will make impossible our ability to lead or guide the people of God. Ultimately, idols of godless thoughts numb our ability to discern the presence or voice of God and make our leadership null and void. We must have our thoughts fully cleansed by the blood of Jesus and allow the Spirit's purging activity to have its way in us. Then we can again find our way and know well and enjoy the presence of the God who redeemed us.

Day 230 | The Hope of a New Heart

August 18—Read Ezekiel 9-12

Christ-focused, softened, tender, and responsive hearts can alone turn a nation toward God, uproot the hatred, greed, and corruption that dominates our culture, and heal our land. "Give us new hearts" should be the prayer of every believer, for only God can do it! Ezekiel 11:19

This great promise of the new covenant came to the people of Israel in their time of stubborn rebellion. God promised that a day would come when their fossilized and impenetrable hearts would be replaced by hearts that were soft and tender hearts of flesh, as opposed to stone, and then they would be able to hear from God, receive the grace of Yahweh, and enjoy the relationship with God they once knew.

We are people of this glorious covenant, a covenant sealed by the blood of Christ. His work at Calvary made it possible that the sin, greed, anger, hatred, and envy that permeates every aspect of fallen culture and is embedded in the sinful hearts of humanity would be rooted out and replaced with hearts that are tender, pliable, and softened to the sweet and loving voice of the Holy Spirit. A new heart can be ours if we submit to His work and allow the cleansing and sanctifying power of the Spirit to renew and remake us.

Day 231 | Idols in Our Way

August 19—Read Ezekiel 13-15

William Cowper wrote these words, "The dearest idol I have known, whate'r that idol be. Help me to tear it from Thy throne, and worship only Thee." We must remove from our hearts anything or anyone that has taken the place that belongs only to God. Ezekiel 14:1-5

The opening verses of Ezekiel 14 unpack the story of Israel's elders coming to Ezekiel to hear from the Lord. As they were coming, the Spirit revealed to Ezekiel that they had idols in their hearts. He inquired of the Lord whether he should even counsel with these men, and the Lord affirmed that unless they dealt with the heart idols, neither they nor the house of Israel would hear from Him. This was the downfall of God's people.

This text is both sobering and deeply challenging. Heart idols continue to plague the people of God. The idols of pleasure, greed, pride, and possessions haunt us and vie for our allegiance. The world tells us we need more to satisfy our hearts, and we far too often believe that lie. When we allow those pursuits to consume us, they become idols that find their place on the throne of our hearts and then threaten our walk with God and hope for divine intimacy. We are called to confess these false idols and, without exception, remove them from our hearts.

Day 232 | The Message We Share

August 20—Read Ezekiel 16-18

The character of God is changeless. He is holy, and that holiness demands righteousness, but He is also eternally merciful and rich in grace. That grace, as has always been the case, offers a new and clean heart and a right spirit to all who come to Him. Ezekiel 18:30-32

The word of the Lord through the prophet Ezekiel was strong, intense, and demanding. The house of Israel must turn from their hardened hearts and wicked ways, repent, and seek righteousness. Yet, though the word was a strident appeal for repentance, it was accompanied by an invitation to receive a new heart and spirit and to know the beauty of divine restoration and forgiveness.

The message we share with a lost world must certainly be one of clarity. To sound the warning of judgment for those who refuse to turn to God is incumbent upon us. Eternity is real, and the possibility of others spending eternity without God should motivate us to action. Yet the message we bring is also, and most importantly, one of grace. A new and clean heart is available, a renewed spirit is offered, and the hope of eternity with Jesus, a result of His mercy, is ours to share.

Day 233 | The Name of the Lord

August 21—Read Ezekiel 19-21

Since the lavishness of God's grace comes to us because of a divine determination to honor His own name, it becomes us to give ourselves to ensuring His name is revered and honored. Ezekiel 20

This prophecy of Ezekiel carries with it a strong word that describes clearly the motivation of God in His acts of judgment and blessing. As He speaks to the people of both Judah and Israel, He reminds them that His divine judgment came because they and their fathers had rebelled against Him and forced His hand. *"I acted for my name's sake"* is a thrice repeated declaration of the Lord. The integrity and reputation of His name was behind His activity with the rebellious people in the wilderness as well as those who rejected Him many centuries later. Interestingly, even the restoration of His people when they repented was an act that God carried out for His name's sake.

It is important for us to remember that God is very jealous for His name. His name is a place of shelter for us, a stronghold to which we can run when the world is difficult and our pain is great. It is because of His great name that we are showered with grace and mercy and sustained by His Spirit. For His name's sake, He moves and acts so, His name should be honored, revered, and always esteemed above all others. While other nations walk in the name of their gods, the people of God walk in the name of the One whose name is great and greatly to be praised.

Day 234 | Eternally Rewarded Pain

August 22—Read Ezekiel 22-24

Ezekiel knew that speaking truth to an upside down culture was to be misunderstood. To be serious and measured when society was frivolous and unrestrained was to be marked as harsh, and to be undaunted by personal pain while standing for truth was to be lonely. Ezekiel 24

God called Ezekiel to a ministry that was radical and misunderstood by a culture that had lost its way with God. To make His point, God told Ezekiel that when his wife died, he was not to mourn. This was not a fixed and universal principle imposed on all who served Yahweh. This was for Ezekiel, to be a sign to the people of God. That which they loved and in which they boasted, the temple, was being fully profaned. Because of their disobedience, God would not allow them to mourn that loss. They had brought it on themselves. Ezekiel's life was to testify to how that which is loved can be taken from us, and for Israel, their meted out punishment was deserved.

God has called us, like Ezekiel, to stand out in a world of lostness and darkness. Our standing for radical truth will cost us something, and we will experience pain and possibly loneliness as a result of our stance. Though this pain may never be met with a corresponding reward in this life, we will be given grace to sustain, and we can embrace the promise of eternal reward and divine fellowship.

Day 235 | His Plan Will Be Accomplished

August 23—Read Ezekiel 25-27

The judgment of God will be meted out against all evil and ungodliness, but the sin of the nation's reaping the most exacting judgment is to stand against the people, plan, purpose, and promise of God. His purposes are holy, and His plan will be accomplished. Ezekiel 25

When God called Abraham and promised to make of him a great nation that would carry the blessing of God, He also told him that whoever blessed this nation, He would bless, and those who cursed Israel would be cursed. This was the foundation of Ezekiel's prophecy against the nations. Nation after nation had turned its back on Israel and instead of supporting her, had fought against and profaned the holy city. Now they were being called out by the prophet and promised the harshest of judgments.

Today we still see that God protects His people and blesses those nations that stand with Israel. Beyond merely the protection of Israel, there is still a greater truth. What God plans WILL come to pass, what God purposes WILL be fulfilled, and what God promises, He WILL perform. This is a truth to which we must be committed—for His ways, though beyond our ways, are always righteous and holy.

Day 236 | Only Christ Deserves Our Trust

August 24—Read Ezekiel 28-31

Israel leaned on Egypt to protect them from Babylon but quickly realized they were like a crutch made of brittle bamboo that shattered. C.S. Lewis said, "Relying on God has to begin all over again every day as if nothing yet had been done." We must depend on HIM alone. Ezekiel 29:6

This powerful prophetic word to the people of Israel did not mince words. God was speaking to Israel and telling them that before long the people of Egypt would know that He was the true and living God. Israel had depended on Egypt to protect them from Babylon, but when the pressure was on, they had completely caved. They had looked sturdy, but when leaned upon, they faltered and forced Israel to fend for themselves. Their failure of placing trust that belonged only to God in Egypt, would cost them dearly.

Far too often we put our trust in that which should never have that privilege. The writer of Proverbs calls us to *"Trust in the Lord with all your heart, And lean not on your own understanding"* (Proverbs 3:5 NKJV). When we trust in others or lean on the strength of our own ingenuity or gifts, we will always fail. We must commit ourselves to placing our trust in Him daily, leaving Him our burdens, and allowing Him to shoulder our concerns. This will bring His blessing, and we will know fully the outcome of His mercy and grace.

Day 237 | Hearing and Obeying

August 25—Read Ezekiel 32-34

Let us listen and respond—hear and act when God speaks. God's Word must inspire action and embolden passion. Pretentiousness among God's people will undermine His work. Ezekiel 33:30-33

This chapter ends with Yahweh speaking into the life of the prophet Ezekiel. Ezekiel was discouraged because it seemed as if the people were not changing. They hurried to hear him prophesy and encouraged others to hear the "word of the Lord", but they continued in their disobedience and they dishonored both the prophet and the Lord. Instead of obedience, after their warm and excited welcome, they would disregard the words that the prophet spoke, and their failure would ultimately bring the judgment of God.

There is a serious warning that is clearly stated here. We must not be of the mind that to hear the words of God and not do them is acceptable. It is not. The Word must change us, and it must make an eternal difference in us, or we are hearing it pretentiously. This is far too often the case in the Church today. We hear; but are not changed, we listen; but we do not embrace, and we see; but we do not submit. God is calling us to action, and we must accept that invitation so that we can effectively work for Him.

Day 238 | The Valley of Dry Bones

August 26—Read Ezekiel 35-37

When God asked Ezekiel if the dry bones could live again, he responded appropriately, "Sovereign Lord, You alone know!" It is never the magnitude of the problem or the vastness of the challenge that matters. The sovereign wisdom and power of God make the difference. Ezekiel 37:3

Ezekiel's vision of the valley of dry bones speaks specifically of God's promise to restore the nation of Israel, and take that which was once dead and gone and breathe into her new life. The picture conjures up powerful images, and imaginative songwriters and preachers have made the most of this ancient prophecy with their lyrics and homilies. Indeed, the modern reader finds themselves amazed at the metaphor and captivated by its implications.

At the end of the day, the vision answers the question of the ability of God. A valley full of dead and lifeless skeletons seems to be a picture of certain hopelessness. God asked Ezekiel, *"can these bones live?"* and Ezekiel rightly responded, *"Sovereign Lord, You alone know."* Ezekiel was exactly right, and his declaration hit the bullseye. There is no grave too deep and no life too far gone that God cannot bring restoration. Our impossibilities can always be overcome by His unlimited possibilities and power, and His sovereign grace will trump our most hopeless dilemmas.

Day 239 | The God Who Restores

August 27—Read Ezekiel 38-41

Fourteen years after Jerusalem had fallen, and both city and temple laid in ruins, God showed Ezekiel what the future could be for a repentant Israel. In our failure and fallenness, God gives hope of a restored future and a glorious inheritance to all who will call on His name. Ezekiel 40:1-4

This great vision of Ezekiel took place twenty-five years after Nebuchadnezzar's first incursion into Judah and fourteen years after Jerusalem had been destroyed by the Babylonians, temple and all. God took Ezekiel, by way of a vision, to the top of the mountain overlooking the Holy land and revealed to him what He would yet do for the people and for His holy city. God had not given up, and Judah's disobedience did not leave them beyond the hope of restoration. There was much more He would do, and Ezekiel was to tell the people.

This is such a marvelous and liberating truth. Often we feel as if our failure has forever cast us away from God or made restoration impossible. Even if we are forgiven, we feel as if we can never be used of God, or at least, things will never be the same. This revelation to Ezekiel reminds us of the fallacy of such thinking. God is a renewing and transforming God who can take the shambles of Jerusalem, as well as our lives, and rebuild them to become something great again—something better than ever, and more capable of making a difference than before.

Day 240 | The Law of the Temple

August 28—Read Ezekiel 42-44

It was the law of the temple that the whole area surrounding the mountaintop on which the temple sat would be most holy. Oh, the implications for us—we are the temple of God's Spirit. May our words, thoughts, actions, responses, and attitudes reflect His holiness. Ezekiel 43:12

The Temple Mount has a rich and storied history. It was built by Solomon on the mountain where Abraham prepared to offer Isaac as a sacrifice before God provided the ram in the brush and it was also the place where David purchased the threshing floor of Araunah to make a sacrifice and appease the wrath of the Lord. This place was to be marked off and given supreme reverence. Clearly, the sacrifice provided by God to Abraham and the need for sacrifice to assuage God's wrath speak powerfully toward the work of Jesus on Calvary. This place, the Temple Mount, Ezekiel revealed as holy and not to be profaned.

This revelation of God's law is no coincidence, and it carries enormous implications. What a profound and glorious picture emerges when we reflect upon this reality. We are the New Testament temples of the Holy Spirit. We house the very presence of God, and our lives are to be presented as living sacrifices, holy and acceptable unto God. We are to be holy, engage holiness, and protect it as well. We must not treat either the gift or the power of God's presence in a trite or casual manner. His presence matters, and His glory is to be guarded with the greatest of care.

Day 241 | Invited to the River

August 29—Read Ezekiel 45-48

A small trickle from the temple grew in magnitude, became a mighty and uncrossable river, created life to bordering trees, and made fresh the Dead Sea. This river made glad the Psalmist (Psalm 46:4), inspired John (Revelation 22:1-2), and can be released in us (John 7:38). Ezekiel 47:1-12

The many visions of Ezekiel continue to stump scholars centuries after they were penned, and often their interpretations elude our deciphering capabilities. Many suggestions are made, but they rarely find a strong consensus. This vision reveals to Ezekiel water that flows from the temple's threshold and a man with a measuring reed who is trying to assess the depth of the water. At first it was but a trickle, and then it became ankle deep, then waist high, and ultimately grew to become waters deep enough to swim in.

While the certain interpretation may not be unanimously agreed upon, one thing is for sure—the water pictures the life of God that flows from the temple where His presence dwells. The further out one goes, the deeper the water becomes. God has invited us to taste and see that He is good, to drink deeply at the river of life, and to swim in the depths of His glory and grace. The better we know Him, the more we want to experience Him more and more. This is an invitation we must unhesitatingly accept.

Day 242 | Nothing is Impossible With God

August 30—Read Daniel 1-2

When faced with the impossible, Daniel did not cower, panic, or cave to fear. Instead, he declared, "But there is a God in heaven." This—so rarely seen today. A faith that doesn't deny the impossible but trusts impeccably in a God who DOES the impossible. Daniel 2:27-28

Nebuchadnezzar was a ruthless tyrant and his servants were only pawns in his life of self-indulgent pleasure and ease. When he was a given a dream that he could not interpret, he demanded that his wise men and astrologers not only give the dream's meaning but tell him what the dream was as well. None were able to deliver and all were sentenced to a brutal death and their family and homes were destroyed.

Daniel, the Hebrew who was gifted and anointed by God's Spirit, stood in the gap. With the intercession of his godly friends and the blessing of God, he was able to name the dream and give its interpretation to the king, thus sparing the lives of all the Babylonian wise men. The impossibility did not paralyze him for he knew he served a God of the impossible. This is the faith we must possess. Impossibilities may loom, but with God all things are possible.

Day 243 | Stand!

August 31—Read Daniel 3-6

When the music of Babylon sounded, everyone bowed to the golden image except three young men unwilling to forsake God. Today the world hears the sound of human ideologies seeking to own their allegiance, and nearly all follow and bow. God's people must stand! Daniel 3:4-18

One of the most often repeated stories of the Old Testament, and one of the greatest examples of bold courage is found in Daniel chapter three. Shadrach, Meshach, and Abednego, the three young Hebrew exiles, refused to bow to Nebuchadnezzar's golden image, despite the promise of certain death in the fiery furnace. When the music played, signaling the call to bow, these three, committed to the holiness of Yahweh and convinced of His protection, stood their ground, and in so doing, brought glory to the God of Israel.

Today Christians are bowing to the idols of sports, entertainment, wealth, and pleasure and embracing the ideologies that run contrary to the Word of God. These godless ideas seek to consume the believer's time, resources, and passion. This is a day when those who call Jesus Lord must refuse to bow to the noise of the world, and stand!

Day 244 | Unashamed

Daniel's words were powerfully convicting, and they anticipated the need of Calvary. "O Lord, righteousness belongs to You, but to us, shame of face." Though shamed by our sin and deserving of God's judgment, God, in Christ, has imputed Christ's righteousness to us. Daniel 9:7-9

Daniel's honesty before God about his own life and his own people was striking. He acknowledged clearly their rebellion and their wickedness in turning away from Yahweh and following after the gods of other nations. The only thing that they were deserving of was judgment and disgrace, and the only apt description of what marked them was "shame of face." This was their just reward, but thankfully, in anticipation of the work of Calvary, Daniel was quick to point out that to God, honor and glory should be ascribed because of the gift of righteousness that He would provide.

While Daniel's prayer is for a people living more than two and a half millenniums ago, it still fits us perfectly. Shame of face is what we deserve. Our sin and rebellion have left us undone, unworthy, and incapable of standing before a holy God. But Calvary demonstrates the righteousness of God and reveals to us God's perfect love. Though we deserve shame, Jesus, through His shed blood, has given us His righteousness so that we might stand before His throne of judgment, unashamed.

Day 245 | Prayer—The Only Answer

September 2—Read Daniel 10-12

The prayers of Daniel, on behalf of Judah, remind us that the Church needs, not better tools or plans, but more who will seek the face and heart of God. As E.M. Bounds said, "Men are God's method. The Church is looking for better methods; God is looking for better men." Daniel 10

There is much about the apocalyptic writings of Daniel that stir the hearts and piques the interest of readers. Grand and mystical visions were given to Daniel, and his position in the royal palace of the Babylonian monarch was leveraged to bring great hope to the people of God. Beyond these, Daniel was a man of intense prayer. His refusal to quit praying, despite the edict that would land him in the den of lions, and his intercessory prayer on behalf of his people, marked him as a stand-out prayer warrior. He knew that unless he prayed, Judah had no hope.

This is still the hope for the people of God today. Beyond prayer, there is no weapon, tool, method, or passionate appeal that can turn God's people back to Him and return the nation to hope and holiness. We have for too long sought the creativity of humanity or the charisma of our leadership to do a work that can only be done on our knees. Daniel knew this and gave himself to such wrestling in the spiritual realm to bring the restoration of the people of God. We must not look to our own strength but instead, call on Him who alone can turn the spiritual tide, and seek His face with great fervency and passion.

Day 246 | Grace That is Greater

September 3—Read Hosea 1-3

Despite their wretched rebellion and the gravity of their sin, God promised to redeem Judah from their self-induced bondage. Deliverance would come, not through sword or military might, but through the meek Savior. No sin-created hole is too deep for the grace of Jesus. Hosea 1:7

The southern tribes of Judah had lived for many years in deep rebellion and disobedience and had treated with disdain the law of Yahweh. Hosea was called to prophesy to the backslidden people, and it would be through a lived-out parable that he would convey his message. God called Hosea to marry a prostitute, and despite her unfaithfulness to him, he was to love, restore, and redeem her. This was to reveal to the people of Judah that God would redeem them, even in their unfaithfulness. It would not be by sword or military might that they would experience salvation, but through the steadfast love of God.

This is such a rich and hope-filled truth for us. God does not redeem us through our gifts, talents, or creative strategies. Our redemption and deliverance does not come from others. It is purely and solely God's grace that gives us hope, and there is no place, even of our own making, that is beyond that grace.

Day 247 | Destroyed for a Lack of TRUE Knowledge

September 4—Read Hosea 4-6

Today we are bombarded by information, have instant access to useless trivia by a simple search, and are consumed by new learning (2 Timothy 3:7), but we are presiding over a cultural undoing because we lack knowledge of the true God and disregard imperishable truth. Hosea 4:6

The prophet Hosea prophesied to both the northern and southern kingdoms of Israel and Judah. He warned them of the impending judgment and cried out with a heart of passion, longing to see his people turn back to God. His prophetic work cost him dearly as Yahweh asked him to marry Gomer, a prostitute, to show the people of God the grave danger of unfaithfulness and the great heartache God felt when His people turned their back on Him. Central to Hosea's prophecy was his reminder that the people's failure to hear and heed God's truth (true knowledge) was the reason for their bleak future.

This is still true for God's people. Never have we had access to more information, and never has a culture been greater connoisseurs of knowledge than today. Yet we, like the people of Israel, face a bleak future if we do not return to the living truth of God's Word and embrace the only knowledge that is able to save and secure us in perilous days!

Day 248 | Don't Be A Crooked Bow

September 5—Read Hosea 7-9

God described Israel as being as "useless as a crooked bow," unable to strike their target. They "look everywhere" He said, "except to the Most High." We are called to ONE GOAL—the prize of the high calling—to know Christ—to be like Him. Can we do that? Hosea 7:16

This unusual term, "a crooked bow," speaks volumes about the condition of the apostatizing nation of Israel. A crooked bow points to Israel's uselessness and their inability to fulfill God's purpose. They had turned from God, sought after idols, and lost their potential to make the name of Yahweh known to the nations. They had been called and once full of potential, but their backslidden condition left them impotent and falling short of their destined purpose.

So sad is the condition of the contemporary Church that has turned to other means of fulfillment and pursued selfish pleasure rather than the holiness of God. We are called to press on toward the prize of knowing Christ, to reflect His purpose, His character, and His holiness. Only when that is our pursuit are we able to fulfill that to which we have been called. Only then are we a straight arrow that can pierce the darkness of this world with the life-transforming message of the Gospel. Only then will Hell's gates come crashing down as we carry the truth of Jesus to the hungry, hurting, and broken. Let us press on!

Day 249 | Turn to Him and Be Healed

September 6—Read Hosea 10-12

Like Israel, our nation has the appearance of greatness—rich and envied. But our hearts have been deceptive, and our comfort is being smashed. God pleads with us to sow with righteousness in mind, allow our hard hearts to be broken, and turn to Him. He will heal. Hosea 10:1-2, 12

The opening words of Hosea 10 make Israel out to be prosperous and the envy of other nations. They seem to be blessed, and their cities are marked by luxury and ease. But as one reads the words of the prophet, it is clear that those days are coming to an end. Their hearts had been deceptive, and they were about to take the brunt of God's judgment. God invites them, while there is still time, to turn back to Him, to sow with righteous goodness in mind, and let God break up their stony hearts so they can live.

We, as a nation, are no different than Israel. We are prosperous, and the world envies our position of prosperity and prominence. But we have failed God, turned our backs on Him, and sought after pleasure. We are invited to be transformed by turning to Him and to allow His Spirit to break up our stony hearts, so that as we turn back to Him, we can be healed.

Day 250 | From Prominence to Homelessness
September 7—Read Hosea 13-14

"Besides me there is no savior." This is God's word to the tribe of Ephraim, once blessed and prominent, but because of their idolatry, they had turned from God—they would be cast out of Canaan. It is dangerous to have known God intimately and then turn from Him. Hosea 13

Of all the tribes in the northern kingdom of Israel, Ephraim, which emerged from the family of Joseph, had been the most blessed and had experienced tribal prominence. Sadly, that prominence was not to last. Their rebellion, which was manifest in their idolatry, would lead to their eviction from Canaan. Like their spiritual father, Satan, who once walked in the presence of God but was kicked out of heaven, they too, were cast out because of their prideful folly and had become homeless.

This kind of loss is not relegated only to an ancient tribe in the land of Israel—there is a great warning for us as well. No matter how blessed we may become, and no matter how others view us, it is of serious spiritual consequence to walk away from intimacy with Christ and turn to the world to find satisfaction. Like Ephraim, when we make such a choice, dire consequences will follow.

Day 251 | With Eyes Toward the End

September 8—Read Joel 1-3

"While little is known about Joel, one thing is certain—he had far-sighted vision desperately needed today. He saw clearly to the end of human history, knowing that behind all the frenetic activity was the calm hand of God's Spirit, calling humanity to hear and to proclaim. Joel 1

Scripture says very little about the prophet Joel. His name is mentioned only once, and the only detail given about his life is the name of his father, Pethuel. That fact is found is verse one of chapter one. Apart from that, we know only that Joel's name in Hebrew means "the Lord is God." Despite the minimal information we have about Joel the man, we do know that he had vision that is desperately lacking today. He saw through the ups and downs that history would record and saw beyond it all, the activity of God empowering His people by His Spirit, and preparing them to proclaim the Gospel in the midst of a godless generation.

This is the kind of foresight we need in the Church today. We long for men and women who see through the present struggles and concerning pressures of life to the hope of the Spirit's outpouring on all flesh. With that focus and the determination to keep that hope alive, we can endure the day's difficulties and flourish in preparation for the world to come.

Day 252 | Don't Limit the Ones God Chooses

September 9—Read Amos 1-4

Amos—a shepherd from Tekoa—he was not a prophet nor the son of one (7:14), but he had a word from the Lord and left all to speak it. We must be willing to hear what God is saying regardless of who He chooses to say it, and like Amos, we must be willing to leave all to obey. Amos 1:1

Many of the prophets of the Old Testament enjoyed a heritage of priestly or prophetic origin. Not so with Amos. He was just a shepherd from Tekoa who spent his time herding sheep and tending to the sycamore trees south of Jerusalem, near Bethlehem. There was nothing about him inherently that made him a prime candidate to carry the word of the Lord, but God gave him a word to share and he obeyed.

We often limit God's work in us and who He may choose to speak to us. The story of Amos challenges us to reconsider limitations we may place on God. We may feel ordinary, but God may desire to use us. Will we be willing to leave all to do what He has called us to do and share and speak His word? We must open our hearts to the word of the Lord, even if it comes from an unsuspecting source. The people of Israel were not expecting a prophetic voice in a Tekoan shepherd, but God used Amos. Will we be willing to do the same?

Day 253 | Religion Without Devotion

September 10—Read Amos 5-7

If I stand before God with outstretched arms and declare His goodness, yet do not sacrifice to ensure that others know Him too, my worship is displeasing. If I stand before Him relishing my liberty without concern for the same for others, my worship is not acceptable. Amos 5:1-24

The rebuke of God's people though the prophet Amos was strong and poignant. The once holy and righteous nation had turned from their God and embraced spiritual formalism, void of sincere worship and marked by godless hypocrisy. The people would go through spiritual motions, offer incense and sacrifices, and yet, their hearts would lack any serious devotion to Yahweh. Amos called them out. Their worship was self-centered and their concern for others was forgotten. They loved their own freedom and liberty but made profit off of the bondage of others.

This prophetic word is strong and clearly in need of a contemporary hearing. How often does the modern church pride themselves in their packaged religiosity that is really nothing more than spiritual motions, wholly emptied of deep consecration? How often do we enjoy the luxuries of our houses of worship and the prosperity of our spiritual journeys but forget those who are without? This is a religiosity that will not be accepted by God and that will be met with strong and eternal consequences.

Day 254 | The Coming Famine

September 11—Read Amos 8-9

Israel's sinful rebellion prompted Amos' prophetic word—there would be a famine of God's revealed word. Four centuries of divine silence ensued. America's refusal to bow before her Creator and the Church's lukewarmness is ushering us toward the same. Pursue Him now! Amos 8:11-13

Amos was a shepherd by trade, a commoner with little notoriety, but his prophetic ministry to the northern tribes of Israel was profound. As Israel continued to spiral decadently into spiritual compromise and idolatry, he warned them of the dire consequences of their spiritual backsliding. He warned of a day to come when famine would cover the land—not a famine of bread, but instead a famine of the Word of God. This sounded odd and was indeed tragic for a nation who had been given the Torah and the covenant, yet nonetheless, the warning was fulfilled.

No nation has been so blessed in modern history as has the United States. We have been saturated with the privilege of freedom of worship, inundated by the proliferation of the Gospel, and gorged with the preaching of God's Word. But like the people of Israel, we have become lovers of pleasure and have taken our blessing and our faith for granted. Unless this nation turns to Him, we too will experience a famine of God's holy and prophetic Word, and without that word, spiritual starvation cannot be avoided.

Day 255 | No Place to Hide From God

September 12—Read Obadiah

Pride is damning. When we become comfortable and secure in our wisdom, ingenuity, wealth, or personal skill, we stand in great peril. Edom dwelt in the well-fortified cleft of the rocks, thinking themselves secure. But when you set yourself against God, you are never safe. Obadiah

The prophecy of Obadiah is short but powerful. He prophesied to the nation of Edom, descendants of Jacob's brother Esau, and warned them that the day of judgment was coming. They were living in the clefts of the rock and felt their position was secure from all enemies, even from God Himself. They had worked hard to put themselves in such a secure spot, and in their minds, they were untouchable. Obadiah warned them that their rebellion against God, rooted in pride, would lead to their destruction unless they turned to God. They did not.

So often, we build our own fortresses and work to secure our lives feeling confident that our efforts have put us in a position that is untouchable. Sadly, there is no such secure position when we are rebelling from God. Wealth does not secure us, wisdom or entrepreneurial savvy does not safeguard us, and talent and gifting do not shield us from the penetrating work of the Spirit and the judgment of God. We must shake our pride and find our security in the holiness of God's grace and in the pursuit of His presence

Day 256 | Embracing the Difficult Calls

September 13—Read Jonah 1-2

Too often, we, like Jonah, faced with an unattractive and unrewarding assignment, requiring obedience without fanfare and engagement with those we might otherwise overlook, run away from the call. Attentive listening and uncompromised obedience is what God seeks. Jonah 1:1-3

God called Jonah to preach to Nineveh, the capital of the Assyrian empire, which had treated the Jewish people with ruthless brutality leaving a trail of carnage. Still, Jonah knew that if the Ninevehites repented, God would overlook their evil and restore them. It was an assignment that had no perks and offered no great hope of future blessing. Instead of obeying and leaning into the call, Jonah fled and paid a great price.

God will often call us to the unattractive and the unrewarding places. In a cultural context that demands affirmation, most are reluctant at best and, more often, completely resistant to a call that holds out no hope of true reward or instant gratification. To reject these opportunities will only lead us to more struggle and place us in positions that are even more uncomfortable. God expects us to listen attentively and obey completely!

Day 257 | Leave Their Faults to God

September 14—Read Jonah 3-4

Until we quit managing the lives and dispositions of others and deal honestly with our own prideful, angry, and critical spirits, we will live in the frustration of a divided heart, an unsettled soul, and a joyless existence, unable to embrace God's mercy for ourselves. Jonah 4

Jonah's epic spiritual journey was one marked by hard lessons learned and deep resistance to the work of God in his life and the life of the Ninevehites. Though they were pagans and unworthy, in the eyes of Jonah of God's mercy, God sought to restore them, and in the process, taught Jonah a thing or two about His grace as well. Jonah resisted stubbornly and found himself frustrated with the wind, the plant, and the worm, all things he had no control over, instead of focusing on his own need of growth.

What a powerful picture of so many Christians today, who spend their time criticizing the shortcomings and weaknesses of others while neglecting their own heart attitudes. Then, when God sends some heat or takes away their security so they can learn to trust Him, these same believers turn their attention to the faults of others instead of trying to learn what God might be wanting to teach them. We must learn to leave the faults of others to God and trust Him to change us.

Day 258 | Warning Against Comfort

September 15—Read Micah 1-3

Into a society that bends over backwards to make us feel cozy, comfortable, and spiritually safe in our self-absorbed freedom, the prophet's word comes—warning us of the dangerous folly of ear-tickling messages that are void of truth and exalt blessing over holiness. Micah 2:11

Micah prophesied in the time of Jerusalem's false security, a season when sin was glossed over by false prophets taking advantage of the sensual longings of the apostate people of God. For decades Judah had worshipped false gods, and they were wasting their resources on lavish pleasure and fleshly appetites instead of caring for widows and orphans. They were listening to false prophets who accommodated their sin rather than the prophets of God who were calling them to repentance, but they were comfortable in their sin.

Contemporary culture seeks to lull God's people to sleep and ease them into a sense of false security. Economic prosperity, coupled with the proliferation of pleasure, work to tempt Christians toward a lukewarm and compromised state. The false prophets of prosperity and cheap grace invite us to rest in the comfort of our present state. God, however, is calling us back to holiness, full surrender, and the glory of suffering for His sake.

Day 259 | Hope is On The Way

September 16—Read Micah 4-5

Hope is ahead, said the prophet Micah to a broken Judah—Once great, the envy of all nations, now feeling the heat of Yahweh's discipline. But redemption was coming—Messiah in a manger. In our moment of struggle, in our day of uncertainty, hope is ahead—Christ is coming. Micah 4

Micah, like many of the Old Testament prophets, spoke to the people of Judah in their days of decline. Prophesying before the Assyrians invaded Samaria and destroyed Israel in 722 BC, and two centuries before Judah would fall to Babylon, he warned the Jews of the judgment that was to come because of their continued apostasy. They had once been great, but soon they would be devastated. Yet even in his prophetic condemnation, Micah would remind them that all was not lost. Redemption would one day come through the promised Messiah, the child born in Bethlehem who would save humanity.

We are living in days of great concern, a season when it seems that the judgment of God is looming. As a nation we have forgotten God and turned to do our own thing. A holy God can do nothing but bring correction. We are feeling it now, and it may likely grow darker in days ahead. Yet hope is still on the horizon. A day is coming when the same Jesus who once entered this world as an infant in a manger will return as King of Kings and Lord of Lords, and we shall forever reign with Him.

Day 260 | There is No One Like Our God

September 17—Read Micah 6-7

Self-loathing may cycle you in shame and regret, other people may make you feel unworthy and useless, and other gods insist you earn your way into good graces, but there is NONE like our God. He delights in unfailing love and hurls our sin into the sea of forgetfulness. Micah 7:18-20

It is the intention of Satan to render the child of God useless and powerless, seeking to keep them wallowing in the quagmire of their sinful failures and frequent missteps. This is a strategy he finds quite successful and uses with great precision. Living in shame and regret trying to secure our own redemption through self-denial and embracing false humility and the posture of unworthiness, many Christians sit on the sidelines and fail to engage the Kingdom work to which they have been called.

God is not like that. He forgives completely, He holds no grudge, and He remembers not our sin. His sacrifice of Calvary was not meant to hold us in the bondage of perpetual shame and defeat, but was intended to free us to be used of Him and to bring Him glory.

Day 261 | The Lord is Good

September 18—Read Nahum 1-3

Though difficult times often befall us, and a just God must bring justice where sin has been rampant, the truth is that the Lord is good. In the most challenging of times and in days of deep uncertainty, He is our refuge, and He knows well our thoughts, fears, and pain. Nahum 1:7

God's Word through the prophet Nahum was harsh. Judgment would be unleashed against the people of God, who had drifted and had followed their own way. It would mean unsettled times, an immediate future that was uncertain, and a painful season that would be filled with heartache, trial, and perplexing questions. But that was still not the final word. Nahum reminded the people that God was GOOD.

We are living in a day of trouble and confusion, most of which has been brought upon us because of turning from God's holiness and seeking our own desires, comfort, and worldly dreams. Clearly, we are experiencing the chastisement of a Father who chastises those whom He loves. Still His nature is GOOD—always GOOD, and He is always a refuge to whom we can run and find safety, even when the days are hard!

Day 262 | Choosing to Rejoice

September 19—Read Habakkuk 1-3

While we are not given the choice of what trials we might face or what pain we might suffer, we are given the choice of how we will respond. Like Habakkuk in the face of grave circumstances, we can choose to trust, rejoice, and keep moving forward. Habakkuk 3:17-19

Habakkuk's inquiry of the Lord, wondering why God seemed to be turning a blind eye to Judah's sin, elicited a response even more troubling. God would use the wicked Chaldeans to judge His own people, and that judgment would be brutal. This was not what Habakkuk had expected or what he had bargained for, but still he chose, even in the face of uncertainty, to rejoice in God and His faithfulness.

We will no doubt experience trials and suffer pain that we would have never chosen if given that opportunity. Picking and choosing our life's pressures is not up to us—it lies within the sovereignty of God. What choice we ARE given is how we will respond. Like Habakkuk, we must choose to trust even when we don't see His plan, rejoice when our emotions want to cave, and never stop progressing no matter how rugged the path. This is the posture that invites the aid of God and unleashes the full arsenal of the triune God who is always for us.

Day 263 | Seek the Lord

September 20—Read Zephaniah 1-3

As culture continues its godless trajectory, we must heed Zephaniah's word— "Seek the Lord,"—for in Him is our only hope. "Seek righteousness,"—for without it we are unprepared for God's judgment. "Seek humility"—so that we may provide a voice of hope to this world. Zephaniah 2:3

Zephaniah prophesied to the people of Judah during the days of Josiah before he led the people to spiritual reform. They were quickly slipping away from their covenant relationship with Yahweh, and soon they would be overtaken by Babylon and go into exile. The urgent cry of the prophet was for the people to seek the Lord, pursue righteousness, and strive to be humble. This would be their only hope of restoring their spiritual vitality and living as God intended.

As the culture in America, and sadly, even within the Church, continues to spiral toward great apostasy, the message of Zephaniah needs a fresh hearing. Our only hope is found in a renewed relationship with Christ. The only thing that can make us ready to stand before God is a restored righteousness, and the only means by which we can have a meaningful voice to a lost world is to walk humbly. We MUST again seek the Lord and His Kingdom.

Day 264 | Never Changing God

September 21—Read Haggai 1-2

Twin certainties provide calm and peace in the midst of difficult days. One, when God makes a promise, He always fulfills it. Two, God's abiding presence with us is never inconsistent. As He was with us in past days, He is with us now. Haggai 2:5

As the people of Judah stood over the remains of the temple and contemplated its rebuild, their hearts felt the weightiness of the questions, *"will it ever be the same again?"* They wondered if their failure had disqualified them from experiencing the promise of God, and if they would ever know the glory of His abiding presence again. The word of the Lord, spoken by the prophet Haggai, put both concerns to rest. God's promise stands, and His presence never leaves.

Many today need reminded of those twin truths. Often, when our failure has been great, our doubts have consumed us, or our struggles have left us weakened and we wonder what the future holds. God would have us all know that what He has promised us, He can and will perform, and the sweetness of His presence that we once knew and cherished is never beyond our reach. Even as we stand over what seems to be the shambles of our past, He is there.

Day 265 | By My Spirit

September 22—Read Zechariah 1-4

Rather than cowering hopelessly before the mountain God has called us to climb, or trying to wrestle it to the ground in our own strength—inviting burnout, God calls us to draw perpetually from the reservoir of His Spirit to accomplish great exploits through Him. Zechariah 4:1-7

Zerubbabel was the civil leader of Jerusalem and was tasked with leading the people of God in the rebuilding of the temple that was lying in ruins. The people were discouraged, the enemies nearby were taunting them, and his leadership was being challenged. He was unsure how he would ever be able to accomplish what God had called him to do. He was given a vision of the throne room of Heaven and told that his strength would come from the supply of oil (symbolic of the Spirit of God) that flowed from there. Not his might or power but the power of the Spirit would ensure his success.

Many tasks seem daunting and many spiritual mountains stand in the way of us realizing God's call on our lives. Our enemy taunts us with doubts and fears, and often it is tempting to cower in discouragement or to foolishly try to accomplish spiritual victories in our own power. It is only by the power of the Spirit that we can ever hope to do what God has called us to do and be who He has called us to be.

Day 266 | Get Busy!

September 23—Read Zechariah 5-9

Zechariah charged God's people to lay aside their obsession with enemy opposition, personal ease, and prosperity and finish the task of building the temple. The task of reaching the nations is before us, but every distraction and excuse must be laid aside. Zechariah 8:9-13

The prophecy of Zechariah was delivered to a people who had become obsessed with the reasons why they could not do what they had been called to do—namely focus on their divine call and rebuild the temple. The prophet calls them to turn their eyes away from distractions and hindrances and turn to opportunity. The more they focused on their enemy, the less they would see the rebuilt temple's potential.

We are often of this same mind. We have been called to carry the Gospel to the world and make disciples of all nations, and yet we focus our attention, far too often, on the reasons we cannot. God is charging us to lay down our excuses and stand firm against our enemies who are powerless before Christ and His Word, and finish the task to which we have been called. A world of lost people awaits the Gospel, and we must not neglect our call to get it to them. This will require great faith, steadfast hope, and disciplined focus.

Day 267 | Looking to the Crucified One

September 24—Read Zechariah 10-14

While this text, indeed all of Zechariah 12, is replete with allusions to the last days restoration of Israel, it also underscores the ONLY way to experience God's restoring grace—look to the Crucified Christ, mourn over your sins, and turn back to Him in repentance. Zechariah 12:10-11

Zechariah has long been known as an eschatological book, loaded with great implications that effect the coming of Christ and the establishment of His eternal Kingdom. One day in the final act of this temporal world, the nation of Israel will look on the Savior they crucified and experience His grace and salvation. Now their hearts are hard, but then they will experience restorative grace.

One must not only see future implications in this text. Zechariah's prophecy powerfully informs our spiritual experience today and reminds us that divine grace comes not because we deserve it, but because we look in the right direction. When humanity realizes they cannot procure God's favor through their own works and they have no hope but to look to the Crucified Christ, then they will experience an outpouring of His love and know true forgiveness.

Day 268 | Forever the Same

September 25—Read Malachi 1-4

While secular culture disregards a Holy God and a worldly Church "worships" with a self-centered focus on feelings and personal pleasure—truth will not be altered. One day—from the sun's rising to its setting, His name will be honored, glorified, and praised. Malachi 1:11

The prophet Malachi was the last of the old Covenant prophets to Judah, and he warned them about their continued spiritual decline, capitulation to selfish worship patterns, and the influence of the ungodly. It would not be long before Rome would overtake them and, because of their sin, they would again become bound to servitude. Yet He promised, despite their failure, that their God had not changed, and His plan would not be thwarted.

We, too, are confronted by a culture that has forgotten God and a Church culture that has drifted from her founding moorings. Progressive perversions of the Gospel have gained traction within the Church, and the threat to her is both external and internal. Yet God has not changed. His truth can be denied, but it cannot be changed, His plan can be forsaken, but it will never be stopped, and His name may be abused and blasphemed, but will forever and eternally be honored, bowed before, and exalted.

Day 269 | A God at Work in Our Lives

September 26—Read Matthew 1-3

This genealogy serves to remind us of God's continuous involvement in the story of humanity. He is no absent creator. It also reminds us that Jesus is the long anticipated climax of history: The Messiah…King. Our story can only be rightly lived if HE IS the center. Matthew 1:1-17

So often the genealogies of Scripture are rushed through or overlooked altogether. Many assume that only the great theologians or historic buffs need to spend time poring over their meanings. But to do so is to deny that all Scripture, as the Apostle Paul said, is profitable to us. This genealogy of Jesus is rich in meaning. Those who are included, the women, the Gentiles, even a former prostitute, all speak to the grace of God and the inclusive nature of Christ's redemptive work.

One of the great truths that emerges from this Matthean genealogy is that of divine activity in the story of humanity. Some would argue that God created the world and then left it to run on its own. Nothing could be further from the truth. From the very beginning, He worked together all things, good and bad, used people great and evil, and brought about His perfect plan that culminated in the death and resurrection of His Son. This truth is not limited to the ancient days—that same God is at work in our lives through His Son.

Day 270 | The Essence of Discipleship

September 27—Read Matthew 4-5

Discipleship is to follow Jesus. It is not a LEARNED curriculum but a LIVED journey. It is exacting—it requires leaving things, maybe even people, behind, and it runs against the grain of popular culture because it disrupts self-coddling and expects self-dying. Matthew 4:18-22

In five verses, Matthew records the dramatic calling of two sets of brothers who would form one-third of the twelve-member discipleship band that followed Jesus for three years—Peter and Andrew, and James and John, known as "the sons of thunder." When beckoned by Jesus, they immediately left their nets, uncertain of where He would lead them, and followed Him on a cross-cultural journey of self-emptying and reckless abandon.

Today, we have made discipleship neat and polite. It is cookie-cutter Christianity in a box, intended to create a group of people who can routinely spit out Bible facts, find the books in the Bible, and conform to the cultural norms of the local community. This is not discipleship as Jesus intended. He calls us to give up everything and follow Him wherever He leads us, not with a predestined knowledge of where we are headed, but with a willingness to walk by faith and not by sight.

Day 271 | Citizens of a New Kingdom

September 28—Read Matthew 6-8

The realm to which we once belonged was one of anxious worry—a rat-race—a chronic drive to accumulate, hoping to find happiness but bracing to be disappointed. The Kingdom of God we now seek gives certain assurance that our Father will meet and satisfy every need. Matthew 6:25-34

In this powerful portion of Jesus' discourse from the mountain (*The Sermon on the Mount*), the Savior calls His followers to a life free of worry and anxiety. His examples are many, but He hones in on the folly of seeking after and worrying about material things such as food, clothing, and personal possessions. Pointing to the lilies of the field and the birds of the air, He reminds the crowd that their heavenly Father knows well their needs and will supply every one. His final blow is to tell them that to worry about such things is to behave as the pagan Gentiles did.

This truth is so important for believers today. We are no longer servants of this world, nor are we citizens of a temporary realm. Our citizenship is in Heaven and the duration is eternal. As citizens of our glorious inheritance, we need not revert back to the realm of the temporary and carnal. We can rest assured that as we seek first the things of the eternal Kingdom of God, we need not worry or fret for our Father will supply our every need.

Day 272 | Rest for the Weary Soul

September 29—Read Matthew 9-11

Weary is the soul—heavy is the burden of one trying to forge their own way, secure their own peace, and ensure their own happiness. To them an invitation from Jesus comes—an invitation to come near, submit to His Word (yoke), and rest in the joy of an unburdened soul. Matthew 11:28-30

Jesus' followers struggled to understand that He came to take off the heavy burden of works-driven righteousness extolled by the Jewish religious class. The burden of such expectation led to spiritual drudgery that sucked the very life out of their relationship with God. They found themselves seeking to curry divine favor and earn righteous status before God. It was exhausting. Jesus offered a better way.

Many struggle with the burden of past failures, desperately trying to deserve righteousness or prove their spiritual standing, yet spiritually and emotionally spent. To them the words of Jesus come as a fresh breeze in the scorching heat of the dessert. We need not carry the burden of performance. We don't have to prove ourselves worthy. We simply must surrender to His will, His Word, and His grace. That burden is easy and that yoke is light. Drawing near to the Savior and accepting His grace brings rest to our weary souls.

Day 273 | His Presence is Peace

September 30—Read Matthew 12-14

Whether threatened by a storm, walking by faith over the waves of challenge, or resting in the assurance of His presence—we are safe and secure. He sees us when we are toiling and He prays. He lifts us when we fall. He steps into our upheaval and speaks "peace." Matthew 14:22-23

Matthew records the miraculous feeding of the multitude by Jesus, then notes that He sent His disciples to the other side of the lake on a boat while He spent time alone in the Father's presence. As He was praying, He saw that the disciples had been confronted by a storm on the lake, and He saw them struggling to get across. He made His way down the mountain and onto the lake as He walked on the water toward the boat. Initially frightened, Peter asked to join Jesus on the water and, as long as his eyes were on the Master, he walked on the waves. When Jesus entered the boat, the storm ceased.

Much rich truth proceeds from this narrative. Storms are no match for God. Jesus rides above them all and stands victoriously over every trial we may know. Perceived distance does not limit the hand of God. He sees us when we struggle and moves to our rescue. Our failures do not disqualify us. When we fall, He picks us up and steadies our focus and our step. No chaos or disruption can withstand the peace that His presence brings.

Day 274 | To Be Changed on the Mountain

October 1—Read Matthew 15-17

After the bold, but selfish, offer of Peter to erect three memorials for Moses, Elijah, and Jesus, the Father spoke, "This is my dearly loved Son who brings me great joy." The Father is pleased not by great works or daring claims, but by humility, obedience, and trust. Matthew 17:5

The invitation to join Jesus on the mountain was a high honor to Peter. He, James, and John accompanied Jesus to the top of the mountain where Elijah and Moses were transfigured before them. Peter suggested that three dwelling places be erected for permanent residence on the mountain. God's voice interrupted the misguided fisherman and reminded him that they were there, not to be wowed or entertained, but rather to be transformed.

Too often, we, like Peter, seek the exhilarating and thrilling moments of mountaintop spirituality. It is not to spiritual ecstasy that we have been called but to quietness and life-change. It may feel good in the moment to ask God to stop the clock on those moments when our feet feel as if they are floating in the heavenlies, but what God desires for us is that we listen to His Son and become changed by His Spirit.

Day 275 | Forgiveness—Redeemed and Obligated

October 2—Read Matthew 18-20

Nothing reveals more adequately the heart of God or demonstrates more perfectly His character than forgiveness—while still sinners He died and forgave us. Nothing is more insulting than for those, forgiven by a holy God, to refuse forgiveness to another. Matthew 18:31-35

All of the inspired Scriptures point us to a God of infinite wisdom, power, knowledge, and glory. Every page that is turned reveals more fully the nature and character of the sovereign Creator of all that is and has ever been. However, nothing strips away the clouded vision of humanity as we try to wrestle with who God is, as does His cross. There, the supreme sacrifice was made to forgive and redeem those so unworthy.

With the cross in full view and the devastating sacrifice of Jesus ever before us, forgiven humanity must follow suit. To refuse forgiveness to one that Jesus has died for, or to accept His forgiveness while withholding that same grace from another is to consider unholy the shed blood of God's Lamb and to count His sacrifice as meaningless.

Day 276 | Bearing the Image of the One Who Made Us

October 3—Read Matthew 21-23

The imprint which clearly marks a man or a woman, visibly seen in the way they live and act, can be said to be the heart's possessor. We are people of the King, indelibly marked by the imago dei. Though bearing that image, do our lives reflect that He owns our hearts? Matthew 22:15-22

A great truth comes to us from this famous showdown between the Jewish Pharisees and Jesus over the issue of paying taxes to the state. Their hope was to catch Jesus in a trap that would either put Him in the place of siding with the Romans and denying the Lordship of Yahweh or upsetting the Romans and risking their fury. Instead, Jesus turned the tables. Asking for a Roman coin, He asked them whose inscription was on the coin. When they affirmed that Caesar held the prominent spot on the coin, He instructed them to "render to Caesar what belongs to Caesar and to God what belongs to God."

The truth could not be clearer. It is the one who owns the imprint on the object to whom one must give allegiance. In matters of the state, Christians are to respect and honor the societal systems and world structures. However, each of us is marked by the image of God (*imago dei*), which is passed to all of humanity from the first Adam, and since the imprint of the King of Kings has been marked on each of us, we owe Him our full allegiance, our deepest devotion, and the entirety of our worship. It is the mark of one's piety how well they reflect the character of the One whose image has been stamped upon them since their formation while yet in the womb of their mother.

Day 277 | Extravagant Worship

October 4—Read Matthew 24-26

Her act of devotion was extravagant, her worship costly, and her generosity was extraordinary. But, why shouldn't it be? God's boundless grace and tender mercies demand no less. The restrained expression of day-to-day thanks is an inadequate response to such a gift. Matthew 26:10-13

When the woman of Bethany poured out the expensive perfume on His head as He sat at the table in Simon's home, many were quick to criticize her wasteful expression. How much better it would have been had she sold the precious fragrance and used the proceeds to aid the poor. The disciples themselves were caught in this mindset and were oblivious to the profound depth of her actions. Jesus reminded them that what she did was an act of deepest devotion, one that came with an opportunity that would not always be available. She had done the "good thing," and they should learn from her actions.

No expression of worship, act of service, or sacrificial gift is too great to give to the One whose grace is responsible for our transformation and eternal hope. Obligatory acknowledgements of His love and empty attempts of expressing our thanks will never suffice. We must be people of extraordinary gratitude and extravagant worship. His sacrifice deserves and, indeed, demands such a response.

Day 278 | God at Work

October 5—Read Matthew 27-28

Jesus' death was not evil's victory or a helpless martyrdom. Darkness covered the earth (46), the veil tore in two from top to bottom (51), bodies left their tombs (51), and the earth quaked (54). GOD was at work. The sinless One becoming sin—laying down His life. Matthew 27:45-66

Many see Calvary as a place of defeat, a place of pitiful capitulation by the Nazareth-born carpenter who could not withstand His accusers and could not deliver on promises He had made to His disciples. As He hung on the cross between the two thieves, He appeared beaten and overcome—finally quieted. But we know better. The darkness that covered the earth was supernatural, and it was followed by the ripping of the veil, mass resurrections, and an earthquake. This was no ordinary execution. This was God at work!

Every child of God needs to know that what things appear to be are not always what they are. In our darkness, in our pain, and in our most difficult moments, God is at work. He is able and stands ready to shake the world on our behalf, bring life to what seems dead, and tear asunder the veils that keep us from God's presence. He is at work in every situation.

Day 279 | Jesus and His Family

October 6—Read Mark 1-3

*"For whoever does the will of God, he is my brother and sister and mother."
Jesus' words were not meant to de-value the bloodline family, rather to extol the
profound beauty of the family of faith and encourage its development and
safeguarding. We need one another. Mark 3:35*

The final verses of Mark chapter three have puzzled many for
centuries. As Jesus taught, His mother and brothers paid Him a visit
and sent messengers to ask for Him, hoping to have some time with
Him. The words of Jesus to the inquiry of the messenger reads so
strange to our ears today. *"Who are my mother and my brothers? For
whoever does the will of God, he is my brother and sister and mother."* On the
surface, this seemed so flippant and dismissive. But that was not at all
what Jesus was communicating. Rather than dismissing His human
family, He was expanding His spiritual family to all who obediently
trust Him.

The importance of the family of God can never be overestimated. It
is the greatest of all privileges to be called the *"children of God,"* *"heirs
and joint heirs with Christ."* It is this community of people who is called
upon to share the Gospel with the world, build one another up as we
live in devotion to our brothers and sisters, and display the beauty of
Jesus to a dark would.

Day 280 | Storms Build Faith

October 7—Read Mark 4-6

The Christ-follower's life should not be one of fanciful and elaborate speculating or fearful cowering—rather, having come through life's storms by trusting Christ, we should confront spiritual darkness with God's truth, Christ's presence, and the Father's compassion. Mark 5:1-20

The fourth chapter in Mark's gospel recounts the disciples' experience when Jesus was awakened from a nap in the boat's stern and calmed the furious storm. Though it raged fiercely, Jesus spoke to the winds and the sea and it was stilled. The miracle caused many to muse, "*Who is this man, that the wind and the sea obey Him?*" Immediately after exiting the boat, they were welcomed by the demoniac who lived within the tombs, and they watched as Jesus confronted him and set the man free, on the road to normalcy. Their faith, having just seen the miracle on the sea, was able to grasp this miracle as well.

We need not be afraid of the challenges that face us or the threats of our enemy. To cower in fear or live anxiously is not God's plan for us. Having been powerfully carried through the storms of this life, God's children should rest in the certainty that nothing is too hard for Him.

Day 281 | He Does All Things Well

October 8—Read Mark 7-8

Our most valuable lessons are learned through crushing disappointment, our faith is deepened by agonizing loss, our hope is established through dark nights, and His presence sustains our souls in deep loneliness. We can truly say—He has done all things well. Mark 7:37

As Jesus made his way through the crowds in the region of Tyre and Sidon, the Gentile woman approached Him, begging Him to help her daughter who was possessed by a demon. When He exited that region he moved toward the Sea of Galilee and the region of Decapolis, a region with ten Hellenized cities, where a man was brought to him who was both deaf and dumb. Jesus, moved by the man's need, healed him so that he could both hear and speak. The crowd, astonished by the miracle, proclaimed of Jesus, *"He has done all things well."*

Both the Gentile woman and the man who was deaf and dumb came to know the power of Christ and His true character through their adversity. We often think that we can know Him best through the good times, but it is through the heartaches, the trials, and the crushing that we truly come to know Him for who He is. It's when we get through those difficult days that we can say with confidence, "He has done all things well."

Day 282 | It's Not About Me

October 9—Read Mark 9-10

It can be painful, but it is necessary to authentic discipleship to understand that the Kingdom is much bigger than us, others are to be more important than us, and it all doesn't revolve around us. Mark 9:33-50

One of the most uncomfortable texts in the gospels is found here, where the disciples are arguing among themselves about who would be the greatest. It's uncomfortable because Jesus strongly rebuked them, telling them that the one who hoped to be great or first must be willing to be as insignificant as a child and last in line. It is also uncomfortable because it reveals our own longings to be noticed and our own selfish desires to be great.

The world needs our witness. They need to know about the love of Jesus and the price He paid for their redemption. We are the salt to the earth, the preserving hope of a world out of whack. But if we refuse to be humbled, to set aside selfish ambitions, and to recognize that the plans of God are bigger than us, we will fail in our calling and leave a broken world without the witness it so desperately needs.

Day 283 | The Divine Priority of Forgiveness

October 10—Read Mark 11-13

Forgiving those who have hurt us is so crucial that Jesus instructs us to stop praying in order to forgive them. When forgiving someone becomes difficult, we should focus on the One who forgave us more than the one we need to forgive—His grace enables us to forgive. Mark 11:25-26

The teaching of Jesus indicates that great and supernatural results are available to those who seek God in faith. Mountain-moving faith that makes the impossible possible is the subject matter of this dialogue Jesus had with His disciples. Surely, nothing could be greater than to see God's hand move in response to the faith-filled prayers of His own. Despite the great potential that lies in the power of prayer, Jesus explains that even supernatural acts pale in comparison to restored relationships that come as a result of forgiveness.

Jesus is clear. If, while we are praying, we are reminded that a relationship is broken and in need of reconciliation, we are to stop the prayer and go to that one in hope of restoration. This marks the divine priority of forgiveness and provides us our own forgiveness. What a shame it is that many go about their business seeking the miraculous that only God can do, and yet by failing to make right broken relationships that are within their power to mend, they offend the very God they ask something great from.

Day 284 | The Gratitude of a Forgiven Mess

October 11—Read Mark 14-16

Despite her painful insecurities, she poured out a messy offering on Jesus, anointing the Anointed One because she saw Him for who He was. He gladly welcomed her. Jesus doesn't care how messy our lives or offerings might be. Just stop, recognize Him, and worship Him. Mark 14:3-9

It is hard to imagine a more dramatic scene than this one detailed in Mark's gospel. Jesus was in the home of Simon and was eating dinner with his family and friends. Walking into the open concept house of ancient Israel was a woman who knew that she must find and worship Jesus of Nazareth. While we are not told for certain, the context implies that she had been forgiven by Jesus and wanted to express her gratitude by emptying her most precious treasure on Him as an act of devotion. Her act was judged harshly by the disciples, who felt she was being wasteful, and many surely thought her arrival had only made a scene and most certainly a mess.

Despite the harsh criticism of those in the house, Jesus commended the woman for her worship. He did not care how messy it was, for He knew how messy her life had been. He gave no thought of the cost of the perfume, because soon He would pay the ultimate price at Calvary, and He knew her worship was a testimony to the depth of her gratitude. Jesus is still not afraid of our messy lives, nor is His heart turned away by our sin. He welcomes us to come with our mess, pour out our hearts to Him, and have our lives restored.

Day 285 | Normal Christian Living

October 12—Read Luke 1-3

Those who are truly walking in obedience to God should experience divine activity in their lives as a normal way of life. That divine activity will always witness to those around them and serve as an opportunity to point others to God. Luke 1:57-65

The birth of John the Baptist, as part of the life narrative of his mother Elizabeth, was steeped in divine activity. Her pregnancy was a miracle, the angelic visitor that spoke to Zechariah was supernatural, and the infilling of John by the Spirit, while still in Elizabeth's womb, was clearly a work of God. The gospel writer, aware of the activity of God in their lives, noted that all the hill country of Judea talked about the movement of God and what was happening.

Sadly, such divine activity in the lives of believers today is an exception to the rule. Rare is the supernatural witness exuding from the lives of Christ-followers that might surely make an eternal impression on a lost world. This should not be the case. If we are living lives of obedient holiness, the activity of God in our lives should not be rare, but should mark clearly that we have entrusted our hearts to Him and that His favor is upon us.

Day 286 | The Prerequisite of Obedience

October 13—Read Luke 4-5

Peter was weary, and his own efforts had proven fruitless. All night—not a single fish. Jesus had another plan—Peter followed. Understanding the plan of God for our lives is not a prerequisite for a miracle. Reverent submission to His Word and un-delayed obedience are what move the hand of God. Luke 5:1-11

This text of Luke is the precursor to the call of Peter and his brother Andrew to follow Jesus and be His disciples. Along with these two brothers, James and John, the sons of Zebedee, also became followers of the Man from Nazareth. As Jesus passed by the water, He saw empty boats and asked Simon Peter, the boat's owner, if He could use it as a platform to teach the growing crowd. After He had concluded His teaching, He asked Peter to go out further and cast his nets. Peter protested that he had fished all night and caught nothing, but nevertheless, agreed to obey the Master. The result was both amazing and humbling. The nets were overwhelmed with fish, and Peter fell on his face before Jesus, terrified in the presence of holiness.

This narrative is pregnant with rich truth. Jesus told Peter not to be afraid but to follow Him, and from that day on he would fish for men. The miracle occurred not because Peter understood what Jesus asked him to do, but because he obeyed. Far too often we feel we must understand the way God works. That is not the case. We are called to obey and when we obey, whether we understand or not, God will act on our behalf.

Day 287 | With Hope We Grieve

October 14—Read Luke 6-7

Jesus, to the widow of Nain whose son had died— "do not weep." From One who had Himself wept, this may seem odd or cold. But—He wasn't saying grief or sadness is bad. Instead— "don't weep hopelessly, for I know the rest of the story, and it will turn out for your good!" Luke 7:13

The widow at Nain experienced grief twice over. Her husband had died, and now her son was gone too—she was alone. As grief overcame her, she was found weeping as she encountered Jesus. His words seemed harsh and uncaring on the surface: *"do not weep!"* She was taken aback by His words and no doubt questioned why He thought them appropriate. It becomes clear as the narrative unfolds; Jesus was not saddened by the fact that she expressed sorrow but that she did so hopelessly. He knew His plan—resurrection.

This truth is powerful and applicable to us today. In fact, the Apostle Paul addressed this very issue with the believers in Thessalonica. He did not command them not to grieve but reminded them that their grief was not hopeless (1 Thessalonians 4:13). For the child of God, the grief that comes as a result of death is not hopeless, because Jesus still has resurrection in mind.

Day 288 | The Consequences of Cynicism

October 15—Read Luke 8-11

Many, like the cynics outside the home of Jairus, miss the opportunity to see Jesus at work as they focus on obstacles and impossibilities. Cynicism, doubt, and a negative attitude consumed by the world's evil will lead to missing divine activity right in front of us. Luke 8:49-56

When Jesus arrived at the home of Jairus, the ruler's servants told them it was not worth bothering Jesus, for his daughter had already passed. Jesus, however, dismissed their suggestion and entered the home with the assurance that the girl was only sleeping. His assurance evoked the cynical laughter of the crowds, but also caused them to be shut out of the home, therefore missing the miracle.

So many today miss the work of God's hand and never experience His powerful moving because their hearts are bent on their cynical observations and negative outlook. This indictment is not reserved only for the unbeliever. Many in the Church miss out on what God is doing because they are more comfortable finding fault, doubting the possibilities, or obsessing over the evil that has flooded our culture instead of drawing near to Jesus and pursuing His grace. God stands ready to do a new thing among us and reveal Himself in new ways, but the cynical doubt of His people must be laid aside.

Day 289 | A Costly Decision

October 16—Read Luke 12-14

The message of Jesus is hard but honest. No one who hears should ever feel misled about the cost of following Him or about the necessity of choosing. The way may often be unappreciated, but no other destiny is worth pursuing, and only His way leads to eternal life. Luke 12:49-53

The words of Jesus to His disciples caused them quite a jolt, and His message was strong and direct. His coming to earth and ultimate death on the cross was not going to bring instant peace to humanity, and the disciples would not find people standing in line to welcome them and sing their praises. Instead, the message of Christ and the cross would divide—it would challenge—it would even wreak havoc with familial ties thought unbreakable. To follow Jesus would mean a price must be paid.

This is still true today. Being fully surrendered to the Lordship of Christ is not for the faint of heart. It is exacting and costly. While the grace that brings salvation is free, the cost of receiving that grace and choosing Christ as the exclusive means of salvation will bring resistance. The world will reject the claims of the exclusivity of Christ and will recoil from the notion of eternal judgment, but though the way is hard, the choice to follow Christ is the only choice worth making.

Day 290 | Coming to Our Senses

October 17—Read Luke 15-17

While it is trendy to say that God accepts us as we are, one must come to their senses and recognize that a life lived in the defeat of the pig's slop is not God's intended plan for His own. An intentional move away from that and toward the Father is still necessary. Luke 15:17

The telling of the story by Jesus of the lost (or prodigal) son is, without question, one of the most powerful explanations of the Father's undying love delivered to us in Scripture. Rich and beautiful is the picture of the father, heartbroken by his son's rebellion and departure, still waiting anxiously and expecting that one day his son would return. Finally, that day came—the son decided that the pigpen was not where he was supposed to be and returned home.

Many today live far beneath their spiritual privilege, and too many find themselves separated from the Father, slopping around in the mire and muck of sinful worldliness. Yes, it is true that God accepts us where we are, but He will not leave us there. He wants to place His cloak of righteousness around us and share fellowship with us at His table. That cannot happen unless we come to our senses and move toward Him.

Day 291 | This is Grace!

October 18—Read Luke 18-20

THIS is Grace! The widow in her complete desperation, the tax collector in his honest humility, children in their utter helplessness, and one who is willing to acknowledge they own nothing—ALL is God's. These know the tender and welcoming forgiveness of the Father. Luke 18:1-30

Luke 18 provides a profound unveiling of pure grace, one needy recipient at a time. The widow who had no political pull with the judge gained an audience with him by her perpetual pursuit. She was followed by the tax collector, standing in the shadow of the Pharisee who thought his religious routines gave him access to God. The tax collector knew that divine favor was only a result of grace. Then came the children—escorted by their parents who knew that only if Jesus touched them could they be blessed. Finally, the rich young ruler appeared in Luke's narrative, struggling to understand that only by giving all and owning nothing could he be in a position to experience God's riches.

These texts provide us with great lessons in grace. It is not the religious, wealthy, arrogant, or person of stature that has an in-road with God. It is the one who comes humbly, emptied of self-importance, and readily acknowledging their need that will truly and fully know the grace of God.

Day 292 | Stay Awake

October 19—Read Luke 19-21

Jesus said, "Stay awake at all times." Spiritual alertness to the seriousness of the day, the work and strategies of the enemy; the spiritual complacency of the people of God, the longing of God's heart, and the activity of the Spirit is a greatly needed quality. Luke 21:36

At the end of a long discourse on the signs of the times and the future that awaited the people of God, Jesus told His followers to *"always be on the watch."* It was watchfulness that would allow them to escape the devastation of evil and ultimately enter the presence of God in eternity. Complacency would be their demise, but a watchful heart would leave them with hope and assurance for the future.

Our culture, and sadly the Church, has become deeply complacent and has fallen asleep spiritually. We have lost, in many cases, discerning hearts and spirits that can identify the devices of the enemy and discern his activity and strategies. We must be awakened to the seriousness of the day, the tactics of our enemy, and the certainty of divine judgment. We can no longer afford to slumber. We must become enlightened and inspired by the Spirit.

Day 293 | Hearts that Burn

October 20—Read Luke 22-24

When God's people are in the presence of Jesus, and the Scriptures are rightly divided as pointing to Him, their hearts burn within them with passionate anticipation, and their fellowship with Him is sweet. Luke 24:24-34

One of the great stories of the New Testament is the encounter Jesus had with the two travelers on the road to Emmaus on resurrection Sunday. They had no idea that it was Jesus who was talking to them about the law and the prophets and they recognized neither his appearance nor His voice as He reasoned with them through the Scriptures. But when He broke the bread and distributed it to them, their eyes were opened and they acknowledged that, as He taught, their hearts were burning within.

This sense of burning and longing hearts should mark the gathering of God's people. The Word, the Bread of Life, is living and powerful, and as it is broken and rightly divided to us, our hearts should burn and leap within, as did John the Baptist in Elizabeth's womb when Mary entered the room carrying Jesus in hers. The worship of God's people should be marked with just such excitement, burning passion, and glowing anticipation as those travelers experienced that day long ago.

Day 294 | The Power of the Word Made Flesh
October 21—Read John 1-3

Resident in the Word, second person of the Godhead is all POWER—speaking into existence all that is; LIFE—sustaining all who trust in Him; and brilliant LIGHT—shining into the darkest of situations, to bring hope. The Word became flesh to share our loneliness and pain. John 1:1-14

Few texts in Scripture can compare with the rich majesty of John's epilogue, which describes the glory of Christ's incarnation and articulates His eternal existence. John is careful to help His readers understand that the Word of God, the eternal Son who became flesh, was the creator of all things, the sustenance of all life, and the illuminating light to all humanity.

This text is far more than a brilliant theological treatise. It does more than just stretch the intellect or stir inquisitive spiritual interests. John makes clear that these qualities of the Son of God provide practical benefits as well. His power is able to do more than we could ever ask or think, His life sustains all humanity, without Him no life is known, and His light makes even our darkest moments full of hope, knowing that our path is lit by His presence.

Day 295 | The Lord of the Harvest

October 22—Read John 4-6

It is tempting to become enamored with the joy of harvest, foolishly presuming that our efforts produced success. Never forget the joyless toil of those before us, the essential work of the Spirit, and God's call to sow, even when we ourselves do not see the harvest. John 4:37-38

These words of Jesus are instructive. After reminding the disciples that the harvest field of lost souls was white and ready to harvest, Jesus further elaborated on principles of the harvest. One of those great principles is that often we have the privilege of gathering a harvest that someone else planted before us. This is most often the case on foreign soil and underscores the beauty of the Body of Christ and the important role of every individual.

On an individual level, an awareness of this great truth should lead us to humility, and warn us to walk carefully. One must not presume that the harvest they enjoy is a result of their giftedness or their personal piety. The law of the harvest is a divine principle, and when seeds are planted before us and watered by those who precede us, we may enjoy the resulting emergence of fruit, but we dare not get sloppy in our pursuit of Him. Divine blessing is a result of grace and is not synonymous with favor. We must walk in holiness, consistent devotion, and perpetual obedience, trusting that whether we are called to plant, water, or gather, the Lord of the harvest will ultimately do the work, and it is His glory we must seek.

Day 296 | Deficient Faith

October 23—Read John 7-10

One of the great deficits of modern Christianity is consistency. Our spiritual disciplines are so often on-again, off-again, leading to a roller-coaster spiritual journey. Those who CONTINUE or ABIDE in Him walk in freedom from sin, fear, defeat, and discouragement. John 8:31-32

As Jesus taught His followers about the true depth of discipleship, the notion of continual abiding was at the fore of His admonition. Jesus discounted the idea that one could really be His disciple by just having an encounter with Him or giving Him cursory attention. To be a true follower of Christ and bear the fruit of that relationship with confidence of His keeping power, they would need to remain in His Word and live in obedience to His commands.

Consistency in spiritual disciplines is sorely lacking in the Church today. So much of our worship is an invitation to a feeling, a promise of an encounter, or a call to emotional expression. These things are all good and have a place in the life of the Christ-follower, but only those who remain in a perpetual walk with Jesus and live in obedience to His Word, even in times of challenge and hardship, will be able to live free from the bondage of sin, soar above the looming fear that is instigated by Satan's ploys, rise above the besetting sins that challenge one's faith, and continue in the hope that comes in knowing Jesus. Jesus calls us to follow, but also to abide!

Day 297 | A Life that Glorifies the Father

October 24—Read John 11-14

To have Christ's mind is to live intentionally—to be spent and to reject self-preserving ideologies that, at best, safeguard the single life while forfeiting the harvest of a life fully invested. While the soul may be troubled by such existence, God is glorified. John 12:23-28

This narrative in John's gospel informs so much of our understanding of Jesus' ministry and reveals how He beckons us to follow. Jesus had already been hailed as King of the Jews by the crowd of onlookers who had lined the streets the day before, and reminiscent of the Magi from the east who came at His birth, the Greeks sought to speak with Him just hours before His death. Jesus, moved by the sacredness of the hour and the weightiness of the occasion, spoke of His death. The time had come for the Father to be glorified, and Jesus would, like a corn of wheat, fall into the ground and die. He called those who were with Him to surrender their lives to the Father's will, even if it meant death for them as well.

The words of Jesus still speak to us. Human instinct is to preserve oneself and to ensure that we guard our own lives and preserve our resources. But to follow Jesus is to lay down the security of this life, the control of our destinies in this season, and surrender our desires and future into His hands. Though the thought may seem uncomfortable, it is only when we die to self that we can truly live, and it is only when we decrease that Jesus is glorified in us.

Day 298 | The Divine Exchange

October 25—Read John 15-17

Just hours before the cross, Jesus prayed to the Father these words, "And the glory which You gave Me I have given them..." As the Sinless One became sin FOR US, the glory of His righteousness became ours, accompanied by a promise that we would one day be like Him. John 17:22

As Jesus left the upper room and made His way to Gethsemane, He stopped to intercede for His disciples and beseech His Father. The words of His prayer dripped with an extraordinary pathos that unveiled the deepest longing of His soul. His words spoke of the amazing exchange that was about to take place, the glory which the Father had bestowed upon Him, and the gift that He was about to pour upon His followers through His sacrificial death at Calvary. This prayer looked forward to the most powerful moment of human history.

The great exchange is this—our sin laid on Him at the cross while His righteousness becomes ours. No words can adequately describe this most glorious moment. No song of praise, no act of worship, and no earthly offering could ever begin to match the worth of His sacrifice or adequately respond to the divine love revealed as Jesus laid down His life for us.

Day 299 | The Folded Napkin

October 26—Read John 18-20

John stepped into the tomb—he saw not just a vacated grave but the binding clothes of death laid aside and the shroud that screamed death's certainty believed!" See the empty tomb! John 20:10

Resurrection morning was full of wonder and discovery for the beloved disciple John as he accompanied Peter to the tomb that Mary had reported was empty. They hurried to the garden, but as John entered in, he observed what was clearly a scene that revealed holy activity. The grave clothes Jesus had vacated were there on the tomb floor, and the napkin placed over the face of every corpse, a universal sign of death's power over humanity, was folded neatly in a place by itself.

This folded napkin was a sign to John, and indeed to all of us still today, that a major shift had occurred. What he saw before him was more than a detail for the gospel writer to document. The scene proclaimed a powerful message. Death no longer looms as the dreaded enemy with an awful sting. It has been de-throned and de-fanged by the resurrection of Jesus in splendor and great glory. Death will come, but it does not bring the final word for the child of God. Instead, death is the casting away of the tent made with hands and a welcome reception of our house not made with hands, that is eternal in Heaven.

Day 300 | Night Gives Way to Dawn

October 27—Read John 21

As the dark night gave way to morning, the empty-handed fishermen found that the Master could provide what they thought impossible, and the failed and ashamed apostle experienced restorative grace. We must never let the dark night of our soul define God's best for us. John 21

Few chapters in Scripture are so rich with both profound pathos and overflowing hope as the final chapter of John's gospel. All night long, the disciples had toiled, with nothing to show for it. This humiliating outcome was like rubbing salt in the wounds of Peter, whose shameful denial of Jesus had left him feeling as if his value was gone and his future ruined.

But when darkness was driven out by the Galilean sunrise, a new narrative emerged. The Master, betrayed by Judas and denied by Peter, appeared to them on the shore and told them to cast again on the other side, and the catch was miraculous. Even more amazing was the breakfast of fish already on the coals waiting for them, and the restoration he offered to Peter that included the assurance that he would be used greatly for the One he had denied. Dark moments need not have the final say when Jesus stands near our shore.

Day 301 | No Need to Fear

October 28—Read Acts 1-5

We do well to remember Gamaliel's words to the Sanhedrin, shaken by the apostles' ministry. "If it is from God, you will not be able to overthrow them." Threats, rejection, and godless disregard for truth do not threaten the Church that Jesus promised He would build. Acts 5:39

The Sanhedrin wanted to do away with the apostles, knowing the threat that the Gospel posed to their power and to their religious institution. If they allowed the apostles to continue, they might lose their power and control. Gamaliel, however, knew that to resist God was a hopeless cause, and if this growing band of Christ-followers was really ordained of God, there would be no stopping their progress.

We spend too much time worrying about the tactics of our enemy and living afraid that his attack might thwart the work that God has called us to. Nothing could be further from the truth. Jesus promised that He would build His church, and the gates of Hell itself would never prevail against His work. This should provide great comfort and embolden us in our efforts. What He has promised, He will perform.

Day 302 | Found Faithful

October 29—Read Acts 6-7

Stephen's heavenly welcome as the first Christian martyr was punctuated by Jesus standing at God's right hand to receive him. Whether he was distributing food to widows or defending the faith before an angry resistance, he was faithful. May we be found faithful as well. Acts 7:55

Stephen entered the scene of the early church in Acts 6. He was chosen by the Holy Spirit as a result of the church's prayer, to be one of the first seven deacons of the early church, tasked with distributing the benevolence fund to the Hebrew and Greek widows. His ministry, however, was not limited to his work as a deacon. He was also a great proclaimer of the Gospel, a vocation that led to his being stoned by the Jewish council. As he was being stoned and on his way to becoming the first Christian martyr, Heaven was opened and he saw the Son of Man, standing at the Father's right hand welcoming him into eternal glory.

What Stephen was rewarded for with such a majestic greeting was his faithfulness. Whether he was preaching or serving, he was always faithful. This faithfulness was rewarded by God. God's call to us is faithfulness so whether in little things or big, we should always live to serve faithfully the King and His Kingdom.

Day 303 | The Fuel of Church Growth

October 30—Read Acts 8-12

The Church—facing opposition, stretched themselves in prayer. James was martyred and Peter was thrown into prison. Peter was delivered, Herod was divinely judged, and a funeral was held for James. The Gospel spread. Through tragedy, trial, and in victory, a praying Church will overcome. Acts 12:20-24

This chapter in Luke's narrative of the growth of the early Church is chock-full of fast moving action. King Herod, was on a rampage persecuting the Church, and he seized two of the leaders of the Christian Church, James and Peter. James was quickly martyred for his faith, and Peter was placed in prison. The church gathered and interceded for the apostle, and God miraculously delivered him in the middle of the night. This angered Herod and he took that anger out on the people of Tyre and Sidon. As he spoke before the people and allowed them to praise him as a god, he was struck dead in that very moment. Despite all of that chaos, struggle, and trial, the praying Church still experienced rapid growth.

It is clear that the enemy of the Church cannot thwart the growth of what God has promised to build. When the people of God pray, it does not mean that every trial will disappear or that no crisis will come. James was still martyred despite their prayer. What it does mean is that the Church will prevail, that the enemy's ploys will be exposed and defeated, and that the world will watch as the Church overcomes and expands. This is the assurance in which we can walk and the confidence in which we can stand. Prayer fuels the overcoming Church.

Day 304 | What Else but Sing?

October 31—Read Acts 13-16

We ask of Paul and Silas, bloodied backs and imprisoned in a dark, cold jail, "How could you sing?" They retort, "what else but sing?" They knew their enemy was on the run, reverting to violence, Jesus had risen, and they had been counted worthy to suffer for Him. Acts 16:20-26

One of the great stories of biblical heroism is found in the 16th chapter of Acts. Paul and Silas had experienced early ministry success in Philippi, but their converts were of such consequential status that the community leaders were angered and had the two evangelists thrown into prison after they were beaten. At midnight, Paul and Silas began to sing and praise God, and the divine response was an earthquake that would break their chains and bring the jailer to his knees, crying, *"what must I do to be saved?"*

Many would question Paul and Silas, wondering how in their circumstances could they sing? Their response would be, *"what else but sing?"* They knew that their enemies were desperate, and the only recourse they had was violence. To Paul and Silas, this was reason to rejoice. When trials come our way and the enemy attack seems to be ramped up against us, it is a sure sign that the Kingdom is coming and the enemy is frightened. This is not the time to cower or recoil—this is the time to sing!

Day 305 | The Only Hope

November 1—Read Acts 17-19

The early Church confronted the godless Ephesian culture with bold truth— "the word of the Lord grew mightily and prevailed." A sinful culture won't be won by a progressive, powerless, and Word-less Church, but a Spirit and Word-filled people will see their mission prevail. Acts 19:1-20

As the New Testament Church began to penetrate the pagan world of Ephesus, they did not water down the truth or acclimate their message to the prevailing cultural mores of the Ephesians. Instead they spoke the truth of the Gospel with boldness—Jesus Christ crucified, resurrected, ascended, and coming back! They knew that anything less than that would never turn their world around.

It is quite unfortunate, but the contemporary church seems to have abandoned the bold approach of their first century ancestors. Repeatedly, we water down the truth, seek the least common theological denominator, and dress our message up in the garb of worldly, shallow, and empty maxims. These will never turn our world to Jesus. Only the bold, unfettered, and uncompromised Gospel, that exalts Christ and lifts Him up for a broken world to see and embrace, will ever bring transformation and hope to a dying world.

Day 306 | Finishing My Course

November 2—Read Acts 20-23

The depths and lengths, the ups and down, the trials and the challenges that may await us are unknown. Yet still we embrace the conviction that, unless this life we now have is used to finish our God-given assignment of telling others about Jesus, it is of no value. Acts 20:22-24

There may be no more touching New Testament narrative than Acts 20, the grand farewell discourse of Paul as he addressed the Ephesian elders on his way to Jerusalem for the Passover. He would never see them again. The tears were real, the hugs punctuated by true love, and yet the focus of Paul was never more clear. Paul told them that, as he traveled to Jerusalem, he knew that suffering and even death might await him, but the course that God had placed him on must be finished or all else he had done would be for naught.

This is the focus that must mark our lives. There is much we can do, and many opportunities that will present themselves to us. But the course that God has called us to must be our aim. That course may include great challenges and even disappointments, but its end will be glorious if we have been true to our calling, and if our way is marked by lives who have heard the grand story of Jesus and His love.

Day 307 | Nursing No Offense

November 3—Read Acts 24-26

It is the certain hope of Christ's return that brings both divine scrutiny and eternal reward and should motivate each of us to strive faithfully for a "conscience without offense toward God and men." Our hurt won't matter then, and our bitterness will be judged. Acts 24:10-16

As Paul stood before the governor Felix, he answered charges that had been leveled at him regarding his behavior while in Jerusalem, specifically his alleged attempt at profaning the temple. With a calm reserve Paul spoke, noting that when his ministry was properly investigated Felix would find that he was innocent of such ridiculous charges, and even if not, Paul was certain that one day when Christ returned to judge all humanity, he would before His Lord, be exonerated. Thus his conscience was clear, and no bitterness was harbored.

So much truth can be gleaned from the words of the falsely accused apostle from Tarsus. He would not harbor hate or seek revenge, because he knew that God saw his heart and one day his motive would be vindicated and his reward received. So much pain would be avoided and so much peace would be known if God's people would refuse to nurse their offenses and trust the Judge who always does what is right.

Day 308 | We Need a Word From God

November 4—Read Acts 27-28

Into gloomy circumstances, when navigation seemed impossible and the waves were at full throttle, Paul spoke words of life and faith. Today, we need no more critics, skeptics or faithless pessimists, rather those who know God has stood by them and speak hope over fear. Acts 27:21-26

As Paul headed to Rome, a prisoner of the empire preparing for a meeting with Caesar, the ship on which he traveled was met with a furious storm that threatened to destroy both the sea vessel and its passengers, many prisoners of the state. The crew did all they could to settle the seacraft, but they were no match for the raging storm. While almost all had given up hope, God sent an angel to assure Paul that no life would be lost. He calmed all who were on the ship and told them that God had spoken, and their lives would be spared. It was that word of hope that changed the course of history and the lives of those on board.

Our world is certainly in tumultuous times and the storms of doubt, evil, and confusion are furiously raging. Many are speaking words that discourage and cause the hearts and joy of many to wither. How deeply we need men and women who have heard from God, who will speak a word of hope to this generation and settle the melting hearts and sinking souls of fearful humanity.

Day 309 | True and Powerful Gospel

November 5—Read Romans 1-4

The Gospel IS NOT an invitation to live carelessly beyond the concerns of law and obedience, knowing that a covering of grace is always available—rather IT IS an impartation of power that enables us to live righteously, practice holiness, and walk in obedience. Romans 1:1-6, 16-17

As Paul opened his letter to the Church at Rome, he laid out with clarity the focus of his epistle—the POWER of the Gospel. It is for Gospel proclamation that he was chosen, called, and equipped, and the Roman readers were certain of his passion to live obediently to his calling. Paul calls the Gospel *"powerful"* and tells his readers that, in the Gospel, there is a righteousness imparted to all who believe, enabling them to live holy lives.

This great truth needs to be proclaimed loud and clear into a world and Church that has lost its way. In the face of a new and perverted gospel that allows grace to be gutted, love to be twisted, and sin to become benign, true Gospel preaching will boldly remind hearers that the standard of God's holiness has not been lowered; but the true Gospel is the power of God unto salvation and empowers believers to live holy and say "no" to sin.

Day 310 | God's Ultimate Purpose for Us

November 6—Read Romans 5-7

God's purpose, contrary to false and self-centric teaching, is not to produce spoiled and entitled "King's Kids," but rather mature believers transformed into Christ's likeness. This happens as we rejoice in trials, knowing that they produce endurance, character, and hope. Romans 5:3-5

Paul's letter to the Romans is, without question, his greatest and most exhaustive theological treatise, carrying profoundly rich truths regarding justification by faith. It is also crucial to understanding God's purpose for our lives. Paul describes the important role that trials play in our spiritual formation and reminds his readers that God's purpose for His own is greater than temporary happiness or fleeting pleasure. He wants us to be like Him.

This message is difficult for contemporary culture to comprehend. We live in a very pleasure-driven world where instant gratification is a highly sought after commodity. Many trade long term stability for a momentary thrill. The Spirit's work in our lives is a patient work, one that takes the trials that we face and shapes them so that they produce in us the endurance that begets character, which in turn yields hope. This is the divine goal—hope that we will one day be conformed into the likeness of Jesus.

Day 311 | Beautifully Blistered Feet

November 7—Read Romans 8-10

Across the rocky, dusty roads, ancient messengers carried their news, but their feet would become blistered and bloody. If the message was good, their feet were "beautiful." The sacrifice required to carry the message of hope to a lost world is beautifully worth it. Romans 10:15

One of the great missions texts in the New Testament is the tenth chapter of Romans. Here, Paul makes it clear that humanity is lost without the salvation offered in Christ, and unless that message is proclaimed by someone who has been sent, it is impossible for one to hear, have faith, and believe. The sent messenger who proclaims the Good News is paramount to the heart of the Father. Paul underscores that importance by citing the prophet Isaiah's words, *"How beautiful are the feet of those who bring Good News!"*

In ancient days, messengers would travel miles across rocky, dusty plains and mountains to bring the message to the recipient. Often, when they arrived, large blisters had formed and blood seeped from their feet. But if the message was good, the pain was worth it. This is what Paul was saying. The pain and sacrifice we may experience to carry the Gospel to the ends of the earth is well worth it when one-day people of every kindred and tongue are together around the throne of God in Heaven—because of beautifully blistered feet.

Day 312 | The Goal of Tests and Trials

November 8—Read Romans 11-12

Jesus "learned obedience through what He suffered," says the Hebrews author. Here, as WE present ourselves fully to God, bodies and minds, we, through testing (proving), better discern God's will. The fire of testing makes clear the path we are to take. Romans 12:1-2

Paul's letter to the Romans is two-thirds rich theology and one third practical application of that theology. Having understood the truths of the first eleven chapters, dealing with Christ's work of justification of humanity, Paul challenged his readers to a full surrender of themselves to the Lord by presenting their *"bodies a living sacrifice"* and called upon them to reject the world's attempt to conform them, allowing instead, the Spirit to transform their minds. When that is done, argues Paul, trials and challenges may come, but they become a means by which we can better discern the Lord's will.

Just as Jesus experienced great trials and suffering, but through them became more aware of the joy of walking in the Father's will, so we can know God better through our struggles. As we submit to those experiences, we find that they are a means through which we can know God's plan, His way, and His loving compassion better.

Day 313 | The Tragedy of a Tainted Witness

November 9—Read Romans 13-14

A carnal believer ferociously defends their personal rights. A mature believer gladly forfeits their rights, understanding that their lives are to represent well their God, and that their rights are tempered by the responsibility they bear for the weaker believer. Romans 14:19-23

Paul's words to the Roman Christians were designed to aid them in maintaining a spirit of peace and unity within the church, so that their witness to the pagan world bound for Hell would in no way be tarnished. In matters of conscience, he instructed them to be mature and not allow their own convictions or rights to dictate how they treated others. He placed the greatest responsibility on the one who understood their Christian liberty, calling upon them to forfeit their rights so that the unified witness of God's people would effectively touch the lost.

It is easy today in our individualized western mindset to demand our own rights and overlook the potential harm that our liberty might bring to others whose conscience may be weak. Mature Christians will always be willing to forsake their own rights for the sake of those who may not know Jesus, and who might be hurt or even lost if the Church's unity is destroyed, or their witness tarnished by boasting in their personal liberty.

Day 314 | Refusing to be Divided

November 10—Read Romans 15-16

God's heart is a unified and peaceful Church. Satan seeks to disrupt. When spiritual experience is ranked to determine spirituality, motives are prideful spiritual appetites that divide. When serving Christ is the aim, Satan is defeated and God's peace reigns. Romans 16:17-20

The words of Jesus' high priestly prayer, *"that they all may be one"* (John 17:21) reveal the Father's heart. His desire is that we all be unified, lay down our divisions and disagreements, and provide a united front against a raging enemy for a lost world. Too often, we are divided over doctrinal minutia and spiritual experiences that are distinctive and argue for an elite layer of Christianity. This is detrimental to the cause of Christ.

The work of Satan is a work of distraction and distortion. He loves to get the focus of believers off of the lost so that he can ensure that they will not be brought to Christ. Sadly, one of his most effective means is to cause Christians to be divided over their own spiritual experiences that they feel make them special or more spiritual. These attitudes are not driven by godly pursuit but self-ambition and pride, and must be rooted out for the cause of the lost.

Day 315 | But We Have the Holy Spirit

November 11—Read 1 Corinthians 1 1-2

While frustration comes easy as we navigate the ever-changing culture filled with empty world views and ideologies—we find hope in knowing that the Spirit we have been given is not the spirit of a futile world but the Spirit of the Holy, living, and all-wise God. 1 Corinthians 1:2-12

The world is full of emerging ideologies, perverted notions of sex, gender issues, and even spirituality, and the hungry heart in seeking for meaning to life, can find itself confused and disturbed. Sadly, those who seek to engage these worldviews, looking to find meaning in their practice, find themselves frustrated and empty. These ideologies become like a mirage, promising the hope of water while all the while making promises that are futile.

As believers, we have a certainty about the truth to which we ascribe and an assurance that what it promises, it will deliver. This truth, found in God's Word, promises that when one places their faith in Christ, they become vessels or temples that house the Holy Spirit. The Spirit that inhabits us is not the spirit of this world that offers nothing but hopelessness. The Spirit that raised Jesus from the dead, enables us to live in resurrection power, and provides a never ending supply of spiritual water to quench our thirst.

Day 316 | Much More than Words

November 12—Read 1 Corinthians 3-4

We must not forget that Kingdom work is not about words spoken, strategies implemented, or programs developed, but the power of the Holy Spirit to transform lives. We will never find satisfaction in eloquent words but only by a sincere work of the Spirit in our hearts. 1 Corinthians 4:20

As Paul warns the Corinthians about those who would seek to distract and persuade them away from the Gospel, he commends himself to them. He does not do this in an effort to brag about what he has done, but to help the Corinthians see the sacrifice he had made so that they would understand just how important the Gospel and the work of the Kingdom really was. He did not want them to settle for a counterfeit message, one that was void of sacrifice or which necessitated no cost. The *"Kingdom,"* he reminds them, is not *"just a lot of talk; but living by God's power."*

This is an important reminder to us today. It has become increasingly popular in the contemporary Church to strategize, posit philosophy, repeat trendy catch phrases, and engage in colorful rhetoric dabbed in some theological jargon. These, however, without the demonstration of the Spirit's power that transforms hearts, amount to a bunch of colorful nothing.

Day 317 | Glorify God With Your Body

November 13—Read 1 Corinthians 5-6

When creationism is mocked and redemption through Christ's blood is discarded, self-worth and meaningful purpose are obliterated. Truth says- "God made you, He redeemed you, and lives in you." Our CALLING is GREAT and our PURPOSE is DIVINE! 1 Corinthians 6:19-20

Into the pagan world of Corinth, informed by philosophies of fatalism and chance, Paul entered with the Gospel of Jesus Christ, rooted not in wishful thinking or mystical fate, but in absolute truth, fixed in the historical death and resurrection of Jesus Christ. The body, argued Paul, is not an evil and expendable cloak that lacks purpose and requires no restraint. The human body was redeemed to house God's Spirit and designed to glorify God.

Our world today, profoundly influenced by philosophies that reject a Creator and divine design, disregards life, gives no thought to the sanctity of the human body, and seeks no restraint to unbridled lusts and perversions of our culture. As believers, we affirm our bodies are jars of clay, housing the treasure of God's presence, and redeemed by the purchase price of Christ's blood, to fulfill His purpose and bring Him much glory.

Day 318 | Marks of the Mature

November 14—Read 1 Corinthians 7-8

Marked by self-absorption and motivated by personal rights, the modern Church's standard of holiness has sagged to a miserable low and the responsibility to care for and guard the souls of others for whom Christ died has all but vanished from her core values. 1 Corinthians 8:9-13

In this text, the Apostle Paul is teaching a crucial component of mature discipleship—that is, mature believers must be willing to lay aside their rights and privileges of grace if their liberty could bring potential harm to someone young in the faith or threaten the spiritual foundations of the spiritual novice. Liberty must be forfeited for the higher call of our brothers' or sisters' spiritual growth.

This kind of selfless living is sadly absent from so much of the contemporary Church. Having become liberated in Christ and now aware of the depth of grace, many have set aside all previously embraced standards to enjoy their freedom in Christ. This unchecked freedom, named "Christian liberty" has produced serious harm to many young believers and has gutted the potency of the Church's witness.

Day 319 | Our Eye on the Prize

November 15—Read 1 Corinthians 9-11

We are suffering from having lost our focus, running hard in many directions but running aimlessly. The prize is the heavenly calling and ensuring that all hear and can run for the prize too. Discipline. Diligence. Focus. Sacrifice. All must be reclaimed! 1 Corinthians 9:24-27

In this ninth chapter of 1st Corinthians, Paul is addressing the ease in which those pursuing Christ can become distracted and get off-course. He wants his readers to understand that the calling he had demanded his undivided attention and his disciplined focus. If he failed to diligently commit himself to a grueling and self-denying focus, he could ultimately see all that he had done for the Kingdom come to naught.

This failure to be self-disciplined is sadly a symptom of a self-absorbed and pleasure-pursuing culture, and these tendencies have worked their way into the church, creating disastrous results among congregants and clergy alike. This, in turn, undermines the church's witness and community impact. We cannot afford to miss out on God's best, lose the prize that awaits us, or fail to reach the ones to whom we have been called. We must give ourselves to a focused and disciplined pursuit of Christ so that we can claim the prize.

Day 320 | Truth and Love

November 16—Read 1 Corinthians 12-14

Peter exhorts us to grow in knowledge and truth (1 Peter 3:18). Paul commends us to mature in love. Truth emphasized over love can make one harsh. Love trumping truth may produce compromise. Both virtues must be brought into mature balance. 1 Corinthians 14:11-13

In a world so truth-impoverished, it is incumbent upon God's people to be propagators and defenders of truth. Likewise, in a culture that seems to so often pit people and groups of people against one another, love is a commodity that is desperately lacking. How must we balance the twin necessities of truth and love?

We must take great care never to promote a love that requires no truth or a truth that is devoid of love. When all energies are brought to bear on declaring truth, but love fails to undergird the proclamation, truth critiques and crushes. When love is embodied but truth is disregarded, a sloppy and worldly spirituality emerges. Passionate defense of the Gospel's truth, proclaimed in the unconditional and grace-filled love of Christ, is transformative and brings hope to the hopeless.

Day 321 | Always at Work

November 17—Read 1 Corinthians 15-16

Securely anchored in the absolute truth of Christ's resurrection, we should labor, serve, and give for the sake of the Kingdom, with no restraint or hesitation, for we can be confident that investment in the Kingdom always produces certain and eternal reward. 1 Corinthians 15:58

Our culture certainly makes discouragement easy and fosters cynical and apathetic disengagement. When we look to those who lead, we despair, and when we consider the trending godlessness and lust for pleasure that so dominates, it becomes easy to retreat to the sideline. Such is the posture of many who once engaged the work of the Kingdom.

It is incumbent upon the Church to remember the truth upon which her call is established and the power that resources her activity. It is Christ's triumph over the final enemy—death—that assures us no adversary can withstand the Gospel's power, and it is His promise— that a kernel of wheat that dies will produce much fruit—that emboldens our witness. There is no time for inactivity, no excuse for cowering, and no reason to shrink back. The resurrected Christ reigns, His Truth still liberates, and His Kingdom is still coming!

Day 322 | A Fragrance of Life and Death

November 18—Read 2 Corinthians 1-2

The task of spreading the fragrance of Jesus to a lost world, knowing that our words, behaviors, and attitudes communicate a clear message to both believers and the unsaved, is a daunting reality—one mediated only by the sufficient and abundant grace of Jesus. 2 Corinthians 2:14-16

One of the greatest truths we can ever learn is the enormous impact that our words, attitudes, and actions have on those around us. Paul made this emphatically clear to the Corinthian readers as he explained that their lives exuded a fragrance matching the quality of the life they lived. Godly living would emit a fragrance that encouraged and challenged other believers to pursue a deeper walk with Christ, and it would simultaneously cause unbelievers to sense that they were undone and in need of a Savior.

This responsibility is one of our greatest but most challenging duties. To fail in this by living lives empty of sincere godliness is to cheat fellow believers out of an encouraging witness and to leave unbelievers with an impotent understanding of biblical holiness. While the task is great, the grace of God is sufficient to enable us to live faithfully.

Day 323 | Called to Truth

November 19—Read 1 Corinthians 3-4

The ministry we have should not discourage. We are His instruments and we are not called to produce results. Ministry is measured, not by creative strategy, but commitment to truth. Gospel rejection is a rejection of God, not us, and is a result of spiritual blindness. 2 Corinthians 4:1-6

Paul's ministry was met with strong resistance in many places, but a faction in Corinth that disputed the apostleship of Paul was one of his greatest challenges. His unorthodox methods, refusal to take their money, and insistence on the purity of the Gospel message kept him at odds with this group of dissenters. Despite the hardship and attacks, Paul stayed true to his calling, knowing that his responsibility was not to change lives, but to be obedient to the truth. If his message was refused, it was God they were rejecting.

This is an attitude that should permeate the lives of all who feel God's call to ministry. We are merely vessels—jars of clay—through which God desires to work. When our message is shut down, we must not take offense, for it is God that is being resisted. God has called us to preach and teach the truth, and when we do that, transformative results must be left to Him.

Day 324 | The Glory of Suffering

November 20—Read 2 Corinthians 5-6

A deficient theology of suffering is plaguing the Church. Suffering should be the believer's expectation and rejoicing through that suffering should be our unwavering determination—confident that God transforms the worst for His glory to reach the lost. 2 Corinthians 6:3-10

After decades of the health and wealth gospel, the American Church has lost its understanding of the crucial role of suffering. We have been taught, either explicitly or implicitly, that suffering is a curse at worst, or sorely beneath the privilege of the Spirit-filled believer at best. This vein of teaching is not only spiritually bankrupt, but has created a generation of selfish and entitled believers, ill-equipped to live out the Great Commission.

The biblical record stands in stark contrast to this deficient theology. Throughout the pages of Scripture, suffering is the means to our fullest spiritual development, the catalyst to crystallized faith, and the unspeakable privilege of those who call Christ "Lord" to share and fellowship with Him in the power of the cross. Greater still, it is through suffering and our response to it and through it that a lost world may see the grace and love of Christ and make Him their Lord.

Day 325 | Godly Sorrow

November 21—Read 2 Corinthians 7-10

Grief felt over pain caused to God and others by our sin produces repentance that leads to fullness of life without regret. This pain we should foster and embrace. Grief felt only because of the consequences of being found out fails to bring transformation. 2 Corinthians 7:10

Paul here reminds the Corinthians of his previous letter and how the last one he had sent had been painful. He noted that his correspondence to them on the previous occasion had made them grieve. He was clear, however, that the grief that they felt was not something he regretted because he had seen that their grief had produced a turnaround, fostered by repentance for the sin he had called out in the letter. In the mind of Paul, grief or pain as a result of conviction leading to repentance was well worth it.

It is not uncommon for people today to grieve or feel pain when they are caught in their sin or when their sin produces hard and challenging consequences. This kind of pain is not to be commended according to Paul when he writes to the Corinthians. Commendable grief is that which flows from a heart gripped by the conviction of the Holy Spirit and has turned from its wickedness back to God. This godly sorrow should be the hope of us all.

Day 326 | The Examined Faith

November 22—Read 2 Corinthians 11-13

Paul calls us to examine our own faith—is it genuine? Do we KNOW that Jesus Christ is among us? Do we make choices with that awareness? Do our words reflect that understanding? Would Jesus be comfortable with the way we live and be willing to participate with us? 2 Corinthians 13:5

As Paul closes his second letter to the Corinthians, he gives them a series of strong but clear warnings. One of those is here—he charges them to examine carefully their own faith to measure its authenticity. The measuring standard by which they were to examine their faith was the life, nature, and character of Christ. Ultimately, he was asking them if their lives were lived in such a manner that others would see in them a demonstration of Christ. If not, they should reconsider and ask God to help them be restored.

The notion of examining our faith is important for today. Many live their lives as professed Christians, but the evidence does not bear out their confession. Their lives neither resemble Christ nor do they point to Him. Unless our lives do, we cannot with integrity claim our faith is genuine. We should heed Paul's call, and make certain that our faith is both demonstratively holy and indeed replicable by those who follow in our footsteps.

Day 327 | The Gospel We Preach

November 23—Read Galatians 1-3

We do well to remember that the Gospel we preach is not a human construct—it came by revelation of Jesus Christ. It must not be altered, manipulated, or deconstructed. Jesus died for our sins, according to the Scripture, was buried, and raised. That's it. No more. Galatians 1:11-24

Paul's letter to the Galatian churches was a strong word of confrontation because of their failed fidelity to the Gospel that he had preached. He was shocked that they had so quickly removed themselves from the truth he had proclaimed, and they were following after new messages that had proliferated through the Galatian area of Asia Minor. The message he had preached had come directly from Jesus Christ, and it was the simple truth of Christ's death, burial, and resurrection. Paul wanted no part of a gospel that sought to add or take away from these truths.

Pluralism, syncretism, and biblical illiteracy have all plagued today's Church. Too often the unadulterated Gospel is dismissed and traded for new and more modern versions that gut the truth from the message of Scripture. We must guard against any effort that removes the truth from our message or waters down the claims of Christ and its clear implications. The Gospel is enough! Anything less will not do, and anything more is not the Gospel.

Day 328 | The Price of Preaching Truth

November 24—Read 4-6

"Have I therefore become your enemy because I tell you the truth?" This was Paul's question to the Galatians, and this paradox is seen clearly in our modern culture. Truth is the enemy of a godless and self-absorbed culture, and its propagators will feel resistance. Galatians 4:16

The heart of the apostle was broken as the people of Galatia, a people he had poured himself into, turned on and rejected him because of the message he proclaimed. The one who was willing to give himself for the people and who committed to sticking with them until Christ was "fully formed in them" (Galatians 4:19) had become their sworn enemy.

Paul's experience is not unlike what we know today as we seek to uphold the truth of God's Word. In a world where right has become wrong and wrong has become right; and where society is confused by the lies of the "prince of the power of the air,"—speaking truth, and embracing a Gospel of grace, manifested in the cross of Christ and received by faith alone, outside of works, often makes us enemies of a culture that demands its own way and wants desperately to carve out its own way of salvation. This battle we are called to engage!

Day 329 | Nothing Can Replace Unity

November 25—Read Ephesians 1-4

Before addressing spiritual gifts and commitment to sound doctrine, Paul described walking worthy of Christ's calling as humility, long suffering toward others, and determination to maintain unity and peace. Gifted orthodoxy without godly relationships is worthless. Ephesians 4:1-3

The Apostle Paul was a stickler for sound doctrine and the passing on of truth. His instructions to Titus and Timothy in the pastoral epistles were chock-full of exhortations to maintain biblical integrity and be committed to proclaiming the Gospel. He also was passionate about teaching the correct use and potential benefits of the exercise of spiritual gifts within the church body. Yet he understood that all of the orthodoxy in the world and the manifestation of spiritual gifts within the church would be meaningless if they lacked unity and failed to reflect Christ's character in the community. Their witness would be ruined and the Gospel would be deemed shallow and useless.

No greater truth could be underscored today. Solid biblical teaching is crucial to the life of the church, and spiritual gifts enable the Church to build one another up. But if the relationships within the Church are marked by selfishness and conflict, the witness within the community will be stained, and the power of the Gospel annulled.

Day 330 | Divine Love vs. Worldly Love

November 26—Read Ephesians 5-6

A godless culture has hijacked the notion of love as a cover for sin and reduced God's nature to this one quality. The distinction between worldly love and divine love is sharp and clear. Worldly love is sensual and selfish—divine love is sacrificial and selfless. Ephesians 5:1-6

In the final three chapters of Ephesians, Paul builds on the theological foundation that he established in the first three chapters, namely the truth that in Christ we are redeemed from our life of sin and brokenness and are now firmly rooted in the new life. One of the primary features of this new life is an understanding of what it means to love. As Paul opens chapter five, he reminds the Ephesian believers that love in Christ is not about the sensual and carnal ways of the old man, but is to be modeled after the love Christ revealed to us through His sacrifice on Calvary.

Our culture desperately needs to be reminded of Paul's words. Love has been cheapened in contemporary society to mean any form of self-aggrandizing pleasure or sensual relationship, whether or not it falls within the principles of God's Word. Most only want to speak of God as love, and that as a perverted love that knows no holiness. The love God calls us to is the love Jesus demonstrated that is sacrificial and selfless, NOT sensual and selfish.

Day 331 | Embracing Our Adversity

November 27—Read Philippians 1-2

It was the spiritual depth and the patient steadfastness of the early Church that saw great moments of adversity as opportunities for their witness to shine and the Gospel to advance. This missing component of our modern Church—we must determine to recapture. Philippians 1:12-14

The early Church was far more resilient than the church today, and no was more resilient than Paul. He told the church in Corinth that he had been beaten and shipwrecked three times and was stoned and left for dead. Additionally, on multiple occasions, Paul found himself chained to guards as he lay in prison awaiting trial. But he saw these occasions not as times of defeat to be despised, but as opportunities for the Gospel to advance that should be cherished.

This spirit desperately needs recaptured in the modern Church. We seek to shake ourselves from every possibility of suffering and cast out all possibility of knowing pain. Surely, says our shaky and selfless theology, God could never mean for us to be experiencing this. Those musings fall well short of the biblical paradigm. Suffering should not be viewed as a cross to bear, but a privilege to share; for in our suffering and chains, physical and otherwise, Jesus can be seen as exalted, and when He is lifted up, all humanity is drawn to Him and His grace.

May we embrace the suffering and cling to the crosses that come our way.

Day 332 | That I May Know Him

November 28—Read Philippians 3-4

When our focus is attaining success, overcoming weaknesses, or placating emotions, we will live on a spiritually anemic roller-coaster. When we rest in our position IN HIM and make our grandest pursuit knowing Him better, we will experience resurrection power. Philippians 3:8-10

Paul had much to brag about in the flesh. He had accomplished much and had experienced the grandeur of elite academia and religious position. His heritage was unblemished and his pedigree unparalleled. Yet he knew it was all worthless and must be laid aside if he was to pursue the only One that mattered. It was all meaningless garbage in comparison to knowing and experiencing Christ Jesus.

When we pursue the things, riches, and prestige of this world, our lives will be mired in the rut of disappointment, unmet expectations, and an insatiable lust for more power, wealth, and notoriety. Emotions will drive us, and highs and lows will mark every day. When we know who we are in Christ and settle into that assurance, the power of the risen Christ will sustain us. The only lingering passion will be, not for more of the world, but more of the Christ who saved us, more of His character revealed in us, and more of His love to put on display for a lost world.

Day 333 | The Worthy One

November 29—Read Colossians 1-2

He is knowable and powerful—the firstborn of all creation. He is Creator and Sovereign over all things—the One who holds it all together. He is the founder, builder, and Lord over the Church and the One we worship. In Him is all we need—His name is Jesus! Colossians 1:15-20

The opening chapter of Colossians is famously known as one of the richest theological texts and an example of high Christology. In majestic language, Paul points his readers to Jesus, the One who made all that is made, holds it all together by the Word of His power, and reigns as the *"firstborn from the dead"* and the *"Head of the Church."* The words of the apostle make it clear that Jesus is eternally existent, fully God, and yet, in His Incarnation, fully human. Truthfully, this description of Christ surpasses all others in providing an accurate and full picture of the divine Son of God and Son of Man.

Beyond its rich theology, this text gives us practical truth that we can heartily embrace. As the image of the invisible God, Christ made God knowable. We can experience His love and grow in relationship with Him. Still, this God who we can intimately know is the Creator who holds not only universes together, He holds our lives together as well, while at the same time, building His Church and managing its affairs. He alone is worthy of our worship.

Day 334 | An Upward Call

November 30—Read Colossians 3-4

For those who are united with Christ in His death and resurrection, there is to be an upward gaze, an upward movement, and an upward determination. It is His presence we must seek, His vision we must enjoin, and His perseverance we must emulate. Colossians 3:1-2

Much of Paul's letter to the Colossian church was geared toward challenging his readers to understand and live out their identity in Christ. Many other ideologies threatened the fledgling church, located in the Lycus Valley near both Hierapolis and Laodicea. It was tempting for new believers to avoid the prospect of persecution and to settle for false doctrine and worldly pursuits, but to do so they would have to disavow their relationship with Christ and forsake their identification with Him. Paul calls on them not to and reminds them of their identity and their responsibility to an upward call.

Today believers are also tempted to lay down a radical and passionate pursuit of Christ in order to avoid being ostracized or risk potential persecution. Paul's words to the church in Colossae still call us to a great responsibility and give us assurance that obeying that call is worthwhile. With our spiritual eyes focused on His presence, we can move deeper into our walk with Him and carry His vision of a world that knows and embraces the Truth with the confidence that He will sustain us in our uncompromising and unbending devotion to Him.

Day 335 | Joy for Mourning

December 1—Read 1 Thessalonians 1-4

Grief is part of a broken world—experienced by those who love. But hopeless grief is not the lot of the child of God. Our grief is transformed by hope in a person Who has Himself conquered death and Who promised to return for us. Our hope is in Jesus. 1 Thessalonians 4:13-14

All who have lived have experienced grief, and the Thessalonian believers were no exception. Loved ones had passed, their hope for Christ's return had diminished, and their fledgling faith was being tried. Paul's pastoral heart ached for those he loved, so he penned his first letter to them to sort out their theological misunderstanding and offer them, not a grief-free life, but a life that knew Christ's power to transform grief into hope.

Many today struggle just like the Thessalonians. Their loss has been great, and the pain continues to mount. Repeated loss leads to a sense of hopelessness and often stifles the faithful anticipation that should mark the believer. These words of 1 Thessalonians remind us that we do not grieve as those who are hopeless, but rather we stand in the assurance that Christ's return will bring joy for our mourning.

Day 336 | The Most Frequent Command

December 2—Read 1 Thessalonians 5

GIVE THANKS! The most often repeated command of Scripture. The psalmist says THIS is good. Good because it is the only appropriate response to a good God. It leads us into His presence where joy is full (Ps. 100:4; 16:11), and it is His will. 1 Thessalonians 5:16-18

Though some would argue that Christianity is just a burdensome and overwhelming mountain of rules and mandates, the reality is that the most often repeated command of Scripture is not pejorative. It is not a "thou shalt not!" Instead it is the command to "Give thanks!" For as the psalmist says— "It is a good thing to give thanks unto the Lord." It is good, because He is a good God and good, because giving thanks is the appropriate thing to do.

The believer who longs to know the presence of God and sincerely desires to walk in the blessing of following God's will should practice often this command. Giving thanks is the means by which we enter the gates and courts of God's presence where fullness of joy can be experienced, and it is an act that declares our deepest desire to align ourselves with His will and, in so doing, makes us recipients of the blessings that come to those who walk obediently before Him.

Day 337 | The Evidence of Faith

December 3—Read 2 Thessalonians 1

In radical opposition to what is often called "gospel," promising a TEMPORAL life of ease, prosperity, and comfort, God's Word prepares us for trial, hardship, and suffering that produces faith and patience, counting us worthy of the ETERNAL Kingdom of God. 2 Thessalonians 1:4-5

As Paul wrote his second letter to the believers in Thessalonica, he spoke of how proud he was of them and how they had become a boasting point as he made his way to churches throughout the region. The focus of his boasting was their steadfast faith, despite their trials and suffering, which he called "evidence of the righteous judgment of God, that you may be counted worthy of the Kingdom of God for which you suffer." Paul considered their suffering as evidence of their solid faith.

This understanding of integrity of faith is far different than that which has been propagated in the contemporary Church. Too often, it is prosperity, success, and health that for some have become indicators of righteous and faith-filled living. Clearly, that is a misconstrued notion. The life of sincere faith will indeed be marked by trial, suffering, and hardship, but will one day give way to that which will make it worth it all.

Day 338 | Hold Fast and Held Fast

December 4—Read 2 Thessalonians 2-3

Deconstructing societal values, historical truth, and personal faith is the sport of a godless agenda aimed at lawlessness and demonic rule. Our call? Unshakable holiness and tenacious defense of truth. Our promise? Christ will hold us fast. 2 Thessalonians 2:15-16

Paul's letter to the Thessalonian church was meant to calm, steady, and encourage them. They were being challenged by those who were making false claims about the coming of Christ and re-interpreting the apostolic doctrine that they had been previously taught. The attack from the false prophets was difficult to endure for the young church, but Paul assured them that God would keep them if they would stand for truth and not compromise their faith.

The situation the church in Thessalonica found themselves in is being replicated in our Church culture today. Great challenges to biblical orthodoxy are being mounted, and a progressive and ungodly approach to biblical interpretation is being embraced, even by those who have been immersed in truth. God is calling us to stand firm, to hold truth high, and defend with all intensity the Gospel in its purity and clarity. If we do—God promises to establish us and keep us in His faithful hand!

Day 339 | Let the Word Change Us First

December 5—Read 1 Timothy 1

The end goal of biblical literacy is not to achieve theological superiority, nor to have answers to all of life's questions. Rather, it is to grow in love, develop a deeper purity, more tender conscience, and a more steadfast and sincere faith.
1 Timothy 1:5

Much of Paul's advice to Timothy in this letter and indeed all three of the pastoral epistles has to do with the propagating of truth and the defense of the Gospel in the face of false doctrine. Paul was very direct with Timothy and Titus in calling on them to be diligent in knowing truth and fighting against all perversions of its tenets. This kind of readiness would only come if they devoted themselves to study and literacy in the inspired writings.

Today, the world sits in a morass of biblical illiteracy, and worse yet, the Church is devoid of any sense of competent biblical literacy. It has sorely deluded the message we proclaim as well as the effectiveness of our discipleship. An intense passion for truth and a vigorous defense against false doctrine must be employed, but in the end, we must not forget that God's primary reason for wanting us bathed in His Word is to be changed by it, made more like Him, and to live our lives before a sinful world as an apt witness to the love, purity, and grace of the One we proclaim.

Day 340 | Love in Action Still Makes a Difference

December 6—Read 1 Timothy 2-4

While uncertainties abound, God's people must do what they know they are called to do—intercede for all authorities, asking God to help them, seek to live quiet and peaceable lives marked by godliness and dignity, and never fail to speak God's truth. 1 Timothy 2:1-2; 3:14-15

Paul wrote his letters to Timothy to instruct him how to best lead Ephesian believers, despite the fact that the culture around them was uncertain and under siege by the brutal and tyrannical Roman imperialism. Paul's advice to Timothy was to teach the Ephesian Christians to stand for truth, but pray for those in authority and seek to live quiet and peaceful lives, being noted for their godly character rather than their vitriolic rhetoric.

This advice needs a fresh hearing in the American Church today. Sadly, we are known more for what we oppose than what we uphold, who we are against more than whose name we exalt, and what we abhor more than whom we cherish. Truth must never be compromised, and confrontation is often necessary. However, as followers of the One who endured the contradiction of sinners without a word and yet changed the course of human history through His conduct, let us not forget that our greatest impact is found, not in the points we score with our words, but with the love we display in our actions.

Day 341 | Our Highest Aim

December 7—Read 1 Timothy 5-6

Paul is clear—no matter how noble the cause, how passionate we are to confront an injustice or false ideology, or how certain we are that God is on our side, our priority must be God's honor. ANY action that would lead someone to reject the Gospel must be forsaken. 1 Timothy 6:1-2

The directives of the Apostle Paul to those who were living in servitude would not go well in today's culture so consumed by self-interest. While Paul no doubt opposed the institution of slavery and abhorred the practice of treating another human with little dignity, the eternal Gospel still trumped all, and his warning was to never let anything, not even attempts to bring social justice, hinder the Gospel.

This message needs to be heard today. Christians should do all they can to ensure that systems of society are just and treat all fairly. But our efforts to secure social justice in this temporal world must never hinder the opportunity to share the Gospel message that provides hope for an eternal peace. Balancing the values of justice and Gospel proclamation may be challenging, but the discerning Church must commit themselves to that end. The honor of God and the propagation of the truth of Calvary must always be our highest aim.

Day 342 | Stirring Up the Gift of God

December 8—Read 2 Timothy 1-2

No matter what challenges lie in wait or what obstacles may appear, God calls us to re-kindle the passion we experienced when He first called us. Fear need not distract or sideline us. God's love, power, and peace have equipped us and will accompany us every step. 2 Timothy 1:6-7

Paul's letters to Timothy are filled with telling and instructive pathos. Writing from a Roman prison, Paul knows that Timothy, insecure about his youth and given to some level of anxiety, may consider the thought of prison or martyrdom too great to imagine. He reminds Timothy that fear does not originate with God. God had given him a great capacity to love, a power to endure trials, a deep peace, and gifts that He expected to be used for Him.

The evil of this world can unnerve us, and the opposition we face can induce spiritual anxiety, leading to spiritual paralysis. But God has equipped us to overcome. We are to love when hated, stand when pushed back, rest in Him when the burden is heavy, and fan into flame the passions and gifts we know God imparted to us when He called us.

Day 343 | Focusing on a Better World

December 9—Read 2 Timothy 3-4

Demas, "in love with this present world," tragically deserted Paul and the Gospel. When we lose focus on the yet unseen, but eternal prize of our heavenly inheritance, we are in danger of becoming enamored by the tantalizing and temporary offerings of this world. 2 Timothy 4:10

As Paul neared the end of his ministry, he spoke of the loneliness he felt in the Roman prison while writing to his young protégé. He told Timothy that no one had defended him when he stood before Caesar to give his defense, but despite the fact no one rallied around Paul, he was glad to report that the Lord had been with him. He asked Timothy to send Mark to him and provides a few other directives. In the course of these final comments, he mentioned the tragic story of Demas, one who had previously served God, but had forsaken Paul and the Gospel because of his love for the present world.

The story of Demas is sadly repeated time and time again today. The world, with its sensual power to entice our fleshly desires, has great power to wreck the faith of those who fail to keep their focus on their eternal pursuit. The visible allure of the world will loom great before the eyes of those who have neglected to shore up the loyalty of their soul through deepened faith and greater surrender.

Day 344 | Be True to Your Confession

December 10—Read Titus 1-3

"Such people claim they know God, but they deny Him by the way they live."
These words should haunt, challenge, and convict every believer. When our actions
do not align with our confession, we do great harm to the cause of Christ and His
Kingdom. Titus 1:16

In his short letter to Titus, Paul describes false teachers that would worm their way into the church body with the intention of doing harm to the believers who were young in their faith. Paul had assigned Titus to the island of Crete where he was to appoint elders to serve the church. As he laid out the qualifications for the prospective elders, he also took time to warn him about the potential infiltration of false teachers. The tell-tale sign of a false teacher, according to Paul, was when their confession was not backed up by their lifestyle.

This description of false teachers should serve as a strong challenge to all believers to take great care with their own lives. What we confess must be what we live. If we say we know and love Him, we must live lives that reveal His work to be our priority. Great consequences will befall the false teacher, but also the hypocrite whose confession is undone by their lifestyle.

Day 345 | Chains for Christ

December 11—Read Philemon 1

Paul called himself a "prisoner FOR Christ Jesus." He didn't despise his sufferings, wish away his hardships, or seek rescue from his chains. Each had a purpose—they shaped his witness and intensified his passion. He was in chains for the Gospel. His master was Christ. Philemon 1:1

Paul's letter to Philemon asks him to welcome back Onesimus, his former slave who had stolen from him in the past but now wanted to return home. Paul believed that Onesimus had been transformed and was profitable to Philemon. In the opening words of his correspondence, Paul identifies himself as a *"prisoner for Christ Jesus."* These words are pregnant with significance, speaking to Paul's willing surrender to the purpose and plan of God. Calling himself a prisoner for Christ was, to Paul, an honor he gladly embraced. It was a privilege of the greatest magnitude.

This kind of willing surrender is sadly lacking in the Church today. We want to avoid sufferings, do all we can to bypass hardship, and make it a matter of faith to stay clear of enemy persecution. This was not the posture of Paul. He knew that his suffering would lead to a deepened walk with Christ and eternal reward that would outshine any present difficulty. We must not despise our present pain but gladly share with Christ in His sufferings.

Day 346 | One Day!

December 12—Read Hebrews 1-3

At present, the world seems to be anything but subject to Christ, but we see, with eyes of faith fixed on Him, that one day every knee will bow before Him and every tongue will confess Him as Lord, and the world's kingdoms will become His forever. Hebrews 2:8-9; 3:1

Quoting the psalmist who in Psalm 2 anticipates the coming Messiah, who will reign in glory with all kingdoms, rulers, thrones, and powers subject to Him and under His feet, the author of Hebrews points his readers to Jesus, the incarnate Son of God, perfect Man, and Son of God. The salvation made available to humanity through Jesus must not be overlooked; how can one escape if they refuse and neglect the salvation offered through Him?

While the hope of this glorious and eternal salvation, where Christ rules and reigns, buoys the hearts of believers today, an honest appraisal of our culture leaves us shaking our heads wondering "will it ever be?" Yet as we heed the words of the Hebrews author and fix our eyes on Jesus, we, with great assurance and hearts leaping in faith, look and work for the day that the "the kingdoms of this world become the Kingdoms of our Lord and of His Christ, and He shall reign forever and ever" (Revelation 11:15).

Day 347 | The Agony of the Garden

December 13—Read Hebrews 4-6

Gethsemane was not a box-checking experience for Jesus. There, let down by His friends, Jesus faced the prospect of becoming sin for us, being forsaken by His Father, and bearing the cross. He won by refusing to blame God and by submitting fully to His perfect plan. Hebrews 5:7-8

For some who seek to lessen the intense struggle that Jesus felt in surrendering His will to the Father's plan, Gethsemane was just part of the play—an act that had to be completed. To believe this is to undermine the rich truth of Christ's dual nature: fully human—fully divine. Those who would argue this point reject the notion that Jesus really had a choice, and suggest that He was merely going through the motions and realistically could have made no other decision than the cross. This, however, is not only untrue, it stands contrary to the words of Jesus Himself who said of His life, "*I lay it down.*"

Jesus did indeed struggle, and He did wrestle with the decision to surrender to the Father's will. To surrender meant He would become sin for humanity and bear the full force of God's wrath against sin on the cross. In Gethsemane, the deepest love and greatest sacrifice known to man was revealed. Forsaken by all and facing His Father's desertion, Jesus still chose to bear our shame, pay our debt, and experience our pain so that we might be free.

Day 348 | Deepening Our Resolve

December 14—Read Hebrews 7-10

Challenging days call for greater, more fervent commitment. This includes an unwavering passion for God's presence, an uncompromised confession of devotion, and a selfless loyalty to the body of Christ—its gathering, its effectiveness, and its edification. Hebrews 10:22-25

The Hebrews author is warning his readers of difficult days to come. The pressure would be great, the temptation to abandon the church would be ramped up, and the consequences of staying might be grave. But they must not be like the wilderness generation that fell short of the promise because the giants in the land seemed impossible to defeat. They must persevere.

Oh, how we need that message today. This is not the time to shrink back but to draw near to God's presence with great boldness and to confidently proclaim our trust in Him. Others in the Church need us. In a day when church attendance is waning, and the priority of gathering seems to have reached an all-time low, we must double down on our commitment to gathering as the people of God, and do so not just to be blessed, but to encourage others to stand strong in the face of adversity.

Day 349 | The Just Shall Live by Faith

December 15—Read Hebrews 11

The posture of faith must always be steadfast confidence in God, the experience of faith is often painful, the fellowship of faith includes all who have trusted God and followed His call in the past and now, and the ultimate reward of faith is yet to come. Hebrews 11:39-40

God has called us to live lives of faith, repeating often the reminder, *"The just shall live by faith."* Those listed in Hebrews *Hall of Faith* lived their lives with a steadfast focus on God's promises and their gaze upon the Promiser. While they lived lives of shining and godly confidence, they were often marked by painful trials. Still, they drew strength from those who went before them. They knew that if in this life, the promise was not realized, a reward awaited them.

It is from these great men and women of God that we take comfort. We too can shift our focus and laser in on the promises of God to steady our walk. While struggles will come, we can find strength in reflecting upon those who have gone before us and find solace in knowing, whether now or in eternity, that what God has promised, He will perform.

Day 350 | A Kingdom that Stands

December 16—Read Hebrews 12-13

Buildings crumble, leaders fail. and empires fall, but the Kingdom of God to which we have come will never end. Despite the turmoil around us, we can be thankful and worship, for while our temporary home may be shaking, our permanent home is sure and steadfast. Hebrews 12:28

The world today is desperately lacking strong and godly leadership, and the foundations upon which we have built our security for so long are being sorely threatened. Integrity and wisdom are both commodities frighteningly absent from the landscape of societal organization and political figures. Many find themselves fearful and living in dread. The joy and hopefulness of our culture has been overcome by cynicism and anxiety.

This need not be the case. While kingdoms and kings come and go, the Word of the Lord endures and prospers. The Kingdom toward which we journey is a Kingdom that is eternal in the Heavens and never loses its authenticity or its power. It is an unshakable Kingdom that will outlast and outshine them all.

Day 351 | Trials and Joy

December 17—Read James 1-2

"Pure joy" is to be the believer's reaction when confronted by multiple trials. How can this be, and where has this response gone? Trials are the ONLY means to developing spiritual endurance, a quality once highly valued, but now sacrificed on the altar of comfort. James 1:2-4

James writes to first century believers who had been forced to scatter because of persecution they were experiencing as a result of their faith in Christ. Many had lost their lives or livelihoods because of their devotion to Jesus. James' call to them was not to compromise, cower in fear, or bemoan their fate as those who had been treated unfairly and forgotten. Instead he called them to *"count it all joy."*

Counting as joy the struggles, trials, and discomforts that come our way as a result of following Christ is not a popular ideology in today's modern Church. We speak more of entitlement, privileges, and power. That is not the way of the cross, no matter how trendy and welcomed such thinking has become. We are to rejoice when difficulty comes, because through that pain we are shaped, made stronger, and endowed with spiritual endurance.

Day 352 | Godly Strategies

December 18—Read James 3-5

A strategy, no matter how creative or impressive it appears and no matter how promising its results, that is not soaked in gentle humility and peaceful self-surrender is not God's way. His plans promote peace and humility and produce righteous, not worldly, fruit. James 3:14-18

James calls his readers to cherish and nurture wisdom so that their lives can bear fruit and reach their divinely appointed destiny. He indicates that wisdom to fulfill their calling and realize their destiny can be found by asking God to impart His wisdom to them. With His wisdom, strategies for success and fruitfulness can be developed, and true fruitfulness can be enjoyed. God's wisdom is available, but appropriate strategies must emerge.

No matter how wise one may feel they are, they do not walk in the wisdom of God, nor are they employing divine strategies, if their lives are marked by envy, bitterness, or self-seeking. If not present in the life of the believer, efforts will be to no avail, and fruit will not remain. The antidote to sensual and self-serving wisdom that stands contrary to the will of God is to sow peace. That peace must be sown into relationships prone to conflict, hearts that have been wounded and broken, and opportunities to show God's glory.

Day 353 | A Grace that Expects

December 19—Read 1 Peter 1

The modern notion of Christianity under grace that eliminates any expectation for holiness, implicitly promotes worldliness, and decries calls for obedience is clearly debunked by Peter's call to action, his warning not to slip, his charge to be holy, and his challenge to grow. 1 Peter 1:13-2:10

When Peter wrote to the early Church, he wrote to a people who understood that holiness was not a gift of divine grace that required nothing on the part of the recipient. Such a concept would have been foreign to the thinking of those who were threatened by persecution, driven out of their homes, and forced to live lives of exile. They knew that their faithfulness in response to the grace that redeemed them was still necessary if they were to gain their ultimate prize.

Cheap grace is the favored commodity of the contemporary Church. Living lives as one wants, bent on personal pleasure and a disdain for a life of trial and hardship, seems to the preferred path for postmodern believers, but this is not the call of the Gospel. What Peter preached was what Jesus taught him—one must take up their cross, diligently pursue the Kingdom of God and its righteousness, and not give way to the temptation to look back.

Day 354 | True Righteousness

December 20—Read 1 Peter 2-5

Spiritual growth and Kingdom usefulness come only through emptying oneself of attitudes of self-protection and personal vindication, surrendering to God's righteous judgment, and an ever-deepening desire for spiritual nourishment.
1 Peter 2:1-2, 21-23

Peter called his readers to a righteousness that was modeled after Jesus. If they had any aspirations of making Kingdom impact, they must lay aside attitudes contrary to the way of Jesus and willingly submit themselves, as did Jesus to the Father's will, even if it meant discomfort or trial. There simply was no other way in Peter's mind. Telling is the tradition that informs us that Peter did just that, surrendering to martyrdom as one who thought it an honor to follow his Lord in that manner.

The American Church has become spiritually soft and has gravitated toward selfish ambition and personal preservation. It is a Christianity of comfort that is most often sought today. We want a life of ease, minimal cost and challenges that do not stretch or threaten our personal ambitions. But this is not the call of Scripture. Instead, we are called to lay aside selfish tendencies to pursue the pure milk of God's Word, the truth that sets us free from ourselves by demanding we submit to the Father who is forming Christ in us.

Day 355 | Building On Our Faith

December 21—Read 2 Peter 1-2

The notion of grace void of personal responsibility was foreign to early believers. Strenuous effort to respond faithfully to God's promises, moral development, diligent devotion to prove sincerity, and attentiveness to His Word are all expected of Christ-followers. 2 Peter 1

Peter addresses the early believers, sojourners of faith who had been forcefully removed from their homes because of their faith, and reminds them of all that God had done for them. In no uncertain terms, he speaks of the precious promises they had been given from God and reminds them that they have been given by God's grace, "all things that pertain to life and godliness." But as he goes on, he makes it clear to his readers that the blessing of God's grace does not exempt them from pursuing spiritual growth and assuming personal responsibility for the same. They are to *"add to their faith"* virtues that exemplify Christ.

Sadly, it has become all too frequent for Christians to rest in the assurance of their salvation by grace and assume there is no responsibility beyond that. This leads to carnal Christianity, a watered-down gospel, and ineffectual evangelism. We have been saved for responsibility, not merely privilege, and each of us bear the responsibility to grow in grace and pursue spiritual maturity.

Day 356 | The Motive of the Scoffer

December 22—Read 2 Peter 3

Though fanciful arguments are made, and intellectual integrity is claimed, most deny creation by a holy God, not because of intellectual arrival, but rather because of a lust for self-indulgence and a disdain for the notion of accountability to God on judgment day. 2 Peter 3:3-7

When Peter addressed the last days scoffers who would trivialize those who embrace the hope of Christ's coming, he lumped them in with those who deliberately overlook the truth of creation, the judgment of God through the flood, and the divine fiat that spawned creation. The point Peter was making was not that they were ignorant or unlearned, but that they had a motive that led them to intentionally dismiss such serious suppositions, knowing that they carry with them implications that demand a response.

The godless world today is full of these scoffers. Their motive in rejecting the theological construct of God as Creator is driven by lust and the desire for pleasure. To acknowledge an all-powerful Creator, and One who is both Judge and returning Savior, is to acknowledge that we must submit and surrender to One who is greater than us, and that is a position that a sinful humanity refuses to embrace.

Day 357 | The Life He Wants for Us

December 23—Read 1 John 1-2

The joy of following Christ transcends the assurance of Heaven. It's the privilege of spiritual growth—to move from knowing forgiveness to knowing the forgiving Father; to grow from knowing His will is good to finding it acceptable, to experiencing it as perfect. 1 John 2:14-16

As the elderly apostle John writes to believers in Ephesus, it is apparent that he longs for them to experience a development of their faith and not to be mired in the stupor of spiritual stagnancy. His words describe a sort of faith escalation that begins at infancy, passes through adolescence and young adult living, then arrives at spiritual maturity. It progresses from knowing that one's sins are forgiven to knowing intimately the One who has forgiven those sins. This is where John has been, and this is where he longs for others to go as well.

This spiritual maturity is sorely lacking in the church today. Too many settle into spiritual infancy, and their growth is stunted by their worldly love and selfish ambition. Christ wants us to know Him better and to move from the fruitless existence of spiritual babes to the overcoming and fruitful life of godly and mature Christ followers. He desires us to be those whose lives teem with spiritual gifts and whose character is marked by a deep love for God and neighbor.

Day 358 | Demonstrated Love

December 24—Read 1, 2, & 3 John

Behold! Reflect upon the profound love God has shown to us in Christ, calling us His children—LOVE WAS DEMONSTRATED. Then, like our Father, if we say we love, we too must demonstrate love in action to those who are in need physically, emotionally, or spiritually. 1 John 3:1, 16-17

John opens the third chapter of the first of his three letters with a powerful invitation— *"Behold what manner of love the Father has lavished on us, that we should be called the children of God."* He calls his readers to reflect on this truth, the truth that the holy and perfect Father has bestowed upon His flawed and sinful children, undeserved love and the greatest of all blessings—to be called His children. This is indeed a marvelous love. Later in the same chapter, he reminds his readers that they cannot just SAY they love, but they must demonstrate it with ACTION.

The Father surely demonstrated HIS love—He did so by sending Jesus to be born and to die for our sins though we had nothing to offer Him. This is demonstrated love—this is love in action. As His children, we too, are called to demonstrative love: love that does more than just *say* it loves, but *shows* that it loves. May we be true children of our loving Father and apt representatives of His love by demonstrating that love to others, even if undeserved.

Day 359 | Fight and Pray

December 25—Read Jude

Jude called believers to "contend earnestly" for truth. He also cautioned them about being so consumed with contending that they fail to maintain their own devotion. This is prudent advice—pray in the Spirit, stay deep in God's love, and seek ways to share His mercy. Jude 20-21

The opening words of this very short letter of Jude call the people of God to contend for the faith and for orthodox truth. False prophets had permeated the Church, and Jude's concern was that the foundations of truth were being shaken. He called upon believers to fight. This was not, however, all that Jude said. Knowing that a fight not grounded in a solid and ever-deepening relationship with Christ would end tragically, he called them to strengthen their spiritual disciplines, especially that of prayer and showing mercy.

Today the Church is certainly threatened by false teaching and a culture of shocking godlessness. We must be on our guard and contend for the truth that we have received and upon which our faith and hope are based. At the same time, our energy must not all be spent defending and fighting for truth. We must also devote ourselves to fervent prayer, ever-growing faith, compassionate love, and showing mercy in every opportunity. Without these, we run the danger of a pure orthodoxy that lacks spiritual power and grace.

Day 360 | The Danger of Losing Our First Love

December 26—Read Revelation 1-2

Jesus' rebuke of the Ephesians reminds us of the real possibility and great danger of being bold for Jesus, exacting in our self-discipline and expectations of others, and tirelessly busy with Kingdom work, and yet having our love grow cold. Of this we must be aware. Revelation 2:2-5

"But I have this against you, that you have abandoned the love you had at first." These were the words of Jesus to the church of Ephesus. They had done much, their doctrine was solid, and their influence and reputation among the churches of Asia Minor was stellar. But the risen Christ saw beyond all of that and saw a people who were growing cold and drifting from the passionate pursuit of Him they had once made a priority. If things did not change, they would find themselves void of His manifest presence.

This is a warning that the contemporary Church must heed. It is easy for the Church, especially a busy and productive one, to get caught up in doing ministry and slowly slip from the passion and intimacy they once enjoyed. It is not enough to plan clearly, strategize aggressively, and teach correctly. The priority of authentic intimacy with the Savior, for whom we labor, must never be forgotten.

Day 361 | Holy and Forever He Reigns

December 27—Read Revelation 3-4

Thrice holy is the One who sits on the throne. Holy=hagios—set apart and unlike any other: to be revered, adored, and worshipped. He REIGNED HOLY on His throne before our trial, REIGNS HOLY as we go through our trial, and will REIGN HOLY when we have come through. Revelation 4:8

As John is granted a momentary glimpse into the glory of Heaven and the majesty of God's throne room, he observes angelic activity. In the Spirit he is able to experience perpetual worship of the One who sits on the throne as they declare and worship, the immutable nature of His character, *Holy, Holy, Holy*. This holiness not only marks Heaven's atmosphere but penetrates our world as well.

Often, we feel our situations are hopeless, and the trials before us are overwhelming. This is easy to do when our perspective is earthly and temporal. This is why Jesus revealed Himself to John while exiled on the island of Patmos—to provide us with a heavenly and eternal perspective. Our trials neither affect nor change the character of the One who promises to walk through these with us. He WAS, IS, and ALWAYS will be holy!

Day 362 | What's Really Going On

December 28—Read Revelation 5-10

Revealing what's really going behind what's going on, John provides a solemn reminder to us all—despite global unrest, political clamoring, and prideful rebellion against God, one day it will end—the Lamb will give rest to the faithful and judge those who rejected Him. Revelation 6

One writer famously quipped, *"The Book of Revelation is an invitation to see what's really going on behind what's going on."* These words are never more accurate than in Revelation's sixth chapter. Here we see the unleashing of global conflict that leads to unthinkable bloodshed, famine, and death, a cycle that continues still in our world. But at the end of that chapter, the curtain is pulled back as the Lamb brings all evil to an end, vindicates those who lost their lives for Him, and makes available eternal rest for all who have trusted Him.

The world may have you anxious and afraid. You may be uncertain about what your future holds, or whether you can survive the evil onslaught brought on by the spirt of this age and the sin of the world. Be encouraged! God is not oblivious, and the Lamb is seated on the throne. Soon all evil will be banished and righteousness will reign; what is really going on is that the Bridegroom is preparing, and the Bride is making herself ready!

Day 363 | The Kingdoms of Our Lord

December 29—Read Revelation 11-16

The sustaining hope of those who abide in Christ is this truth—one day we will hear the throng of Heaven announce, "The kingdoms of this world have become the kingdoms of our Lord and of His Christ, and He shall reign forever and ever!" Revelation 11:15

Throughout the course of John's Revelation, the scene of judgment and divine wrath that will be poured out on the world and a system that has systematically rejected God and His holiness moves toward a grand crescendo. As it reaches that climactic moment, the seventh angel blasts a trumpet and announces that rebellion and sin will finally be confronted in an eternal manner, and those kingdoms, formerly dominated and manipulated by evil, will fall into the hands of the King of Kings and Lord of Lords.

Today's world is filled with cause for anxiety and fear, and often, even the people of God find their hearts gripped by their power. Media reports of evil, political upheaval, and heartaches that seem to have no answer threaten the peace of God's children. All of this can leave one's hope withered and their joy sapped from them. But those who know Jesus know that this is not the final chapter. We look forward to that day, the sound of the angel's trumpet, and the announcement of our King's coronation.

Day 364 | Blood-Dipped Robe

December 30—Read Revelation 17-19

John describes the cloaks that will be worn by both Jesus and His saints at His coming. Even in His return, Calvary's necessity will be on display. Jesus will wear a blood-dipped robe of sacrifice, so that we might wear white and clean robes of righteousness. Revelation 19:13-14

John's description of Christ's return in glorious splendor piques the imagination and stirs the souls of those who know Him and long for His return. The majestic picture painted by the revelator is matched only by his description of Jesus in the opening chapter of his apocalyptic vision. As he describes the cloaks worn by both Jesus and the redeemed, a marvelous truth emerges. He wears the blood-dipped robe while the saints who follow with Him are robed in bright white, gloriously pure robes of righteousness.

It is both beautiful and amazing to see that even in the depiction of this world's final scene, the necessity and power of the cross are demonstrated; and its essential work highlighted. Without the sacrifice of Jesus and without His spotless robes becoming stained by sacrificial blood, our robes would remain soiled by sin, tattered by our failures, and unfit for the presence of our Creator. But because Jesus allowed His robe to be stained by His blood, we have been granted robes of righteousness and given access into His presence.

Day 365 | There Will Be No Temple

December 31—Read Revelation 20-22

Marvelous is the reality of the City of God—there will be no temple. Temples reveal separation—Jews from Gentiles, worshippers from priests, and sinful humanity from a holy God. Christ has made us holy, and eternity will reveal that separation has been eliminated. Revelation 21:22

Though the mystery of John's revelation while on the Island of Patmos is eschatological in nature and unveils the divine workings behind the scenes in preparation for the return of Christ, it also offers incredible insights that illuminate our understanding of salvation. It is in the final chapter that one of those insights grabs our attention. In the holy and eternal city, the New Jerusalem, there will be no more temple, despite the fact that it is the temple that is the centerpiece of worship throughout the ages for God's people.

Temples, however, have rooms or spaces that have barriers. Some can only go to one part of the temple, while others are granted deeper access. The cross, the present working of the Holy Spirit, and the ultimate glorification of God's people that will occur when He returns will transform us all, and there will be no more separation. We will ALL be like HIM, because we will see Him as He is, and all of us will be welcomed into His glorious presence.

ABOUT THE AUTHOR

Kevin has been the senior pastor of Glad Tidings Church in Muncie, Indiana, since 1999. Glad Tidings is part of a four-campus network in east central Indiana and Kevin serves as the network director. Prior to serving in Muncie, he pastored Morocco Assembly of God (Morocco, Indiana) from 1985-1989, and First Assembly of God (Winchester, Indiana) from 1989-1999. He earned his undergraduate degree at Central Bible College (1985), and his MTS (2009) and D. Min. (2012) from Anderson University School of Theology. He was ordained with the Assemblies of God in 1989. He married his wife, Sheila, in 1983, and they have two children and five grandchildren. In addition to this book, he has authored two other books, *Relevant* (a study of the pastoral epistles) and *The Poetic Books: A Pastoral Perspective*.